Killing for Innocence

C.L. Sutton

Chapter One

TEDDY

Mummy says I smell like shit.

I think shit means "poo". She says it with a wrinkled nose, so I know I must smell bad.

Daddy throws a roll of kitchen paper at me, and it hits me on the head.

My bedroom smells like shit, too; but I don't know how to fix it. My bucket is clean. I washed it in the shower this morning when Mummy and Daddy went to the shops. Maybe the smell is coming from the sock I have hidden under my bed. I need to clean that too, but I don't know how. And I have to wipe my bum somehow. It hurts when I don't.

I look at the roll of kitchen paper on my lap. Is that what this is for? Are they going to let me take it upstairs?

Am I allowed upstairs now?

I shift my bum to the edge of the chair. They don't look at me, so I wiggle it some more. The hairs on my arms are all sticking up and I can hear my heart beating in my head.

I stand up, holding my breath.

Mummy shifts her head to the side, making me wince, but I don't dare bring my hands up to my face like I want to.

'Get the fuck upstairs then,' Mummy spits at me. Daddy bites his fried egg sandwich, dripping yolk onto his top. He doesn't look up.

My legs won't move.

I've waited too long, and Mummy karate chops me on the back of my neck. I shriek and run as fast as I can to the stairs, but Mummy is quicker than me and sticks her leg out. She laughs at me as I go flying into the door frame. My head crashes against the wood and it really hurts. I hold back the tears. If Mummy sees me cry, she just gets more mad.

She laughs at me as I crawl up the stairs. I swallow my cries and rub my head where I just whacked it.

My bedroom really does stink. I curl up my nose to try to make it better, but it doesn't work.

This is a really boring room. The most boring room in the house. I've got my bed, but it's only the big mattress bit. I have three books stacked on my windowsill: *Dear Zoo*, *Peppa Pig*, and a book about planet Earth. They're boring too. I think I've read them a million times already. I like the maps in the planet book though, they're pretty.

I also have my bucket. It used to be red, but it's pinker now where it has been sitting in the sun. I wish I could close the curtains, but Mummy took them away one day after she fell out with a lady in the hairdresser's.

I look at my reflection in the window. My blue eyes look dark, like I'm really tired and I push my hair behind my ears to try and tidy it up a bit. I blow air into my cheeks to make them look less scary. It looks like they're caving inwards.

I push my door closed too, careful to shut it properly and not break the rules. I throw myself onto my bed and stare upwards, squeezing the kitchen paper I took from downstairs. The ceiling is brown where water used to come through. Daddy fixed it on the roof, but he didn't fix my ceiling. I'm glad. I like to make pictures in my head out of the brown splodges. I can see a lady's face. She's pretty, like a princess. She looks down at me, smiling. Her eyes are wonky, but that's okay.

The princess on my ceiling knows everything. I tell her all my secrets. She knows I stole a chocolate biscuit last week. She knows I cry in my sleep. She knows about my friend Robert.

Robert is my best friend. He lives in the house next door and, sometimes, when he sees me standing in the yard out the back, he comes to talk to me.

We met in the wintertime. I was standing outside in my pyjamas and I heard the neighbours' back door open and close. I tried to hide by pushing my body against the wall. The little stones in the wall scratched my back.

'Are you okay?' Robert asked me from over the wall. I said nothing. I was too scared.

'I know you're there. I saw you from my bedroom window.' He sounded annoyed, and I was worried that if I didn't say anything, he would get more angry. Louder. And Mummy would find out that I am talking to someone.

'I'm okay,' I blurted out. 'Please leave me alone.'

Robert didn't say anything for ages. I knew he was still there, because I didn't hear him open the door to go back inside.

'Would you like to be my friend?' he asked me. 'You've got blonde hair, like mine.'

From that moment on, Robert was my bestest friend. He would come and talk to me when Mummy and Daddy had gone out and shut me outside. He's the bestest person I have ever met.

Last week, he asked me if I was home alone. I said 'yes' and he threw an actual ball over the wall. It was black and white and rough to touch, but it was so much fun throwing it backwards and forwards over the wall. We tried counting each throw, but Robert was better than me. I can nearly count to ten now – or I think I can. Sometimes I get muddled up. Robert can count all the way to twenty.

I really like Robert.

My hands are sweaty so I wipe them on my T-shirt that's too small for me. There's a little hole in the bottom that I like to poke my finger through.

I can hear Mummy and Daddy turn the TV on now. They laugh when the people on TV laugh. They'll sit there until dark.

I roll onto the floor and slide my hand underneath the mattress, waving it around underneath until I feel the piece of paper. My fingers wrap around it, and I pull it out. I open it up and look at it.

Robert told me it says 'Bob', which is what his friends call him. He said I can call him Bob now too, but I still call him Robert. I like the name Robert the best. There's a smiley face next to the word, which makes me smile, too. I hug the letter.

One day, when I can write, I will throw a letter over the wall, too. I'll tell Robert about the bedroom I want to have with a big bed and a cupboard with clothes inside. I'll tell him about the toys I want, like the car garage I see on the TV advert. The one with the swirly ramp. He'll like that. Robert likes cars, too. Maybe one day we can play together. I'm sure Robert won't mind sharing his toys with me. I bet he has loads of cars to play with.

'What the fuck is that?' Mummy's voice comes from the door behind me. Her voice is all scratchy, like she's just woken up. She's leaning against the door frame with her arms crossed. Her face is all dark and scary as she looks at the paper in my hands.

Without thinking, I stuff the letter in my mouth. She *can't* know about Robert or she'll take him away from me, too.

'What do you think you're doing, you little shit?' She runs at me with her hands out, and she grips my chin, digging her fingernails into my skin. Her face is really close to mine, and I can smell the cigarettes she likes. The minty ones.

'Open your mouth!' she screams. Thick blobs of spit hit my face, so I squeeze my eyes and mouth shut. I hear Daddy drop his plate on the floor downstairs, the cutlery rattling as it falls. But he doesn't come upstairs. I picture him listening on the bottom stair. He likes to know what is going on, but never bothers to help me.

I'm chewing the paper as fast as I can. It's going all sloppy in my mouth and my tummy tenses like I'm going to be sick. I know Mummy is going to hurt me because of this, but that's okay. I know if I show her the letter, she's going to hurt me way more. So I keep chewing.

Mummy pinches my nose and tries to wriggle her fingers between my lips. Her dirty nails scratch my chin. I squeeze my mouth shut tighter. My face feels all hot. I'm panicking. I need to breathe.

I've run out of air. My heart is beating superfast. I pull at Mummy's arms, trying to make her stop. I want her to let me breathe again. But she doesn't let go.

I'm all dizzy and swaying backwards when Mummy finally lets go. I fall onto my bed and open my mouth, gulping in lots of air. Mummy shoves her hand into my mouth. I gag as her fingers tickle the back of my throat and she takes out the piece of paper.

I push myself up onto my elbows and watch Mummy pull the paper open. I wait, my throat burns, and I gag again. What will she do to me?

I'm not allowed to talk to other people. I'm not even allowed to look at people in the shops. And I have to walk with my head down, looking at the floor.

But Robert doesn't mind how much I stink of shit. He doesn't mind if I am dirty. He just wanted to talk to me. And be my friend.

If I can't play with Robert, I will have no one to talk to. My sad tears mix in with the tears from not being able to breathe. Snot drips from my nose and I wipe it away with my sleeve.

Mummy screeches really loud and I cover my ears. The paper has fallen apart; it's too wet and chewed up to open.

'What is this? What did it say?' she screams at me, throwing the paper against the wall where it sticks for a moment before sliding down and landing on the floor with a splat. 'Tell me the truth, you little shit.'

My words won't come out. I shuffle backwards, press my back against the wall, and shake my head.

Robert said he can hear my mummy screaming through the walls. He said mummies aren't supposed to scream like this. He said his mummy buys him sweets and tucks him into bed. But my mummy just screams.

She grabs the hair on the top of my head, and pulls me along the floor so that she's kneeling next to me.

In her really deep, scary voice she says, 'Tell. Me. Now.' She breaks each word up, making her voice sound even more angry.

Everything feels wet and hot. My face is soggy, my throat is burning. I don't know what to do. I don't know where to look.

'It was my name,' I whisper. 'Just my name.'

Mummy waits, but I have nothing else to say. She swallows. 'And who wrote it?'

'Me. I did it.'

She laughs at me and pushes my face into the carpet. I see a clump of light-coloured hair in her hand, my hair. 'You can't write. Don't talk shit to me.'

'I've been learning. I saw it on the TV. Ted. Like a teddy bear. T. E. D.' Words are just spilling out of my mouth, but they seem to work. Mummy stops pushing me down onto the floor and I can feel her watching me as I cry into the floor with my arms wrapped around my head.

'You watch too much telly. You can stay in your room for a week for that.' She stomps across my room, her foot nudging the top of my leg as she leaves.

I *really* cry then. I'm just so glad Mummy believed me. I'm glad she didn't hit me this time.

Then I notice my trousers are wet. I don't think I will stop crying ever again.

Chapter Two

MICHELLE

Once again, sleep has evaded me. As I rouse myself from semi-slumber, my nightmare plays across my mind.

My mouth feels coated in fluff with the bitter aftertaste of bile. I reach out for the tumbler on my bedside table, and it wobbles as I grapple around. Peeking through tiny slits, I try again and grasp the glass, touching it to my lips. I hesitate, take a deep breath, then down the remaining red wine. A couple of mouthfuls won't hurt. It counts as one of my five a day, right?

I force my eyes open with my fingers and face my surroundings. Dirty clothes lie piled up at the end of my bed, plates caked with food remnants are strewn across the floor, and my muddy boots lie where I flung them in front of the wardrobe. It's a mess. My room is an accurate representation of my entire life.

I shrug it off, place my empty glass back down, and roll over to face the wall. My bed is so warm and cosy, and I feel my muscles relax into the soft mattress. Another ten minutes won't hurt.

Just as the world is starting to float away again, there's a tap on the door. I am jolted back to reality, and I groan.

'Morning, Michelle!' Kelsey's voice calls out from behind the door. It's way too early for Kelsey's chirpiness. She's like a character on Sesame Street. 'You've got work this morning, right?'

I roll onto my back and squeeze my fists. She knows I'm going to work today. She's only been reminding me every day for the last week. What is the polite way to tell your only friend to fuck off?

Before I can formulate words that don't contain an expletive, she bursts into my room.

'I've brought you some toast. And coffee.' She steps towards me and hesitates. Her eyes are immediately drawn to the bottles scattered by my bed. She scans my room and her lips curl in distaste. I should really clean up in here.

'Rough night?' she asks, her disdain quickly replaced by concern. 'I heard you in the night. You were shouting something. The nightmares are really getting to you, aren't they?'

Rough night? Try *rough life*. But Kelsey knows that more than anyone, so I keep quiet and just pull the covers over my head.

I hear Kelsey place the crockery down on my chest of drawers, and she perches on the end of my bed. I shuffle my feet over to stop them from rolling under her arse. For such a slim build, Kelsey sure seems to weigh a ton when she invades my space.

'Have you thought any more about seeing a therapist, like we talked about?'

I peer at her from behind my duvet. Actually, I have thought about it. A lot. But I can't do it, and I don't know how to get that through to her. Kelsey thinks talking through things fixes everything, and while that might work for little miss sunshine, my problems are too deep. Too complex. I wouldn't know where to start and I don't think I can open those wounds. They would never stop bleeding.

'Yes,' I tell her, and guilt gnaws at my stomach as I see her face light up with hope. 'But, Kelsey, I just can't. Can you please just try to understand that? Can you please get off my back?'

I shouldn't have snapped. An apology lurks in my mouth, but pride holds it in. I curse my stupidity.

She doesn't even bother to respond. We've had this conversation far too many times, and she knows the outcome. Instead, she slowly closes her eyes and sighs before re-facing me. The look of pity on her face makes me shrivel up and die inside.

I know she means well, but she's morphing from a friend into a mum, and it's driving me insane. I don't need a mum. Not now, not ever.

I met Kelsey when I was just six years old. We were placed in the same temporary foster home and we immediately had each other's backs. We were split up a number of times, but our lives became so entwined that we always found a way back to each other. We stuck together like glue.

What I need now is coffee. The bitter smell is wafting towards me and it's tickling my taste buds.

Kelsey has helpfully placed it out of reach on the chest of drawers, and I am naked. Fuck you, Kelsey.

Dammit. I'm tempted to throw back my duvet and reveal my full naked glory to her, dimply thighs and all. At least she'd scarper in embarrassment. But, modesty wins; besides, I don't have the energy.

'How do you feel about going back to work? Excited?' she asks me, oblivious to the urgent requirement of my caffeine fix.

I peel my eyes off the steaming mug. 'Not really. What is there to get excited about?'

Kelsey's eyes light up. 'Seeing your colleagues? And your clients? I bet they'll be over the moon to see you again.'

She's right there. I love my clients. Most of them, anyway. Some of them are a bit whiny, but their hearts are in the right place. That's the best thing about dogs. They love unconditionally and are happy to accept whatever you can offer in return. Even the damaged ones.

Kelsey beams at me and I realise I'm smiling. 'See? I knew you couldn't wait to go back.'

That's a massive overstatement, but I nod anyway. I really want that coffee.

There is a moment of silence before Kelsey slaps her knees and stands up.'Well, I had better get going. I need to finish get ready.'

'Ready for what? It's your day off.'

For the first time I notice something different about Kelsey. Her normally wavy hair bounces in thick, brown curls. Her already smooth face is coated in makeup, eyeliner flicks the corner of her deep brown, beautiful eyes. I glance down at her long legs that peek out of her dressing gown; she's shaved. There's something fishy going on here.

'I have a life outside of work, you know.' She scoops up the two empty wine bottles off the floor and flounces out of the room. I'm perplexed. Where is she going today, acting all coy? She's hiding something from me, which is weird, because Kelsey is a megaphone personified.

Whatever. It's coffee time.

I step out of bed, into the freezing cold room, grab the coffee, and despite my better judgement, climb back into bed. The coffee is black as the ace of spades – just the way I like it.

I give my armpits a sniff and get only a slight musty whiff, so I decide to skip the shower today. I'd rather spend a few more minutes in my nest.

***

I'm ten minutes late to work, but my boss, Maggie, acts like it's ten hours.

'What time do you call this?' she barks at me. 'Mr Davis and Bugz have been waiting fifteen minutes for you, and you waltz in here looking like you've been dragged through a hedge backwards. Sort it out, Michelle. And come and see me during your lunch break for a catch-up.'

She glances down at my Metallica T-shirt before storming into her office, slamming the door behind her. She can complain all she wants. I don't care. I just want to see Bugz. He's my absolute favourite client.

I walk into the reception area, raking my fingers through my shoulder-length hair. I head over to the section reserved especially for my grooming clients.

Maggie is particular about keeping my clients separate from those here to see a vet. Maybe she's worried my clients will catch some sort of disease or something. Or, perhaps she just wants to keep me apart from the higher-paying customers. Considering what happened last time I was here, I totally get it.

Bugz sees me first and bounds over, yanking his lead out of Mr Davis' hand. 'Bugz, come back!' he calls, but it's too late. Bugz has me pinned to a chair, and he's dragging his nose and tongue over my now slimy face. He's whimpering like he hasn't seen me in years. His butt sways side to side with the force of his wagging tail.

'Hey, boy. You missed me?' I run my hands over his long back, into his coarse fur. Bugz is an Irish wolfhound and his personality matches his size – big, bold, and beautiful, with a hint of chaos. Joy lifts me and my heart swells. This is what I needed.

'You bet he's missed you,' Mr Davis laughs. I like Mr Davis. He's down to earth and fun, unlike some of the other pompous bitches you get in here (the owners, not the canines). 'Where have you been? Bugz really needs a wash. He stinks. I haven't brought him in since you left.'

I clutch Bugz's massive head in my hands. 'I just had some time off to sort myself out.' Mr Davis nods knowingly, but I know he doesn't have a clue, really. 'I'll have him done for you in an hour, yeah?'

'Thanks, Michelle. The insides of his ears need a good clean, too,' Mr Davis calls over his shoulder. 'They're all manky from playing in the river.'

I hear Sharon, the receptionist, tut at our rowdy exchange and I beam at her, giving her a wink to emphasise the sarcasm. She just shakes her head and goes back to clacking her pointy fingernails on her keyboard.

'Come on, stinky boy. Let's give you a makeover.'

Bugz trots by my side as I lead him into the grooming room. Maybe I have missed work after all.

My hour locked away with Bugz offers me the perfect distraction from my fatigue and thoughts of my recurring nightmare. It seems that no matter how many years pass, I cannot let go. The abuse, the pain, the horror of it all.

If I stop for one second, I still see her face looking over me. Screaming. She's pointing at the back door. I am shaking at the thought of walking through it.

Bugz shakes himself off with such ferocity that water splatters onto the ceiling, snapping me back to the present. I laugh and he slurps my cheek in delight. 'No, Bugz. No kisses.' I push my forehead against his neck and give him a hug, and he quietens down, letting me linger against his warm fur.

***

Lunchtime arrives with little drama. A Labradoodle came in needing a trim, and Roxy, the Yorkshire Terrier, visited for her weekly skin treatment. My buddies. By the time I have them all pampered, my heart feels lighter.

My rare happiness all comes crashing down, however, when Maggie's head appears through the gap in the door. 'Time we had that chat, don't you think?' She has pulled her hair into a tight bun, giving her a dodgy facelift. Her pink lipstick is smudged on one side, making her lips look wonky.

'Sure, Mags,' I say, dropping the soggy towels onto the floor. She bristles. Mags hates it when I leave stuff lying around. She also hates being called 'Mags', and I stifle my laughter as I pass by her, heading out of the grooming room.

I enter her office and sit in one of the nasty blue plastic chairs that litter every room in the building. Maggie sits in the plush wheelie chair behind her desk.

'We just need a quick catch-up,' she says, pushing her fingers together like an evil headmistress. I feel intoxicated from my busy morning, escaping my past; or is it the wine I had with breakfast? I fight the urge to laugh, but a grin fights its way through. I bring my hand to my mouth to hide it.'I'm assuming a month off has allowed you to gather your thoughts?' she asks me.

If Maggie had given me a decade off, I still wouldn't have gathered my thoughts. The same thoughts spin around in my head like a merry-go-round. It's like my brain enjoys homing in on my past. On her. My heart, however, does not, and it makes me feel like I'm going crazy.

'Yes,' I lie. I really don't need any more agro. Kelsey has been on my back since Maggie kicked me out, and I can't be bothered listening to it anymore, especially from moaning Maggie. 'My thoughts are well and truly gathered.'

'Good.' Maggie crinkles her nose at me. 'You should know I've given Mrs Mason free monthly grooming for the next six months, so expect to see her soon.'

A groan slips out of my mouth.

'I wouldn't complain if I were you, Michelle. If it wasn't for Kelsey, you would have been fired a long time ago. You're lucky you have that girl in your corner.'

She's right. When we were teenagers, we were inseparable. We would have done anything for each other. But now, Kelsey has been watching me slip away for years and I know I am skating on very thin ice.

'Six months though?' I whine. 'Seems a bit drastic.'

When Maggie gets angry, she presses her fingertips together. Right now, she's pressing so hard it looks like her fingers are going to snap off. It's no surprise that she's mad. I nearly got the practice sued, and if it wasn't for Maggie working her magic with Mrs Mason, she could have reported me for assault. I should thank her. But I won't. I'm sure she knows deep down that I'm grateful.

'Look, Maggie. That woman is a well-known puppy farmer. And she was goading me,' I tell her for the hundredth time.

'Yes, yes. That is no excuse for hitting her, Michelle!'

'Hit?' I laugh. 'It was more of a tickle. I barely touched her.'

'Call it what you want. I'm pretty sure the police would disagree with you.' Maggie sighs. She's had enough. 'This is your last chance, Michelle. If I get a whiff of your bad attitude upsetting any of my customers or staff ever again, you can kiss your job goodbye.'

I know all of this already. I've pushed Maggie so many times and I'm still surprised she's kept me on. I guess being best mates with the top vet has its advantages.

Chapter Three

MICHELLE

I leave the practice feeling energised. It turns out that returning to work was good for me. Who knew? Playing with and snuggling up to my clients again has fed me a good dose of happiness, allowing me to let go, even if just for a little while.

To forget.

I decide to walk the long way home past the park. The evening is warm as summer clings to the air, and it's humid like a storm is brewing. Looking closely, I can see autumn beginning to peek through. The trees are touched with red and a few leaves are drifting to the floor. There's an earthy smell to the air that offers a sweetness associated with decay.

I love it.

I breathe in, letting the air fill me with a sense of calm. Today is a good day. Good days are rare, so I try to commit this one to memory with forced positive affirmations.

I am calm and at peace.

I am calm and at peace.

The park is full of screaming children, their parents praying they can tire them out for a prompt bedtime, so they can then spend the evening scrolling through their phones and ignoring their partners.

I slow down to watch the chaos. The twirly blue slide is proving a hit. Five children are queuing for their turn. Some are shoving each other, as their parents stand around chatting. A girl is crying about her friend squishing a bug. I smile, picturing Kelsey and myself at that age. Kelsey aggrieved and crying; me – the murderer.

'Jason!' a mother calls out from near the gate. A young lad with a mop of curly black hair spins his head to look at her from the roundabout. He doesn't move. He has a look of defiance on his face that makes me chuckle. This little guy isn't moving anywhere.

'Jason. Time to go.' The mum is bundling a tiny baby into one of those carrier things strapped to her body. Her cheeks are red, and she has massive bags under her eyes – the kind owned only by the mother of a newborn.

Jason crosses his arms, shakes his head and, to top it off, stomps a foot.

I wince and feel my pulse quicken and my eyes widen. I lean against the fence to watch how this scene plays out. Unless Jason gets his shit together pretty quickly, this will not end well.

The flustered mum calls out one more time, glancing around to see if anyone has noticed. Realising that all eyes are on her, she stomps over to her son, the baby bouncing against her rotund belly. Terror reaches Jason's eyes as she approaches him, and I gasp.

She grabs his arm and pulls him towards the gate. 'Mummy, no! You're hurting me!' Jason squeals. His voice pierces my ears. He tries to yank away from her, but I can see her fingers pinching into his tiny arm.

Jason screams and tries to pull away. His mum whips him around to face her. 'Don't you dare scream at me like that.' She doesn't raise her voice, but her tone cuts through the air. Everyone pretends they're not looking, but I know every eye is watching the scene unfold.

Someone do something to help him, I think. Should I intervene? To my horror, I find a tear running down my cheek. I brush it away and head towards them. I'm not sitting back and watching this shit. The kid is, what, five? Someone needs to stand up for him.

The gate squeals as I push it open. 'Hey!' I call out. 'Is everything okay here?'

Both Jason and his mum spin around to look at me.

'What's it to you?' she spits at me.

'I'm just checking if your boy's okay.' I shrug. I cannot take my eyes off Jason, who is now cowering behind his mum's chunky thighs.

'Oh, back off, lady. Come back when you've had some kids of your own. Of course he's fine.'

She takes Jason by the hand, and he jogs by her side as they head to the carpark where her Prius awaits. I feel everyone's eyes on me, but when I look around, they all quickly avert their gazes.

I watch the woman drive off before I leave the park in a hurry and continue my walk home, my good mood completely destroyed. Should I have intervened? Was it my place to say something? Is Jason going to be okay?

Shame overwhelms me. Doubt swirls in my stomach. Did I just step out of line? Is that what normal parenting looks like? I scuttle away as quickly as I can. Jason certainly looked okay. He was clean, happy, and he squeezed his mum's hand on the way back to the car without a care in the world. I just made a massive tit of myself.

When I was a kid, I dreamt of a knight coming to save me from Mum, or a superman or something. He never came. He didn't save me. I know I'm no superhero, but I also know that if I hadn't said anything, I wouldn't have been able to cope. My guilt would have gnawed away at me like every other crappy thing that has happened to me. No, I'm glad I stood up for the little guy. Even if all I did was embarrass myself.

Love was not a prominent feature in my childhood home. My parents didn't love me. Damn, I don't even think they loved each other very much. We all just existed in the same space. I was their human stress ball, only there to ease the pains of the daily grind. Eventually, our tenuous ties were severed, and I could let go. Only I never did. I'll forever remain haunted by their evil.

I could never understand my parents' attitude towards me. How can you hate a child so much? I often wondered if I had done something bad, something to deserve my punishment; but now I know the only 'bad' lived inside my parents. It was theirs to own. I just wish I could let go of that, instead of having the same shit thoughts dance around my head non-stop.

I once again contemplate Kelsey's suggestion of seeing a therapist, but I quickly shake it off.

I round the corner onto my street, and being a creature of habit, am drawn into the corner shop. Incense wafts into my nose, encasing my sinuses in the thick, heady smell. Items line each wall, seemingly at random, and touch the ceiling – from tins of beans, to Brillo pads and plastic kites. It's surely only a matter of time before the tower of tea bag boxes collapses onto some old biddy's head. How has Ravi never been sued?

'Alright, Ravs?' I call out to the large backside poking out from behind the counter. Ravi turns to face me, his usual smile planted on his face. I like Ravi. He has an innate ability to cheer me up.

'Shelly,' he calls over, plonking a box of lighters on the counter. 'Here for the usual?'

'Only if they're still on offer?' I wink at him.

'For you, always, my flower.'

I clunk two bottles of merlot onto the counter and throw a bag of peanuts on top. I'll need dinner at some point, and I'm a crap cook, so peanuts will have to do. Just like last night. And the night before.

'Eleven pounds forty please, love.' Ravi pushes the card reader toward me, and I tap it with my card.

'See you tomorrow,' he says as he rips off the receipt, a hint of laughter in his voice.

I throw a wave at him as I exit, taking my evening activity with me.

***

I walk through the front door and see Kelsey sitting on the sofa, waiting for me. She's pretending to watch some doctor drama on TV, but the second I throw my keys into the designated bowl, she turns to look at me, feigning surprise.

'Michelle! Hi. How did today go?'

'Fine.' I pull my boots off and realise I've tracked mud across the hallway. Kelsey follows my gaze and frowns.

'Any ... problems?'

'I was well-behaved, if that's what you're getting at.' Bloody hell, I've just walked through the door, and I'm already getting the third degree.

'Well, that's good. Maggie told me all was fine.'

She's spoken to Maggie? Then why the fuck did she bother asking?

'Coffee?' she asks, sensing my annoyance. She jumps off the sofa and claps her hands together, then skips through to the kitchen. Her black leggings exaggerate her long limbs. She looks like a horse navigating the hurdles.

'Not for me, thanks.' I follow her into the kitchen and hold up my bag, the glass bottles jangling together.

'Oh, Michelle. Not again,' she groans.

'It's fine. I'll just have one and save the other for another day.'

Kelsey huffs. 'No, you won't. I've heard that far too many times. You're lying to me and to yourself.'

Who does she think she is? My mum? What business is it of hers? I know she just cares, but sometimes it's just so ... suffocating.

'Look, you have a shift tomorrow. You need a clear head. You're just so angry, and the booze makes it worse. Why don't you have a cup of coffee and a biscuit instead? I've got Jammie Dodgers ...'

'It'll be fine. Stop stressing, will you?' What I long to say is that I *have* to drink. It numbs me. The nightmares still come in droves, but I just care that little bit less when I drink. She should be grateful that she has no idea what it's like to hurt so much that a bottle of wine is your only escape.

'Michelle,' Kelsey complains, her cheerful mask slipping. She points a teaspoon at me. 'I vouched for you to Maggie. My neck is on the line, and I can't save your arse again. Maggie is already being weird with me. I happen to like my job, and I don't want to lose it.'

Because of you ... The unspoken words dance between us, but I push them away.

I take a clean glass from the draining board and unscrew the cap on a bottle. The crimson liquid glugs noisily into the glass, and I feel my tongue moisten with anticipation.

'Oh please, you're her golden girl. She would never be mad at you. Please just back off, will you? I didn't ask you to speak up for me.' I know I sound like a complete brat, but I can't help myself. Truth is, I'm so glad I still have my job. When all is said and done, I need to pay my rent.

'No, but someone has to stick up for you before you self-destruct.' Kelsey sighs and pours the now-bubbling water over a tea bag. 'Michelle, I'm worried about you, that's all. You need to figure this out. You can't keep living like this. This isn't a life.'

Tears prickle my eyes and I look away. I walk back into the living room to put some space between us. She's right, of course. She always is, but she needs to realise that there is no way out for me. This is my life. This is me.

Wait a minute ... what's that? I pluck out a rogue sock tucked behind a sofa cushion. This is odd. Kelsey isn't one for leaving laundry lying around, and I'm damn sure it isn't mine.

It's black with lime green stripes, and it's huge. A man's sock. I look up at Kelsey, who is now peering over my shoulder. She's blushing over her mug and her eyes are wide with shame. Our argument evaporates.

I grin at her. 'Had a bit of sofa fun, have we, Kels?' I can hear the sneer in my voice, but I don't care. This is so out of character for Kelsey. She's so straight-laced she's practically a corpse, and I'm enjoying having one over on her for once. 'What was it? Doggy style? Reverse cowgirl? A little ... blow job? Must be a true gent if he took his socks off for you.' I grunt with laughter.

'Oh, Michelle, grow up,' she snaps and sips her tea. She breathes deeply before taking the plunge. 'I've met someone, actually.' Her tone is so serious that I swallow my sneer, sharpish. She sits gently on the sofa and folds her legs underneath her.

This can't be good news. I've always felt safe knowing that Kelsey would never kick me out, because she needs someone to share the rent. Now though, if this is serious, she may have found someone else to take on the financial burden. And Kelsey doesn't do casual, so this does not bode well.

I perch on the edge of the sofa next to her. I take a big gulp and the wine slips down my throat with ease.

'His name is Travis. We met at the Vet Show in Birmingham. He was there accompanying his sister, who is studying for her veterinary science degree, and we just got talking over a dog toy stand.'

Shit. That was months ago. She's kept this secret for a long time. This isn't looking good. 'So, it's serious then?'

She nods. I shift my legs to get more comfortable and slosh some wine onto my shirt. I glance at the stain, but choose to ignore it. Kelsey's hands twitch at the mess.

'You could have told me.' I sound like a petulant child and, as much as I will myself to just stop and be happy for Kelsey, I just can't. Kelsey deserves better than me. She deserves this Travis guy who makes her smile from ear to ear.

'I want you to meet him,' she says, and I groan into my wine. I know it's rude, but I really don't want to meet Kelsey's boyfriend. Living with Kelsey has always offered a simplicity that I crave and now I worry things have suddenly become so much more complicated. I don't want to introduce someone new into our lives. Three is a crowd after all.

'Please, Michelle. This is important to me.'

And I owe her. The words hang over us. Kelsey has supported me through so much. All the dramas at work, my nightmares, the fits of rage. She has stood by me throughout, and now I need to stand by her.

'Fine,' I agree. Though I'm lying – and she knows it.

I take my wine to bed.

Chapter Four

MICHELLE

Pain rips through my skull and pierces my eyeballs. The wine bottles sit empty on my bedside table, along with the whiskey bottle I had stashed under my bed. I don't even remember drinking that.

My bedside clock is yelling at me, forcing me into consciousness. I made a promise to Kelsey last night that I would pull myself together. Find a counsellor or something. Drink less. Oops – I think it's safe to say I fell at the first hurdle.

Oh, well. Today is a new day.

I pull myself out of bed and stagger into the bathroom. I brush my teeth in record time and pull on my jeans and a clean top, kicking yesterday's wine-stained shirt into the laundry pile.

It's ten past eight. I have exactly twenty minutes to walk the mile to work. I can do this. Even with an angry hangover weighing me down.

***

'You're late,' Maggie calls over from the reception desk the second I walk through the door. I look at my watch: 08:33. Oh, please. I walk straight past Maggie without even a glance and head into the grooming room, pushing the door closed behind me. I hear Maggie tittering with Sharon, no doubt about how useless I am. Screw it, my first client isn't even here yet. What is there to stress about?

Bile burns the back of my throat, threatening to make a spectacular piece of art on the grooming room floor.

The water cooler in the corner of the room screams at me and I glug three cups, refreshing my senses. I blow air out through pursed lips and with my eyes to the heavens, scrabble around for a strength I know must be in me somewhere. My breaths come in short, sharp pants and even I can smell the alcohol sticking to the back of my throat. I get myself another cup of water and sip it more slowly.

Why do I do this to myself? Drinking always feels like a good idea at the time, but then my hangovers dish out a massive dose of regret.

I brace myself, getting myself ready to take on the day. I can do this. Providing Maggie leaves me the hell alone.

I thank God when my first client doesn't show, giving me ample time to sit and muse over Kelsey's revelation last night.

If she met this Travis guy at the Vet Show, then they've been seeing each other for four months. She's obviously been sneaking him into the house, as evidenced by the sock. I moan with shame. It's Kelsey's house, but she's sneaking guests in. Does she really think I can't handle guests? Or is it because she's embarrassed by me?

Kelsey is right. I have to change. It's one thing to ruin my life, but I can't go ruining hers, too. Kelsey is a pain in my arse sometimes, but she has a heart of gold. She deserves to be happy. She doesn't deserve me fucking things up for her.

I pull my phone out of my pocket and Google therapists in the local area. I get over one hundred hits. I didn't realise there were that many messed up people in this town. It's scary if you think about it.

I click on a few and I'm met with smiles and empathetic eyes. It makes me feel nauseous again. I cannot do this. I cannot have those eyes bore into me while I expose my inner pain. It just isn't me. I'll find another way.

I slam my phone down on the table and pace around the room. I can't change. I know that. and I refuse to get sucked in by false hope. There must be a way to make Kelsey think I'm trying. If she thinks I'm trying to change, she might not kick me out. I mean, I could give up the booze, but that's as likely as Maggie turning into a nice person.

Sharon pokes her head through the gap in the door. 'Michelle, your nine-thirty appointment is here. You are going to love this dog. He's a big slobbery mess – just your type,' Sharon scoffs. She's a cat person.

I leap up, ready to meet my new client.

Sharon was right. Felix is a thing of beauty. He's a two-year-old boxer packed with so much personality and swagger I want to take him home and keep him forever.

'He needs a good wash,' his owner, Pamela, tells me with the poshest accent I've ever heard. She clearly didn't grow up with a silver spoon in her mouth. It was the entire cutlery drawer. 'He's rolled in something disgusting, and I can't shift the smell. And could you clip his nails while you're at it?'

Her eyes bore into mine, not once drifting away, even when Felix tries his hardest to get her attention with his best singing voice.

I just nod. Suddenly, I feel very aware of my council estate accent.

Pamela drifts off to do a 'spot' of shopping, while I massage Felix with a skin-soothing shampoo. He smells all citrussy, and he groans when I drag my fingers through his chocolate-brown fur. When I stop, he paws at my hands, his blazing eyes eager for me to continue.

'Oh, Felix.' I laugh at him. 'We need to dry you off before Mummy gets back.' On cue, Felix shakes droplets of water all over me and I lunge at him with a towel. I wrap it around him and can't resist giving him a big hug. He stands still, accepting my affection.

This is the therapy I need. Maybe Kelsey will let me get a dog. My stomach tingles with desire. But, my hope is immediately dashed when I remember the last time we had this conversation. 'Until you can take care of yourself, I just don't think taking on extra responsibility is a good idea.' She was, and is, probably right.

I'm sitting on the floor in front of Felix. He's kneeling on his front legs, his butt in the air as if he is about to pounce, tail wagging furiously. He's waiting for my next nose-boop, but the door opens, ruining our fun.

'He's fond of you,' Pamela says, creeping up behind me. 'He barely noticed my arrival.'

'He's a good boy. We've had a great time together,' I say, giving Felix one last head scratch. I head to the hook by the sink to collect his lead, then attach it to his collar. Pamela reaches out and takes the lead off me, her eyes not leaving my ever-reddening face. I feel exposed.

She squints at me. 'He smells divine, too. I'll be bringing him in more often. Maybe then my house will smell less dog-like.'

I fake a laugh. I don't really have much to say. Pamela clearly comes from wealth. She's well-spoken and dressed in a cream suit, accented by a crisp rose-pink blouse underneath. Massive diamonds hang from her ears. I can't pick her age exactly. She has the skin of a woman in her forties, but the air of someone with vast life experience, so I put her in her early fifties.

'I'd better head off. Things to do, people to see. But, can I give you one of these?' She slips a business card into my hand. No wonder she's rich, touting her business wherever she goes. 'We're currently looking for volunteers, so if you know anyone looking for some experience, tell them to dial my number. Though I think you might find it somewhat beneficial for yourself.'

I nod, give her a shy smile, and push the card into my back pocket. I don't want to bin it while she's still in the room.

She heads to the door, but just as I am about to release a sigh of relief, she pauses at the threshold and drums her fingers on the doorframe. It feels like she's reading me. I shuffle over to the table and pick up Felix's towel. The table stands between us, a shield against her scrutiny.

Then, without another word, she takes off, Felix trotting by her side.

I stand frozen to the spot. What just happened? I pull the card out of my pocket and start towards the bin, but curiosity gets the better of me and I glance down at it. Let me guess, lawyer? Business analyst (whatever that is)? Maybe some sort of life coach? Something that earns mega money.

I raise my eyebrows.

SPEAK UP – Giving All Children a Voice

Underneath the words are a web address and a phone number. I flip the card over and emblazoned on the back are pictures of children smiling up at me, their arms wrapped around each other like they're sharing a private joke.

Intrigued, I take my phone out of my coat pocket and punch the website into Google.

The website is a concoction of yellows and oranges. 'NEED SOMEONE TO TALK TO?' one banner asks. 'HAVING A HARD TIME?'

There are images of cowering children. Children in floods of tears, clutching teddy bears in their tiny hands. Every single muscle in my body tenses up.

The messages encourage children to call the helpline if they want someone to vent to. Someone to spill their secrets to; someone they can trust. It's a safe place for children living in trauma. I tremble as I scan the words. I don't understand how this service should need to exist. We live in such a messed up world.

Behind all the PR chatter, Speak Up is essentially a call centre for children who need someone to talk to.

The helpline provides a shoulder to cry on. They offer advice and a sounding board. All in the hope it will equip the child with the confidence to act boldly, stand up, and break the chain of abuse, knowing there are people out there to help them.

And all of this is led by Pamela Greene. Founder.

What a woman.

Tears are pouring down my cheeks. Where was Pamela when I was a little girl? I needed this. An outlet. Somewhere safe.

This is perfect.

I shove the card into my back pocket again and continue with my day.

I try to focus on my afternoon clients, but my thoughts keep bouncing back to Speak Up. I can't shift the feeling that this Pamela woman knew I needed this. Is this the salvation I've been looking for? My therapy?

***

I leave the grooming room at 4pm to head home just as Kelsey comes bouncing out of consulting room one. She's wearing her navy blue scrubs and pulling her coat on. She's on a later shift today, so I'm surprised to see her leaving.

'Hey, Kelsey! Where are you sneaking off to?'

Kelsey stops in her tracks. 'Hardly sneaking, Michelle. It's my lunch break.' A smile creeps across her face and she cocks her head to the side. It's her signature move when she thinks she's got one over on you. 'You seem chirpy. Good day?'

'Do I? Oh.' I don't think anyone has ever referred to me as 'chirpy', and I don't like it. 'Just in a good mood, I suppose.'

'Fancy going for a coffee? I've got just over an hour until Jasper comes in for dialysis.'

'Oh, poor Jasper. I miss that crazy Cocker.' Jasper used to come to me for regular grooming, but his owners can't afford it now that he's been diagnosed with kidney disease. I glance at my watch. Who am I trying to kid? I've got nowhere to be and I don't want to go home just to sit on my own. I know it, and Kelsey knows it. 'Sure,' I say, surprised by the enthusiasm in my voice. Maybe I *am* chirpy this afternoon.

Today feels good.

We walk in the blustery weather to the coffee shop around the corner. It's one of those places that stinks of grease, and there's grime smeared across the walls, but the food is so bloody delicious that the general grossness is forgivable.

We each grab a stool at the breakfast bar in the window. Kelsey orders a tuna salad and a carton of Ribena, and I opt for a bacon and egg sandwich and a can of ginger beer. I can't remember the last time I ate properly and my mouth waters when I place my order. It's the perfect antidote to my lingering hangover.

We wait for our food in silence, watching the world pass by. Kelsey leans back on her stool without a care in the world. I am envious of her relaxed demeanour. I chew on my nails and contemplate the yin and yang of our relationship.

Finally, I break the ice.

'Sorry for how I acted yesterday. I should have been more supportive about the whole boyfriend thing.' I cringe at the memory of our conversation. After agreeing to meet Travis, I then stormed off like a petulant teenager. I avoided Kelsey all night after that.

'He isn't my boyfriend.' Kelsey blushes.

'But you want him to be?'

Kelsey drums her fingers on the table and avidly watches a man walk across the road, the wind whipping his coat around him. 'Yes,' she finally admits. 'Michelle, I really like him. I think you will, too – if you just give him a chance.'

'Well, if you like him, he must be a really good guy,' I say, attempting to give Travis the chance Kelsey deserves. Or, at least pretend like I am. 'So, I like him already.'

Kelsey bites the inside of her cheek and continues to stare out of the window. Finally, she makes eye contact with me and smiles. She looks stunning. Unlike me, Kelsey never wears make-up, but she just doesn't have to. My eyeliner is my armour, and my shell is so fragile I have to apply it thickly. Kelsey looks so fresh-faced next to me. Her Bambi eyes are enormous and her lashes flutter like a fucking Disney princess. She's such a lucky cow.

She squeezes my hand in my lap. 'Thanks, Mich,' she squeals into my ear.

The waitress dumps our plates on the table and walks back to play on her phone behind the counter. I rub my hands together at the prospect of my piping hot food.

'What's happened to you today? You're different.' Kelsey pokes me on the shoulder, making me bristle.

'Different?'

'Yeah. Like, enthusiastic.'

I chuckle. It's ridiculous that my happiness is a shock to her. I need to work on that.

'You know you keep telling me to find something that will help me heal? Well, I think I've found it.' I shovel more sandwich into my mouth.

'You're seeing a therapist? Oh, Michelle, that's amazing news! I knew you would sort something out.'

'No, not a therapist.' Egg yolk drips down my chin and I lean across Kelsey to grab a napkin. 'I'm going to volunteer at a local charity.'

There's a pause while Kelsey processes what I've just told her. 'Doing what?'

Good question. I hadn't actually thought about that. My thoughts have primarily been on the charity itself, not my role within it. I pull the card out of my pocket and slide it across the table to Kelsey. She picks it up and turns it over a few times, taking it in.

'This looks perfect for you,' she finally says, a smile spreading across her face. 'Oh, Michelle. I'm so pleased for you. This can be the new start you desperately need.'

Chapter Five

TEDDY

Mummy told me to go outside and get some fresh air. So, I'm standing in the backyard.

I wish we had a bigger garden. With grass. And room to run around a bit.

It's drizzling outside and so cold it makes my skin sting. The clouds are really dark grey and low down. I think it's going to tip it down soon.

I go to sit in the corner by the shed where I like to count the slabs on the floor. Fourteen. I've counted them over and over, and I get bored quickly.

One time, when Mummy was swaying from side to side and in a really good mood, she took me to a park. It was dark outside and really quiet, so I think it was nighttime, but I had the best fun. I can still remember the whooshing feeling in my tummy when I went down the slide.

Mummy can be a good person sometimes.

Just not very often.

Sometimes I like to imagine I'm back at that park. I'm thinking about it now. I think about what would happen if I was to open the garden gate and leave. Would they even notice if I escaped for a little while to play on the swings?

That's a stupid idea. I don't know how to find the park on my own.

'Thick twat,' I mumble to myself, smacking my forehead with my hand.

'Oh man, it's chilly today,' the whisper comes over the wall. The weather is our secret password. Robert thought of it a little while ago. He's really clever. You must learn lots at school.

'It's okay,' I whisper back. 'They're sleeping on the sofa. Just be super quiet.'

'Okay. Mummy wants to talk to you. Hang on.' I hear his feet skip across the slabs in their backyard. I tuck my feet in and hug my knees to my chest. Why does his mummy want to talk to me? Is she going to tell me off for speaking to Robert? She probably doesn't want someone like me talking to Robert.

My heart is beating really fast. I hope she's quiet. I hope she doesn't ask to speak to my mum. I stand up again and wait, hopping from one foot to the other.

I wish I had somewhere to run to. Somewhere to hide. I think about hiding in the shed, but it's dark in there and I really don't want to get bitten by a spider. I really hate spiders.

Suddenly, a lady's head pops over the wall. It's the first time I have ever actually seen someone from the house next door. The wall is taller than Daddy. I imagine Robert's mummy is standing on a chair or step.

I like her face; she looks prettier than my mummy and has less lines on her face. Her hair is brushed into a nice bump on the back of her head and bits of hair have fallen out round the front of her face. She looks friendly. Nice.

I step back against the shed door, trying to put some space between us.

'You must be Teddy.' She's whispering. Robert must have told her to keep quiet, so my breathing slows down a bit. 'I'm Stacey. It's lovely to meet you at last. Bobby has told me all about you.' She smiles at me, but her eyes look sad. 'Your mam and dad not around?'

'They're sleeping,' I say.

'Sleep a lot, do they?'

'Only after they've had a drink or their medicines.' I don't like the look this lady is giving me. She looks angry. Is she going to tell me off?

But, she just tuts at me and glances at the house.

'Take their *medicines* often?'

I stare at the ground. I feel wrong talking to this lady about Mummy and Daddy.

She carries on talking, and it makes me want to cry. 'I hear them through the wall sometimes. Screaming and shouting. My fella, Barry, told me not to get involved, but I've got to do something. You know?'

But, I *don't* know. I don't know what's happening. I just want to go inside. I don't want this lady to talk to me anymore.

'I called them but social services were bloody useless. My sister told me they take a while, not enough resources apparently, but this is just ridiculous. They're doing absolutely nothing.' She looks down at where I think Robert must be standing.

I don't know what she is saying. Who are social services? What should they be doing? Has she told them about me?

'I'll keep pushing for you though, you poor boy. I'd take you myself if it wasn't considered kidnapping.'

There's a sound inside the house and my stomach goes all twisty. I snap my head around to see what made the sound. Please don't let my mummy see this lady.

There's no one there.

The lady is watching me, her eyes all squinty. 'We'll make this quick,' she says, throwing something over the wall at me. I stare down at it. I don't want to pick it up. It's just a little card with a big number on it. 'Call these guys if you need help.'

My body jolts into action and I pick up the card. I stare up at her. I don't know what to say.

'You got a house phone, right?'

I nod, but I don't know why. I'm not allowed to use it.

'Well, copy those numbers on that card there into the phone, then someone will be on the phone to help you. You need a professional to talk to. Someone who might be able to get you out of this shithole.'

'Mum!' Robert mutters from the other side of the wall.

Stacey looks down at him and smiles. 'Sorry kiddo, I shouldn't have said a naughty word.'

I glance at the house. There are no sounds coming from inside; no one is moving. If I squint to look through the net curtains, I can see my mummy leaning back in her armchair, her mouth open, probably snoring.

I remember Mummy and Daddy getting a letter a few weeks ago. Mummy opened it and her face went bright red. 'Did you tell someone about us?' She gave the letter to my dad, who read it, his mouth moving as he read. I knew the letter was about me, because he kept looking up at me. I tried to squish myself into the back of the sofa to hide, but it was no good. They beat me anyway.

'Teddy!' Daddy calls out from the house, making me jump out of my skin. He must want me to get him a beer. I look at the lady, praying she'll leave before he comes outside.

'Keep safe, won't you kid? I can't bear to think of what they're doing to you in that hellhole.'

'See you later, Teddy,' Robert calls out from over the wall. I imagine him holding his mum's hand as they walk back into their cosy house where they keep their toys and hugs.

Footsteps.

'Where are you? You better not be ignoring me, you little shit.'

I run back to the corner where I was sitting before, shoving the card into my pants just as Daddy clicks the door open.

'Oi! What do you think you're doing? I might as well get my own fucking beer now. Get in here, now!'

I don't need telling twice. I squeeze past his massive body in the doorway and take my place on the edge of the sofa, waiting for my next orders.

The card digs into the top of my leg, and I feel excited and nervous at the same time.

I just have to wait for them to go out, and I'm going to call this person. I'm going to be brave.

Chapter Six

MICHELLE

I feel dizzy. My mind is running a hundred miles an hour. Talking to Pamela on the phone about volunteering was overwhelming. Her voice went up an octave when I introduced myself, and I found myself quickly making an appointment to meet up just to end the cheeriness. I then spent two days in a fit of nerves, anticipating what tonight might bring.

The Rose and Crown Pub is just down the road from the Speak Up offices, and I can't resist popping in for a quick glass of wine to soothe my nerves. After one, my stomach still feels queasy, so I have a swift bourbon before I leave. I still feel like shit, but I'm going to be late, so I throw my bag over my shoulder and head out into the rain.

As I approach the building now, I'm so nervous I worried I might bite through my lip. I didn't know what to wear, so I opted for my smartest black jeans and a plain dark green T-shirt under my leather jacket. I don't have any other decent shoes, so my boots had to do.

Where the hell is it? The address Pamela gave me is a second-hand furniture shop. Is this a joke? I pace up and down the street a few times and I am on the verge of giving up and going home to a bottle of vodka, when I hear Pamela call my name.

'Michelle, over here!' Her voice is sing-songy, like she's auditioning for *The Sound of Music.*

I head over to her, and she greets me by a tiny grey door tucked into a little alcove next to the furniture shop. She's wearing a knee-length dress of the palest blue, her tiny waist tucked in with a wide golden belt. I feel scruffy in comparison.

To my embarrassment, she welcomes me with a hug which I cannot bring myself to reciprocate, so she clings to my limp form, unaware of my unease. She smells like she's bathed in Chanel No. 5.

'I am so glad you made it. Come upstairs and meet the team,' she says, leading the way.

We head up the rickety stairs and enter the offices that sit above the furniture shop. The reception area is light and airy, and I'm surprised to hear a hubbub of noise greet me as we near the main office. Pamela opens the door to an open plan room painted a vibrant shade of yellow. It's a stark contrast to the dank weather outside.

There must be twenty people in here, all sitting behind desks and wearing headsets either on their heads or pushed down around their necks. Some are between calls, so give me a cheery 'hello'. Others wave to me, chatting away on the phone. A couple don't look up, seemingly too engrossed in their conversation.

In the centre of the room, a girl with bright red hair sits with her head buried in her hands. My heart goes out to her. I can feel her anguish from over here. But, then a bearded man who resembles Father Christmas wheels his chair over to her and puts a hand on her shoulder.

The atmosphere is supportive and kind, and I feel my hardened shell crack a little. Pamela leads me into her office at the other end of the call centre. She plops into the seat behind her colossal desk and motions for me to sit opposite her.

'Thank you so much for coming this evening. We really appreciate the support.' She leans back in her swivel chair and presses her manicured hands on the desk. 'I have a couple of volunteers heading back to university soon, and I'm worried we'll be too short-handed to make the impact we've become accustomed to.' She smiles at me, waiting for a response, but I don't know what to say.

'Erm. No problem. What is it you need me to do?' When I first asked this question during our phone conversation, Pamela was vague and brushed me off with a lot of charity buzzwords – something about *guidance* and *impact*.

'You'll be taking calls, of course,' she says, shrugging. 'We need more telephone counsellors to listen to children in trouble.' She says it like it's obvious, but alarm bells are ringing loud in my head.

I'm not qualified to talk to abused kids. I thought I'd be doing some filing or something. No, this isn't me. I can't do this. How do I get myself out of this? I shift in my seat and point my feet toward the door.

Pamela senses my unease. 'Michelle, you can relax. I will personally provide appropriate, thorough training.' Her smile eases my discomfort a little, but my stomach is still doing cartwheels. Does this woman usually take such a personal interest in all her volunteers? Something tells me she doesn't. She's far too important, surely?

'I assume you have read about Speak Up and what we do?'

I nod. I have read through the website over and over. Pamela has won awards for her charitable excellence.

'So, you know the sort of cases we handle?'

'Yeah, I think so. Kids being hit and stuff.'

'Yes, but not always. Abuse comes in all forms, sadly. They might be neglected, they might be sexually abused; or yes, physical harm is a common denominator, like you say. We want to be an ear for children when they need to talk. We offer advice and kindness. And we always promise confidence. A child can always remain anonymous until they're ready to either speak up themselves, or let us speak up on their behalf.'

Advice? Kindness? Where is the action? Where is the actual help?

'So, you don't actually help them, then?' I bark. I cannot keep my tone neutral. What's the point of this if they don't get them out of there? Stop the abuse. What good does talking do if they don't take action?

'We help them, Michelle. We just realise these things take time. I've reported over one hundred cases to social services since I started this project twenty-four years ago. That's over one hundred children who would not have been helped otherwise. Not to mention the children who have found the courage to seek help themselves. Or sometimes we just have to be satisfied knowing we have made a child's life better for the few minutes we were on the phone with them.'

I sip the glass of water in front of me, my hands trembling. My throat is dry, and I have difficulty swallowing, but I am hoping the distraction will prevent me from bursting into tears. It's like Pamela has poked at my pain points with a sharp pin.

'Will you help us, Michelle?' Pamela asks. 'I really do think you will be an asset to the team.'

I want to run and never come back. But, a bigger part of me wants to wrap my arms around every child going through what I had to endure, and this would be a start. I can talk. Offer kindness.

I can help get them out.

Plus, maybe this is my chance to fix the mess Mum left of my heart.

I nod. 'Okay. What do I need to do?'

***

Pamela gives me a whirlwind tour of the office. I'm introduced to the team. They all chat cheerfully to me, like this office isn't full of misery and devastation. I admire their ability to disconnect themselves from each phone call, and I pray I have the strength to do the same.

Pamela takes me over to a desk tucked away in the corner where a woman resembling Shrek is sitting. 'This is Lisa, our Office Manager. As well as taking calls, she manages everyday office duties and takes care of the team rota. If you need anything, feel free to speak to her.'

Lisa pushes away her headset. 'Pleased to meet you,' she says with a startlingly girly voice. 'We could use another set of hands.' Her eyebrows remain knitted together and her mouth pinches up in a sneer. She doesn't look pleased to meet me. She looks like she's stepped on dog shit.

'Hiya,' I mumble. My cheeks feel warm. Lisa's arms are as thick as trees. I reckon she could chuck me across the room like a javelin, and I have to fight the temptation to hide behind Pamela.

To my relief, Pamela thanks Lisa and takes my elbow. She leads me into the kitchen, where she flicks the kettle on. 'Don't worry, Lisa is grumpy with everyone. It's in her nature.' She takes two mugs out of a cupboard over the sink. 'I'll be doing most of your observations. Lisa is mainly here to keep everyone in line. I can't have people promise me the world and then just not turn up. The children need consistency. Lisa is the muscle of the operation. She does a fantastic job. Are you a tea or coffee kind of girl?'

'Coffee, please. Black, one sugar,' I say, but I could really murder a vodka right now.

Pamela places a *Speak-Up*-emblazoned mug full of steaming coffee on the table and I scoop it between my hands, the warmth settling my trembling fingers.

'I sense you're feeling a little uneasy?' Pamela asks me, sitting down opposite me at the tiny table. Our knees are practically touching, and I inch my body away from her.

The way Pamela looks at me brings a lump to my throat. This woman is caring. Love runs through her veins. She leans forward, as if to grasp my destructive feelings and take them away from me.

And I long to give them to her. I fill my lungs with air.

It's time to be honest. I have been drowning for so long, and every time Kelsey has thrown me a life ring, she's missed. Maybe Pamela, with all of her experience, has a better aim. I've got to at least try.

'I'm not sure I can do this, Pamela,' I admit.

Pamela nods and sips her fruity tea. 'I thought you'd say that. Most people do. But, I think you're more capable than you realise. I see a strength in you.' Her eyes twinkle at me and I want to believe her, but it feels like a massive wall stands between us. 'There's something about you. A certain quality I have been looking for.'

'Pamela ... ' I stall. I don't know how to tell her I am not who she thinks I am. I'm not special, and I'm definitely not strong enough to speak to children who need help. The help I so desperately needed myself, all those years ago. I don't know how to explain how selfish I am for wanting to run away.

'Please, call me Pam. Talk to me. There's no judgement here.' She leans back in her chair, cupping her hot pink tea.

I can't. I can only sit in silence, staring at a brown smudge on the table. It's a stalemate. Neither of us wants to break the silence. Pamela

– Pam – is completely at ease and unaware of my rising temperature. My armpits feel damp, and I clamp my arms down by my side.

Then the noise inside my brain becomes too loud, and I snap.

'I was abused. You know, when I was a kid.' The words spill out of my mouth. I have no clue where they came from. 'From as early as I can remember, I spent most nights sleeping in the garage. My mum would hit me and push me through the back door into this cold, dark box. It was like a coffin.' I spit the words out like they're toxic.

Then they're gone. It's as if a huge weight has been lifted off my shoulders. Tears pierce my eyes and I blink them away before they fall.

Pam just nods at me, encouraging me to go on. She really is good at this.

'And I don't know if I can do this. You know, talk to these kids. If I couldn't help myself, how am I supposed to help them? It would be like I'm pretending. Lying to them.' To my horror, a tear escapes and slides down my cheek. I wipe it away with my sleeve.

'But, don't you see? It's your history that equips you with the exact skills these children need. You know what it's like to be in their shoes, so you know how vital it is to help them. You couldn't escape your parents because you didn't have someone like *you* in your corner. These children need you.

'Michelle, the pain you experienced is your strength. Something good can come out of all that mess.'

More tears slip down my cheeks, but I let them fall now. Heat washes through me and the burden I've been carrying on my chest for my entire life breaks apart a little. The pressure reduces and my head clears. Slowly, I place my mug on the table and then bury my face in my hands.

I sob hysterically. I sense Pam standing up and closing the door behind me, providing us privacy, and allowing me to grieve the childhood I never had. She places a tissue in my hand, and I breathe in its coconut scent.

'Sorry,' I mumble. 'I don't know what's happening to me.' I fold the tissue in half, hiding the snot streaks.

Pam chuckles. 'I think you're supposed to be here, Michelle. I think this is your path.'

She's so corny. But so right. This is my path. For the first time in my life, I believe in fate. It's my fate to be here.

Things are becoming clearer now. I need to do this.

Chapter Seven

MICHELLE

Kelsey shrieks at me as I walk through the door. It's ten o'clock and I'm exhausted and ready to climb into bed, but Kelsey has other ideas.

'How did it go?' she asks, thrusting a champagne flute into my hand. I throw the ring binder Pam gave me onto the sofa, grateful to let go of the physical and metaphorical weight, and take a sip of the bubbly liquid. I think it's prosecco, but something tastes a bit off. Something dodgy is going on here. I take another sip and watch Kelsey's cheeks pinken. For Christ's sake, it's non-alcoholic.

Some celebration.

Kelsey plops onto the sofa and twists to face me.

'Good,' I tell her. 'I think.' I certainly feel a bit more confident now, but *good* might be stretching it a little.

Kelsey looks like she's going to burst. I get it. She's been putting up with my mood swings and downright offensive remarks for years now.

I'm an absolute mess and she has always been there to clean me up. My unexpected change in enthusiasm must feel like bliss to her.

A fire has been lit inside me, and I don't know what caused the spark. Was it Speak Up? Pam? Me?

'What will you be doing there?'

I shrug. If I look too keen, Kelsey will make a massive deal out of it, and I know it will just feed my nerves. 'Answering calls. Counselling. I have a ton of stuff to learn first, though.' I gesture at the folder lying next to her, which contains everything I need to know about Speak Up and my role in it. 'A spot of light reading,' I jest, mimicking Pam.

Kelsey whistles. 'Well, that will keep you busy,' she says. I know what she wants to say, though: something to stop you from drinking. Maybe she's right.

I smile, but sadness washes over me as I watch Kelsey flick through my file. Kelsey looks so relieved at my change in attitude, and I finally see things through her eyes. I've been so unfair to her. I love Kelsey. She's the only person I have on this entire planet, and I've treated her like shit. I've said some cruel things.

My mind casts back to a fight we had a few months ago. I'd left a coffee-stained mug in my room until it grew a gruesome fungus, and I genuinely thought I was helping by leaving it in the sink unwashed.

Kelsey, who is usually so jovial, absolutely lost it with me.

'What the fuck is wrong with you?!' she screamed, launching the mug into the bin. I just stood there, my eyes flicking between the mug shards in the bin and Kelsey with her hands on her hips, her dark, wavy hair wild. I couldn't figure out what had made her snap. Was it something at work? She always gets emotional when she's had to euthanise an animal, but she usually tells me when she needs some space. I couldn't figure out why she was so testy.

I was a fucking idiot.

'Clean up your own shit, Michelle. And while you're at it, sort your fucking life out.'

Then she stormed off with tears in her eyes. I stood there in shock. I'd never seen Kelsey so mad and her outburst had completely thrown me.

I was such a fool. How has she even put up with me for so damn long?

I have an urge to hug her, but shrug it off. Baby steps.

Talking about me makes me feel exposed, so I shift the conversation back to her.

'When do you want me to meet Travis? I have high expectations for this super hunk, you know. I won't just let any old chump be with you.'

Kelsey giggles and looks away. She isn't used to me being nice. Damn, *I'm* not even used to me being nice. It sets my teeth on edge.

'How about next week? He's working nights this week.' She looks at me with eyes wide open. I instinctively start to shake my head, but stop myself. I can't wipe that eager look off her face. Not now that we're getting along so well.

'Sounds like a plan,' I say. I down the rest of my disappointing drink and say goodnight. I want to devour some of this paperwork before I go to sleep. As absurd as it sounds, I want to ace this.

I leave Kelsey looking pleased with herself. Like she's won an epic battle.

I guess she has. I guess we both have.

***

The file is horrifying. It contains case study after case study of children who have gone through so much more than I did – beatings, starvation, rape. Children who have never experienced love. One boy in Scotland had never even experienced light. What the fuck is that about?

According to the file, a little over two years ago, one little boy reached out to Speak Up after finding his mother beaten to death by her ex-boyfriend. She had been lying dead on the living room floor for four days before he found the courage to call. He'd been eating the food in the freezer and slept by her solid corpse every night.

He was four years old.

I'm exhausted. I cannot even bring myself to read the transcripts of example calls made to the charity. It feels like a punch to the stomach, and I don't know whether I can help these children. What do I say to them? Those who work there must be some sort of superheroes, minus the capes.

I'm not a superhero; I'm not even adequate. I'm just your average loser.

Feeling dejected, I push the file to the end of the bed and drift off to sleep.

It's the first night in months I haven't had a drink to settle my nerves. It's also the first night in years I haven't woken up crying.

Chapter Eight

MICHELLE

'Morning,' I call out to the reception team as I head into work. They glance at each other before returning an unsure 'hello'. I chuckle. This happier version of me is hilarious. I get a kick out of confusing people.

I spend my morning scrubbing a dog with mange and fighting with a French bulldog to have a bath. I end up wetter than he does, but at least he's clean and now we are best of friends.

At lunchtime, I decide to head out and get some fresh air. The window in the grooming room only opens a couple of inches, and claustrophobia often sets in.

The sun is uncharacteristically shining for mid-September, and I want to take advantage of the vitamin D boost. As I'm heading across the field over the road from the practice, I hear someone call out my name.

'Michelle! You finished work for the day?'

I spin around and see Pam and a slobbering Felix rushing towards me. 'I'm on my lunch break. You can bring Felix in at two, if that's any good for you?'

'Oh no, he's still as fresh as a daisy. We're just on a little jaunt.' We look at him as he runs off to sniff what looks like curry, but could equally be a pile of vomit. 'Okay, maybe he's not as fresh as a daisy. As fresh as a dustbin, perhaps?' Pam continues without even acknowledging the fact her dog is gobbling up the slop. 'Can I buy you some lunch? To say thank you for yesterday? I appreciate that it could not have been easy for you.'

The vet clinic I work at is in a less desirable part of town, so I highly doubt Pam would just be strolling past. What is she up to? Why is she here?

Curious and not being one to turn down free food, I join them on their walk. At Pam's command, Felix trots perfectly by her side with his head held high. I'm impressed. I wish everyone could dedicate the time to training their dogs like Pam clearly has. My job would be so much easier if they did.

We head over to the park and Pam steers me to the bandstand where a burger van awaits us. To my surprise, she orders two burgers. I would have put money on her having never eaten a burger in her entire privileged life.

'I just wanted to thank you again for signing up with us. We really appreciate all the help we can get.'

The burger vendor hands over our food, and we take it to a bench where Pam instructs Felix to sit by her side. I bite into the burger and enjoy the grease sliding down my throat. Pam pulls her burger apart and starts feeding it to Felix, who sits patiently on his butt, gently taking it from her hand. I knew she wasn't a burger kind of woman.

'I've been reading through the material you gave me,' I say, taking another chomp of my lunch.

Pam claps her hands together with delight. 'Already? Oh, that's great news. With that level of enthusiasm, we can start your training sooner than I thought.'

Butterflies dance around my stomach and to my surprise, I realise it's excitement, not dread.

I slept like the dead last night. Dreams of my hideous past failed to haunt me. I didn't picture my mother gripping my throat; or the face she made when I walked into the room. I don't think I even stirred. It's like something is lifting inside of me. Like I'm on the verge of clarity, and I have a feeling Pam is the person to chase away the fog, if I can just push past my nerves.

'How soon can I start?' The words appear before I even register the thought. But, I mean it. I want to start. My life needs to start.

'When's your next day off from the grooming parlour? You need to do eight hours of training, but there's nothing stopping us cramming it into one day.'

'Monday,' I tell her.

'Monday it is then.' She beams at me. Felix is sniffing around our feet, looking for burger remnants. 'Go and get some exercise, you lazy boy.' Pam lovingly shoves him away from us and Felix trots off, sniffing the ground as he goes.

'Between you and me, I think I've struck gold with you,' Pam says. She turns to me and clutches my hand. I really regret not wiping my burger hands better. 'I love each one of my team, but they lack something, and I sense you will offer it in spades.'

'Offer what, exactly?'

Pam bites her lower lip and squints at me. 'I can't put my finger on it. Your experience, although terrible, might just be the key to making tremendous changes at Speak Up.'

I can't believe I told Pam about my past. It's so unlike me. But, a warmth spreads through me. Pam has shined a light on my suffering, giving it a positivity that I could never have imagined. It feels good – really good.

I squeeze Pam's hands in response. The human touch feels alien, but it's a good kind of weird. Pam nods slowly and pushes her lips together.

'I think you and I are going to work splendidly together,' she whispers.

I think so, too.

Chapter Nine

TEDDY

I am crouching by my bedroom window, waiting for Dad's car to drive away. They take ages. What are they doing in there? It looks like Daddy is hunched over something. I think he's rolling a joint. He's not very fast at it. He says his fingers are like fat sausages, so he usually gets me to do it.

Finally, the car drives down the road. They said they're going to Mark's. I don't know who Mark is, but I know they will be gone for a while. They'll probably be back tomorrow. That's okay. I get to watch what I like on the TV, and I can sneak some food if I'm careful.

Plus, I get to call my new friends.

I go over to the corner of my room and lift the carpet. This is now where I stash my important things, like the birthday card Robert made for me and the now-dead ladybird I found crawling up the side of the house. It's also where I keep my Speak Up card.

It's a bit more rumpled than when Robert's mummy gave it to me, but I can still see the numbers. I think I know them off by heart now, anyway.

I head into the living room where they keep the house phone, and I tap on the little numbers.

'Hello, Speak Up. Pam speaking. How can I help?'

It's Pam. I like Pam. She sounds like a queen, all posh and floaty.

'It's Teddy,' I say into the phone.

'Teddy, what a treat! How are you?'

I tell her about Mummy shutting me in my bedroom. Pam sounds sad, but she doesn't tell me off. I like that. She asks if she can call someone who will help me.

'No,' I say. I'm too scared. What if Mummy finds out I have been using the phone and beats me? She might really hurt me. She might never let me use the phone again and I will be all alone. I don't want to be alone again.

I tell Pam about the paper aeroplane Robert threw over the wall. He'd coloured it in red and written my name on the side in blue. It was amazing. He couldn't fly it very well and it kept floating into the back alley. Robert said it was a fighter jet. I liked that. A fighter jet called Teddy.

Then I hear it. A car engine getting closer. And closer.

I stretch my neck to see out of the big living room window. It's them! I slam the phone down and run back upstairs to my room at super speed. I grunt when I throw myself onto my bed and hit my elbow on the wall; then I sit and try to make myself breathe normally.

They slam the door behind them. Mummy is shouting about something. I can't breathe and the world is spinning.

'Who the fuck does he think he's talking to like that?' Mummy shouts. I hear Daddy mumble something, but I don't hear his words.

'I mean, I know I owe him a few quid, but I'm good for it. How dare he turn me away? He treated me like scum. Did you see that? Actual scum.'

Her voice goes a little quieter as they walk into the living room. I notice my bedroom carpet is still lifted up, and then I can't breathe at all.

The Speak Up card is still downstairs.

I drag my fingernails down my arms. What do I do? *What do I do now*?

I try to think of a plan, my fingernails drawing blood. The panic feels too big. I might explode.

'The little shit!' Mummy screams louder than ever, and I hear her stomping up the stairs. Dad's heavy footsteps follow closely behind. My door slams open so hard the door handle chips the wall behind it.

'Who the fuck have you been talking to?' She is so close to my face I can feel her wet breath against my lips. Her face is purple. I try to hide behind my hands, but she rips them away.

'Answer me!'

Daddy pipes up, 'You better answer her, buddy.' Buddy? Daddy never calls me that. He's only ever nice to me when he's scared, and he's never been this nice to me before.

'No one,' I squeal. 'I was going to. Just to talk to someone. Because I was bored. But, I don't know how. I don't know how to use the phone.' The lie is way better than the truth, even though I know lying can get me in way more trouble.

'You tell anyone about me and you're dead, you hear me?'

I nod my head really hard so she believes me.

Quick as a flash, her fingers reach around my neck. And she squeezes.

'Come on love, he's obviously telling the truth. He's too fucking stupid to use a phone. Let's try Andy, he'll give us some gear,' says Dad. I am so happy he's trying to help me, but Mummy just squeezes her fingers even tighter. I want to cough, but it won't come out.

I try to pull her hands away, but she's too strong. Too angry.

My tears mix up with my snot. Then everything goes bright white. Then black.

I wake up when my daddy nudges me with his foot. 'You alive?' He's laughing, but even through the screaming sound in my head, I can tell he's scared. I've never seen Daddy this scared before, and I feel my breath quicken. My neck burns as the air touches the bruising. I don't know where Mummy has gone.

I've ended up on the floor, and Daddy shoves his hands under my armpits and sits me up, propping me against the bed.

I keep looking around for Mummy.

'Slow your breathing down,' Daddy says. I try, but my chest feels smaller. I can't breathe in quickly enough and I feel all panicky.

'I'm glad you're not dead, lad. Fuck knows what I'd do with a body.'

'Daddy,' I croak.

'Stay out of your mum's way for a while.' He gets up off my bedroom floor and leaves me alone to cry.

Chapter Ten

MICHELLE

Monday couldn't come quickly enough. I spent Saturday working at the vets, my brain constantly firing case studies at me from the file. Then yesterday, I read through the rest of it.

Oh man, that was a hard read.

The second half of the information pack was brutal. It contained example conversations, appropriate responses, and flow diagrams for potential conversations. It was overwhelming, but in a good way. I feel more secure. I'm ready to get started now.

My only concern is that I must report all safeguarding measures to Pam, who will personally make the appropriate calls to the authorities. It seems like an unnecessary bottleneck in the system. What if Pam is off ill? What if she has too much on her plate? The volunteers aren't even given an indication of who the relevant team would be to contact.

Still, Pam must know what she's doing. She's started this charity from scratch, and it has gone from a team of one to a national treasure. It's obviously a system that works.

***

Pam is waiting for me in her office. She's wearing a dazzling smile and an expensive-looking pale grey suit with an emerald-green blouse underneath. She signals for me to sit down, and I wait while she taps away on her keyboard with her manicured nails. The sound cuts right through me.

'We're going to have some fun today,' she says finally, pushing her monitor so it's facing away from us. I nod. Although I'm looking forward to this, I can hardly call speaking to abused children 'fun'.

Pam continues, 'I thought I would let you shadow me this morning, then this afternoon we can do a little Q and A session, and maybe a spot of role play. Then next time you're here, I can chuck you in the deep end.' She presses her hands together like she's about to dive into a pool.

What the hell have I gotten myself into?

***

'This is Speak Up. You're talking to Pam. How can I help you?' Pam says for the second time. She has the call on speakerphone and the line remains silent. Dread fills my stomach. All kinds of scenarios are running through my head, and none of them are good. Maybe the child can't talk because they're too frightened? Too injured? Dying?

Please say something, I silently pray, while simultaneously telling my pessimistic imagination to shut up.

'Okay, can you cough if you need some help?' Pam mutters into her mouthpiece.

Nothing.

'I'm here whenever you're ready to talk. I won't leave you.' There's a softness to Pam's voice that almost makes me want to pour my soul out to her.

Then, raucous laughter fills Pam's office through the small holes on the phone. Pam's eyebrows fold downwards, and her teeth clench together. 'If this is a joke to you, remember, you are wasting precious time I could be spending with a child who needs serious help,' she spits out. Red tinges her cheeks.

The laughter increases in volume before Pam jabs her finger on the 'end call' button.

Pam huffs and leans back in her leather swivel chair. 'I wish I could say prank calls are a rare occurrence, but we get them all the damn time.' She pushes her chair back and brings her hand down for Felix to lick. I didn't even know he was there. He's all curled up in the corner of the room on the comfiest looking bed I have ever seen. Is that memory foam?

'Why do people call in just to laugh down the phone?'

'Because they have nothing better to do, Michelle. Because they're sitting in a place of such privilege, they cannot even imagine what calls I might be missing. Still, I should be grateful for that, I guess.'

'I think it's because they're bell-ends,' I offer, and Pam's tinkly laugh fills the room. It sounds like someone is running their fingers through a crystal chandelier.

'Well said,' she tells me with a little smile.

The phone rings again.

'This is Speak Up. Pam here. How can I help you?'

This time the silence on the line is stuffed with an intensity I cannot explain. 'It's okay. I'm here to listen whenever you're ready to talk. There's no rush.' Pam glances at me and gives me a quick nod.

There is a whimper on the line. Deep breathing. I want to reach my arms down the phone and pull the little mite into my arms.

'It's Teddy,' a little voice squeaks down the line.

Pam's face lights up. 'Hi, Teddy. It's lovely to hear from you again. Is everything okay?'

Silence.

'Mummy got mad at me again.' Teddy takes a deep breath in, and I hear his breath wobble inside his throat. 'I think I was really bad this time.'

'Teddy, you must know that you are not bad. You are a very good, special boy.'

'But, Mummy says I'm a piece of shit.'

My stomach gurgles. Vomit threatens to pour out of me. My mum used to call me the same.

'You most certainly are not a piece of shit. I promise you. Where is your mummy today?'

'Out,' Teddy whispers. He's clearly frightened that she might come back any minute. Pam bites her bottom lip. 'She might be back soon. I will have to go.'

'Okay, Teddy. Have a little think. Is there anyone else you can turn to when you're struggling? Or are you ready for me to reach out to someone who can help you?'

Teddy makes a gurgling sound, then the line goes dead.

I gasp.

Pam stares at the phone for a few moments before turning to me. 'Teddy has been calling most days for about a week now. The calls are always short. He hasn't told me how old he is, but my guess is he's about six, though I think he has a speech delay so he could be older.'

'Can we get him out of there? There must be something you can do.'

'Michelle, I don't even know where he is. He could be anywhere in the country. Right now, we just have to be here for him, to get him through each day. Then we have to pray he will find the courage to step up and let us get him out of there.'

'Fuck.'

The word hangs between us. I go to apologise for my vulgar language, but Pam nods emphatically at me. I want to reach into the phone and grab him, there's something about Teddy that delves deeper into my sympathy. Is it his sweet, soft voice? Is it because he's a mirror of me?

'Come on. Let's take a break and grab a coffee, and I'll show you how to update each case file. We have a file for each child so we can give each call a personal touch, and for evidence just in case the police knock at our door.'

'For when they arrest the bastards, right?'

'Yes. And ... ' Pam looks me in the eye. A chill runs down my spine and I dread the words about to leave her mouth. 'When there is a death – the caregiver, or the child.'

That's it. I excuse myself and run to the toilet. I barely make it into the cubicle before vomit rushes up my throat and hits the toilet bowl.

I can't do this. I am way out of my depth.

'First day?' a voice calls out from over the cubicle wall. I hear the toilet flush and my neighbour walks out to the sink where she washes her hands. 'I threw up on my first day, too. Don't stress about it. It's like your body wants to purge the shit we have to deal with. My first ever call was a little girl called Poppy-Lea. Her dad had burnt her arm with an iron. Who the fuck does that to a kid, right?'

I wipe my mouth with some tissue and flush it away. Then I make sure my vomit has disappeared down the U-bend before unlocking the door to join my comrade.

It's Lisa, the team leader. She's wearing a long skirt today, so she looks more like Princess Fiona than Shrek.

'I just feel so angry. It's like it's bubbling out of every bit of me,' I tell her. 'How can people be so damn cruel?'

Lisa just shrugs. Her nonchalance is shocking. Children are being killed by those they are supposed to trust. Those who are supposed to love them through every tantrum, every nosebleed, every sleepless night. It's disgusting.

'I hate to say it, but you build up a tolerance. Sounds cruel, but you must put up a wall, and fast. Otherwise, you'll crumble, and those kids will still be out there. The only difference is, they won't have you in their corner anymore. Suck it up, new girl. You've got this.'

Lisa pats me on the back, the force shunting my hips into the sink. She nods briskly before marching out of the toilets.

I look into the mirror. A small lump of vomit sits on my chin, and I wipe it away with the back of my hand before washing my hands in the sink. My eyes stare back at me. Her eyes. Whenever I look in the mirror, I see my mum looking back at me. It feels like glass running through my veins. These are the eyes of an evil bitch.

I slam my fists down on the sink and groan.

My breaths are shallow, and the room is spinning, so I squeeze my eyes shut and breathe in slowly. My fingers grip the edge of the sink until my knuckles are sore.

Gradually, my breathing slows down, and the image of my bitch of a mother dissipates. I continue to focus on my breathing until the clouds lift inside my brain.

I loosen my fists and wriggle my fingers, easing the pain of my tight grip.

The door squeaks open and Pam steps into the room. 'Is everything okay in here? Lisa told me you're having a difficult time.'

'I'm okay,' I tell her. And I am. I can do this.

***

I leave the office just after five o'clock, taking the stairs two at a time. I dive into the street and take a gulp of air. Hordes of people are bustling about, trying to get home after a long day, before the heavens open.

The wind bites at me, cleansing me of the bitter taste I have in my mouth, and in my soul. I feel dirty, like I haven't washed in weeks. My sanity has been tampered with and I don't know whether to laugh or cry. I stand in the street, unsure of how to behave in the normal world – a world where everyone isn't constantly surrounded by horrendous acts of abuse.

'Fancy a lift?' Pam appears behind me. She's grasping Felix's lead in one hand and pulling the office door closed with the other. Sensibly, she has an umbrella tucked under her arm.

I look upwards and feel the first drop of rain splash against my forehead.

'Come on!' Pam yells, and yanks me to her personal parking space. By the time we're inside Pam's Mercedes, we are soaked through.

'Well. I wasn't expecting that,' Pam laughs.

I lose myself in the ridiculousness of the situation and allow the day's tension to leave my body. I'm laughing so hard that my tears are mingling with the raindrops. A flash of lightning zig-zags through the sky. Felix barks at the sky and I laugh even harder.

The roads are slow going. Visibility is poor through the rain, and everyone seems to be reluctant to drive faster than half the limit. Why does rain turn everyone into incompetent drivers?

I catch Pam watching me in her peripheral vision. 'The first day is always the hardest,' she tells me. My momentary good mood comes crashing down.

'You could say that.' I try to smile at her, but my cheeks ache with the pretence.

'It'll get easier.'

'Lisa said the same thing.'

A silence settles between us, filling the car with a comforting calm. Felix adjusts himself on the back seat, the leather making a comical fart noise.

Pam speaks first. 'Do you know how I met Lisa?'

I shake my head. 'No.'

'She was part of a team at social services who were involved in the Baby Patty case.'

I know the Baby Patty case well. Damn, I think the whole of the UK knows the Baby Patty case. Patty was the name given by the media to the baby horrifically physically and sexually abused by his parents in exchange for money from people online, who logged in from all over the world to watch his torture. He died at eighteen months old, battered to death. Social services did absolutely nothing.

'I know what you're thinking. Everyone thinks the same when it comes to that case: social services did nothing to help that little boy. They let it happen. But, Michelle, they didn't just let it happen. Lisa really didn't. The only crime social services committed was finding out too late. You don't know what you don't know.'

'But, how can no one know? They beat him to death.'

'And you think his parents cared enough to take him to hospital? To nursery? That baby never left his home as far as they could tell.'

I stare out the window. I spy a woman scooping up her little girl and tucking her coat around her. Then she runs into the shelter of a nearby bus stop.

'He suffered so much,' I whisper.

Pam responds with silence, and we sit in sad contemplation.

'Tell me your story. Tell me more about your parents.' At last, Pam asks me.

My head twists around and I look at Pam. She's staring out the windscreen, her expression soft.

I don't know what to say. I've always talked around the edges of my childhood, knowing that delving too deep would make everyone feel awkward. I always thought it would be too much for me to tell, and too much for someone to hear. It felt too big to fit into a conversation.

Pam, though, seems to shrink it somehow. I don't know if it's because of her experience or her soothing personality. There's just something about her. It's like I've known her my whole life.

'It was Mum, mainly.' I pause and watch Pam's face. She doesn't move a muscle. 'Dad didn't do anything.'

Pam nods. 'But, he didn't help you either?'

'No. He walked away when she got mad. "Out of sight, out of mind" kind of thing, I guess.'

'What did she do to you?' Her question jolts me. I've never known anyone this forthcoming; this brash. I take a deep breath.

'Mum had an anger problem. The slightest thing would set her off and once she was angry, there was only one way that helped her let go of that anger. Blaming me made her feel better about herself, I guess.'

'So, she hit you,' says Pam. It's a statement, not a question, so I do not offer a response.

Felix yips and growls in his sleep, making me jump.

'The hitting wasn't the worst bit,' I continue. 'It was the isolation. She got so fed up of looking at me that she would shove me in the garage for days at a time. It was dark. Cold. I got hungry.'

'That must have been frightening for you.'

My voice comes out as a meek whisper. 'Time stopped still when I was in there. I didn't know if I was in there for hours or days. It was agonising. I'd hear little feet scurrying across the floor. To this day, I don't know if those sounds were real or a figment of my imagination.'

Pam indicates left into Devonshire Street – my street. The tick-tock of the indicator punctuates the tension in the car. I am surprised she knows where to go. I haven't given her any directions, so I figure she memorised my address from my volunteer form.

She jolts me out of my melancholic reverie with a sudden change in subject.

'You should come around for dinner sometime. My son, Aiden, would love to meet you for sure.' A grin plays on her lips.

Is she setting me up with someone? God, I hope not. That's a complication I really don't need right now.

'Don't worry, I mean nothing romantically. I just think he could use a friend. He works so hard, I worry he might be lonely. And you look like you need a good meal in you. Next week. No excuses.' Her cherry red quiver slightly, and there's a cheekiness in her eyes. 'I'm not taking "no" for an answer.' Even Houdini couldn't escape this proposition.

'Fine. Text me the details,' I say, as she pulls up in front of the terraced house I share with Kelsey. I pull the door handle and push the door open. A bracing wind whips into the car.

'Will do. Oh, and Michelle?' I pause as the rain sticks my hair to my forehead. 'What would you say to your parents now, if you had the chance?'

I shake my head. 'There's nothing I can say.' I hop out of the car and go to slam the door shut. 'They're dead.'

I catch Pam's eyes and she nods at me. 'Karma's a bitch, isn't it?' she says as the door closes. And she drives away.

Chapter Eleven

MICHELLE

'Can I have a quick word?' Maggie calls out as I'm heading out the door. I trudge over to her office. My shift finished five minutes ago, and I'm no longer being paid, so this better be quick.

'Everything okay, Mags?' I see her bristle at the pet name I've granted her, but she smiles anyway. Her smile is warm and I feel my shoulders relax. She's in one of her rare good moods. I'm not getting a bollocking.

'Yes, Michelle. I just wanted to commend you on your change in attitude since your leave of absence. You have really turned things around. I think I'm looking at a whole new woman.'

My eyebrows press together as I cringe. I don't think I've received a compliment from Maggie before, and it makes me squirm. In fact, I'm not used to getting compliments from anyone; except for Kelsey, of course. But then, she'd compliment a post box on its bold colour if the mood took her.

'Erm, thanks?'

'You're welcome. I believe in giving credit where it's due. And, Michelle? Keep it up, won't you? Keep doing whatever it is that's making you happy. Or whoever.' Maggie turns to her computer, looking proud of her inappropriate joke. She dismisses me with the clicking of her keyboard.

As I leave the vet clinic, Pam is waiting in her Mercedes on the other side of the street. She's poking her finger in her eye.

'You all right?' I ask her as I jump into the passenger seat.

'Yes. I think I have an eyelash in my eye,' she says, pulling her eyelid down over her eyeball. She lets go and shakes her head. 'There we go. It's gone. Ready?'

'Sure,' I say with conviction, but really not meaning it. As great as I think Pam is, I don't think I want to go to her house. I've spent every day with her this week at Speak Up, but going to her house just seems a little personal – like I'm crossing a boundary.

As she drives, Pam catches me up on a case I'm responsible for (under Pam's close supervision).

'Chloe called today.' Pam's tone excites me. I sense good news.

'Yeah?'

'She's at her aunt's.'

I sigh with relief. She's finally away from her abusive dad. She's safe. 'Is her aunt going to keep her there until the police get her dad?'

'Yes. I spoke to her aunt personally. She's well aware of what Chloe's dad is up to, and she will not let Chloe go back to him. I don't think he'll put up a fight.'

I know he won't. I've spoken to Chloe multiple times this week. She's been calling the hotline for months, but understandably, never had the courage to tell her aunt that her own father was touching her.

When Daddy tells you he'll kill you if you tell his secrets, how can you possibly spill the beans?

'She told me to thank you.' Pam smiles at me, briefly taking her eyes off the road.

'I didn't do anything.'

'You must have done something right. We've been working with Chloe for weeks. You come along, and now look at her. She's safe.' Pam turns the car into a tiny country lane. If another vehicle comes the other way, we're screwed. There's no way two cars can fit through here.

Pam continues. 'I think the callers sense something about you. You understand them. Your empathy is *real*. That's key in this job, and touching to watch.'

I suspect she's right. It's like my past shines a light on everything they're going through. I can feel each tear; each incident is real to me. I hang onto their every word in the hope I can absorb some of their pain. I listen to their stories in the hope I can give them strength to escape.

'Here we are.' Pam's words cut into my contemplation and I gasp. We are driving through two huge, black, metal gates swinging open on their own accord. Before us, atop a small hill, lies the most beautiful house I've ever seen.

'Home sweet home!' I blurt out. Pam chuckles and pulls the car onto a tarmacked drive that could easily fit five or six cars. There's a BMW convertible parked a few metres away, and a motorbike nestled behind that.

'Oh, good – Aiden's already here. I've prepared a beef Wellington. It's a Gordon Ramsay recipe. I've never made it before, but it looks divine.'

Pam keeps rabbiting on about her beef dish as we get out of the car and head to the door.

I admire the grounds. They're lit up with sporadic spotlights that cast beams of light to showcase the natural beauty. It looks magical. The lawn runs down the hill like dark green velvet, and tall oak trees line the bottom of the slope that heads up away from the house. Not a single building or road can be seen from here.

Pam pushes the huge wooden door open and calls out, 'Honey, we're home!' She chuckles, her laugh tinkling happily. 'That'll make him blush.' She winks at me.

Footsteps sound from down the corridor, which leads to a brightly lit room. A man appears with a coy smile on his face. 'Oh, come on, Mum. Don't embarrass yourself.' He catches my eye and grins.

Aiden is much older than I realised. When Pam talks about him, she makes him sound like a grumpy teenager, but he must be in his late thirties. In his black Nirvana hoodie and slightly baggy jeans, he's a complete contrast to Pam who's wearing a white dress and gold heels. He has stubble over his face and the same twinkly blue eyes as Pam. His dark brown hair is pushed back; long overdue a cut, but sexy all the same.

I feel myself blush. He's way better-looking than I expected. He holds his hand out to me.

'Hey. I'm Aiden.' He takes my hand and gives it a gentle shake. 'Whatever my mum has told you about me, ignore it. She's a liar.'

Pam laughs. 'Oh, come on now, Aiden. You really did pee your pants at a school play.'

'Mum! I was four years old and I was, you know, nervous.' He wraps his arm around his mum's shoulders and plants a kiss on the top of her head.

Their ease with each other is warming. There's no resentment between them. Only love. My respect for Pam multiplies tenfold. I only wish my mum could have been a fraction like Pam. Maybe then I could have been happy, and I wouldn't be so messed up now.

'You have a beautiful home,' I say to no one in particular, as they lead me into a lavish living room. The walls are decorated in some sort of gold-coated, floral-patterned wallpaper, and the lush carpet buries my toes.

'It really is beautiful,' Aiden replies. 'It's why I spend all my time here. Plus, I just like to drive her crazy.' Aiden's smile makes it very obvious he knows this isn't true.

Pam taps Aiden on the arm. 'Oh, tosh. You know you can visit me as much as you like. I enjoy having you around.'

Aiden turns to me. 'Someone needs to keep an eye on the old bird. It might as well be me.'

Pam gasps. 'You cheeky so-and-so!' She's laughing, but her mouth has a tightness to it, so I think Aiden has touched a nerve.

A tray of drinks sits on the coffee table. Aiden must have placed them there before we arrived. He's a true gent.

'Wine?' Pam asks me, but doesn't wait for an answer. 'Aiden, do the honours.'

In true British style, we chit-chat about the unpredictable autumnal weather and the state of the roads, whilst Aiden pops the cork and pours us all a generous glass of wine. Pam takes a sip, and eyes us both over the rim of her glass before excusing herself to tend to dinner.

'Mum tells me you're working at the charity with her,' Aiden says. 'Enjoying it there?'

I nod enthusiastically. 'Very much. I really hope I can make a difference there.' I take a long sip of the delicious red liquid. Aiden sits down next to me, clutching his own glass. I notice he's yet to drink anything, and make a mental note to slow down.

'Mum has been singing your praises all week. You're certainly making an impact, from what I hear.' He leans in close. He's so close I can smell his shampoo: cinnamon and something fruity. 'Between you and me, I think Mum set the charity up to take her mind off my dad dying, but for decades it hasn't seemed to work. Then you come along, and suddenly she's all rainbows and sunshine.'

I don't know what to make of that. How can he be so brazen about such a personal detail? 'I didn't know she was a widow,' I say.

'Yeah, don't look so horrified. It's really okay; it was a million years ago. I think it's safe to say that we have moved on.'

'God, I'm sorry.' I want to shove my foot in my mouth to shut it up. I can't believe I'm talking to the guy about his dead dad ten minutes after meeting him.

'Seriously, don't worry about it. It was a long time ago. A distant memory.' He waves his hand at me, pushing my concerns aside.

'Dinner's ready!' Pam calls out from down the corridor.

When we walk into the dining room, Pam is red-faced from leaning over the hot oven. She's wearing an apron and placing the plates on the colossal table.

'There we are,' Pam says, eyeing up the place settings laid with far too much cutlery for one meal. The smell of beef fills my nostrils and my mouth waters.

***

Dinner is fun. Aiden and Pam have a camaraderie that is hilarious to watch. Aiden loves to tease Pam incessantly about her mannerisms and quirks, and Pam pretends to be hurt, but her smile betrays her act. In return, she's over-the-top sweet towards her son, acting like he's a naughty eight-year-old.

After dinner, Pam goes to clean up the kitchen, refusing all help. Aiden leads me back into the living room.

'Mum's a blast, isn't she? How do you like working with her?' Aiden asks me. 'Does she like to crack the whip?'

'It's ... ' I struggle to find the right word, but decide honesty is probably the best policy. 'Inspiring.'

Aiden nods enthusiastically. 'She sure is. She's worked so damn hard in that place. Just don't let her lead you astray, or you'll get sucked in.'

Astray? What does that mean? I figure in Pam's line of work, you have to get results. Now that I think about it, I wouldn't be shocked to hear Pam has had to bend some rules over the years to achieve the success she has. And the more success she has, the more children she can reach.

'Mum told me your parents died,' Aiden says. I jolt backwards, shocked at the sudden turn in the conversation. It seems Pam's confidence in chatting about abuse has rubbed off on her son. 'That must be hard.' We are sitting next to each other on the same cream sofa we were sitting on before dinner. Only this time, he's mere inches away from me. If I stretch my fingers out, I'll be caressing his thigh. I cross my legs to put some space between us, and to stop myself doing something regrettable.

An electricity is running through me; my skin is tingling, and I can hear my pulse beat behind my ears. I feel alive. It's as if all my self-hatred and pain is evaporating from my body. Since meeting Pam, it's like a big shadow has shrunk. Her openness and ease about my past has made me see it doesn't have to drag me down. It doesn't have to impact my entire life. I can breathe.

I think I've had too much wine.

Aiden is looking at me eagerly, and I feel compelled to fill the void in the conversation before I jump his bones. 'It was harder when they were alive. Truth is, I'm glad they're dead. The world is a better place without them in it.' I tuck my feet underneath my bum and lean back against the plush cushions. 'But then, there is a little part of me that wishes they were still here. There are a few things I would like to say, or do, to them.'

Aiden nods knowingly. I gather Pam has told him everything I've told her. I'm glad she's told him. My truth being out there feels cathartic. And I trust him. He takes my hand, my skin tingles where it meets his and a heat washes over me. He gives it a little squeeze before letting go. I can't help feeling disappointed.

Eager to divert the attention from my reddening cheeks, I say the first thing that comes to my head: 'So, your dad died.' I wouldn't call it a seamless subject change, but Aiden goes along with it, anyway.

Aiden takes a long sip of wine, not once losing eye contact with me. It's sexy as hell.

'Heart attack.' He places his empty wine glass on the table and refills it. 'You know, when he died, I thought that'd be the end of my mum. She was beyond devastated. But, despite her devotion to him, or maybe because of it, since he passed away, she's shined. It's funny how these things work.'

He grabs the wine bottle again from the coffee table, closing the subject. I place my hand over my glass, signalling to Aiden not to pour me any more. I feel lightheaded and I want to remain focused. Right now, I'm risking spilling every tiny detail about my life, and I don't want to talk too much about my past in case I open wounds I cannot heal.

'You don't have to answer this,' I say. I have never been one to delve into other people's business, but the Greene family fascinates me. 'How did Pam get the money to set up Speak Up? I'm so impressed with what she's done there.'

'My dad was an investment banker. You can figure out the rest.' Aiden smiles. His teeth are perfectly white and slightly crooked, which adds to his charm. His eyes are so warm and gentle.

'Mum's set up for life, and she wants to help as many children as she can with that. Her money is her superpower.'

'She's an inspiration,' I mutter.

'You wait until she's got you well and truly under her wing. She has high hopes for you, Michelle. You two are going to make an incredible team. There's something about you. Something impressive.'

Chapter Twelve

MICHELLE

With the rain hammering down for the last few weeks, I've been so busy giving my canine friends well-needed pampering to rid them of caked-on mud and matted fur.

I've been volunteering at Speak Up most days, too, so I'm officially knackered. Each phone call leaves me feeling like I've run a marathon at record speed. I have been dragging my heels into the Speak Up office and my irritability has stepped up a notch. I'm close to burnout.

So, when Pam told me to take a break, I felt grateful to be temporarily relieved of all the pain I have absorbed lately. I feel like my brain's about to explode, and I am no help to anyone without a head on my shoulders.

It's Wednesday and my grooming appointments finish early, and when I stroll through the door at home, I'm glad to be greeted by the delicious smell of garlic wafting from the kitchen.

My keys tinkle as they hit the bowl, and I kick my boots into the corner of the hallway. I hesitate. Was that a man's voice I just heard? I stand in the hallway and listen. I hear Kelsey's girly giggle emanate from the kitchen, followed by a man's bellowing laugh.

My stomach drops.

Shit. Travis, Kelsey's boyfriend! I'm really not in the mood to meet him. I've managed to avoid the meet-and-greet for weeks, with Speak Up providing the perfect excuse. The thought of putting on a fake smile and feigning interest in this stranger's life is nauseating, especially with Kelsey cooing in the background. And don't get me started on public displays of affection.

I consider running upstairs and hiding in my room, but my conscience makes me take a deep breath and nudge the door open with my toes. I need to just get this over with. I need to do it for Kelsey.

Kelsey spots me first. 'Michelle! Hi. You not volunteering tonight?'

I force a smile. 'Not tonight. I needed some time off.'

'Oh, good.' She tries to lace sincerity into her tone, but I immediately feel unwelcome in my own home. Have I walked in on something sexy going on?

Her eyes flit between me and the kitchen area, and I realise she's nervous. Of having me here? Wow, I have really done a number on my best friend.

'Michelle, meet Travis. Travis, this is Michelle.'

A humongous man steps out from behind the fridge-freezer, wipes his hands on a tea towel and holds one hand out to me. My hand practically disappears into it when we shake. 'It's good to meet you, Michelle. I've heard a lot about you.'

I cringe at the things I know Kelsey could have told him about me: I'm a useless housemate, a burden; and to top things off, I'm a drunk.

I try to reassure myself: Kelsey is a good person. She's kind and warm. She would never bad-mouth me.

'Well, I haven't heard much about *you*,' I say, though I immediately regret my words. I sound snide. Thankfully, Travis just laughs. His smile completely wipes the stern look off his face – only now do I see the appeal. He seems warm and kind, the perfect complement to Kelsey's caring nature.

He tells me, 'Well, maybe we can fix that tonight. Can I interest you in some of my world-famous lasagne?'

'World-famous?'

Travis shrugs. 'My mum likes it, anyway.'

I laugh. Travis is huge, and he seems to fill the entire kitchen space, but his presence is easy and relaxed. He is totally suited to Kelsey. I glance at her now, and she raises her eyebrows at me. She wants my seal of approval.

And I do approve. 'I'd like that,' I say. 'As long as I'm not intruding.' Kelsey clasps her hands together and a smile spreads across her face. A little yelp escapes her lips. She wraps an arm around my waist and gives me a little squeeze before drifting over to Travis' side.

'Not at all,' says Travis, and he throws the dish towel over his shoulder, kissing Kelsey lightly on the forehead. It's a simple gesture that speaks volumes. This guy is perfect for my friend. I feel guilty that I've avoided meeting him for so long. 'I'll throw some extra garlic bread in the oven,' he says to no one in particular, pulling the fridge door open.

***

Dinner is indeed incredible and if Travis' lasagne isn't world-famous, then it damn well deserves to be. The layers are perfectly proportioned and there's a thick layer of cheese crust on the top. I have to resist groaning into each mouthful.

'What is it you do for a living, Travis?' I ask him, fully expecting him to say he's a chef.

'Detective.' Travis speaks through a mouthful of garlic bread. I'm impressed, though a little intimidated. People in positions of power have always made me feel shy. At school, I was the kid who'd keep their eyes lowered at all times so the teacher wouldn't make eye contact and call on me. I preferred not to exist, and people with power can draw you into the light without warning.

There's something weird about this, though. 'So, if you're a detective, what were you doing at the Vet Show where you met Kelsey?'

Travis laughs and leans back in his chair. 'Good thinking, maybe you should join the police force.' He dabs his chin with a piece of kitchen paper. 'I was there with my sister. She's studying veterinary science at Liverpool uni,' he says, taking a massive bite of garlic bread and speaking with his mouth full. I like that. He doesn't give a shit about airs and graces. 'Her friend let her down last minute and she didn't want to go alone. So, in stepped her big bro – hero.' He taps his chest and we laugh.

I swallow my food, contemplating Travis' job. It must be cool brandishing your badge, being in a position of power. 'What's it like being a detective? Any juicy cases at the minute?'

Travis laughs, and Kelsey blushes. Was that the wrong thing to ask? Is there some sort of police secrecy code I don't know about? I blush. I'm such an idiot. An idiot with a big mouth.

'You know, the norm – dead people, drugs, sex offenders.'

'Sounds intense.' Goosebumps erupt all over my body. This is too close to home. If this is his normal, then I suddenly feel very sorry for him.

'It is. But thankfully, and I guess sadly, you get a bit desensitised after a while. These people just become part of the job, and you just have to go to bed satisfied that you're doing the best you can.'

That is sad. But, I totally get it. I've been there. Numbing to the pain around you is the only way you can throw yourself into the chaos and actually help. I nod knowingly. I feel like Travis and I understand each other. He understands pain.

We all fall into a comfortable silence. My thoughts swirl around in my head. Only the scraping of knives and forks breaks the peace.

'How's volunteering at Speak Up going?' Travis asks me. Kelsey throws him a look. 'Sorry, was that a secret?'

'Not at all,' I laugh. 'Kelsey just likes to tread very carefully around me in case I shatter into pieces.' I turn to Kelsey and give her a warm smile. 'But, I'm okay now.'

I shovel the last of my pasta into my mouth. 'It sounds so wrong, but I'm actually really enjoying it. Making a difference, you know?' I swallow.

Travis nods. 'I know what you mean. It can't be an easy task walking into that place every day, not knowing what you will have to face. I mean, at least I get paid to clean up the mess that gets thrown at me. It's very admirable of you.'

I feel my cheeks warm up and I stuff more garlic bread in my mouth. Compliments always make me feel uneasy. But, I remind myself of Pam's advice: bask in the compliments you receive, even if you don't believe them. It's how you build confidence.

After dinner, I collect the empty plates and take them into the kitchen. I take a deep breath. I did it. I sat and had dinner with a total stranger without acting like a total dick. I'm shattered, elated, and stuffed with Italian food. I feel good.

Moments later, Kelsey bounces into the kitchen carrying the lasagne dish. 'So, what do you think?' she gushes.

I can't help but wind her up. 'It was delicious.'

'I meant Travis, you numpty.' She rolls her eyes at me. 'Though he is pretty delicious, isn't he?'

She sounds so joyful I can't resist pulling her in for a hug. She drops the dish onto the counter and reciprocates, squeezing me tight. I blink away my tears.

'I'm so happy for you. He's nice.' I let go of the hug and turn to wash the dishes.

'"Nice"? Is that it?'

I laugh. 'Okay, okay, he's *really* nice. You're so well-suited.' It's the truth. They emanate happiness and I couldn't help being sucked into it. 'And a detective?' I mock. 'You'll have to watch yourself now. No cocaine binges on a Saturday night.'

Kelsey rolls her eyes and giggles. She takes a plate off the draining board to dry it. 'Don't be an idiot. And don't tell him I told you, but he's so good in bed.'

'Kelsey!' I always thought she was a thirty-four-year-old virgin. I could have sworn Kelsey's vagina was dried up and long forgotten about. We giggle together, and I realise for the first time in a long time – possibly ever – I'm happy.

'There is something I want to tell you, though,' Kelsey says more seriously. 'When I told Travis you worked with Pam, he went all weird on me.'

'Weird?'

'Yeah, all quiet and wouldn't look me in the eye. Michelle, I think he knows something about her.'

'But what?' She can't leave me hanging like that. What does Travis know about Pam?

Kelsey shrugs and says, 'I don't know. I'm sure it's nothing.' She gives me a small smile but I know she's just trying not to worry me.

I press my lips together. I know Pam has ruffled some feathers within social services and is known by the police as being forceful in her bid to save children. It's how she's achieved such great results and, if you ask me, a necessary evil. Whatever it is, it doesn't matter. Pam is a kind soul. That's all I need to know.

Kelsey heads back out to Travis with a cup of coffee, and I pull my phone out of my pocket. Being with Travis and Kelsey and seeing them together has made me feel soppy.

My finger hovers over Aiden's number. When we swapped numbers, I spent the next few days waiting for his call. When it didn't come, I figured he just wasn't into me. But now, basking in the glow of Kelsey and Travis' affection, I can't resist sending him a text to test the waters.

Thanks for dinner the other night. I really enjoyed it. xx

I hit send and immediately cringe. Yeah, okay, he gave me his number, but I bet he never actually expected me to message him. He was just being friendly. Or was he?

He replies instantly.

I enjoyed it too. I can't wait to see you again. xxx

Butterflies play in my stomach. I really am happy. It feels strange, but I like it. Maybe we can double date with Kelsey and Travis. Kelsey will piss herself with excitement. I chuckle to myself as I put the last glass away.

CHAPTER THIRTEEN

TEDDY

I haven't seen Robert in ages. Not since Mummy found the card. I wouldn't tell her how I got it, so I haven't been allowed outside since. I knew if she found out, I would never be allowed to see Robert again; but, I'm still not allowed to see him anyway.

I miss him.

Sometimes, if I listen really carefully, I can hear him in the garden. Has he forgotten about me? I bet he's playing with his other friends – his better friends from school that can count and play football.

A man came around the house yesterday. He wanted to come inside but Mummy and Daddy wouldn't let him in. I watched him get out of his car from my bedroom window. It was a big, black car and it was shiny with massive wheels. It was a really nice car. It looked like it would go really fast.

Mummy kept saying my name, so I stood at my door and took deep breaths, trying to find some bravery. I peeped around the corner. The landing was empty, so I felt a bit braver. I crawled to the top of the stairs.

Mummy and Daddy were standing on the front doorstep talking to the man. The door was nearly shut, but I can just about see them through the crack.

'I've already told you – Teddy isn't here right now. What's it to you, anyway?' said Mum.

'As per our letter, I'm here to conduct an investigation of the welfare of your child.'

'What letter?' That was Daddy answering. I heard the swishing of paper being handed over.

'Another copy for you. As you can see, I dated it two weeks ago, clearly stating that I would arrive today.'

'Who called you?' Mum's voice was deep, gruff, and super calm, so I knew that meant she was really mad.

'That is confidential information. Now, can I see Teddy?'

'He isn't here,' growled Mum. 'Now, fuck off.'

'Now, now, there's no need to be offensive. You're not in any trouble. I just need to see your son.'

'Fuck off!' Mummy yelled, making the birds in the tree fly away. Daddy grabbed the back of Mum's T-shirt to hold her back. Did he think she was going to hit the man, too?

The man they were talking to was a lot shorter than Daddy, so I couldn't see him very well. And he was a bit taller than Mummy, but not much. His head was super shiny, and he looked a bit like a mole. I was scared Mummy would hurt him.

'Don't make me call the police,' he said to her. Big mistake.

'You what?' said Dad. His fists were squeezed tight, and the man took a step back off the doorstep. 'You have no right coming 'round here with your accusations and threats. I suggest you piss off the way you came from.'

'Look, I can see I've upset you. How about we start again? I will come back next week for another visit. Maybe Teddy will be in then.' He hopped off the step and walked back to his car. I didn't stick around to see what would happen next. Quickly, I crawled back along the landing to my bedroom. I didn't need to see this, anyway. I reckon the whole street could hear them shouting.

All I could do was wait. When they're that mad, I know what's going to happen. I leant against the corner of my room, my knees bent under my chin and my arms wrapped tight around my shins.

'Who called social services?' Mummy was shrieking. She sounded crazy and I pictured her ripping the ginger hair out of her head.

'How the fuck am I supposed to know? I bet it was that dickhead next door. She's a right nosey bitch,' Daddy answered. He meant Robert's mum. I think he's right.

Their voices went all muffled. I think they were still talking about Stacey, but they were being quiet so that she couldn't hear them through the wall.

Then I heard the dreaded stomp. It was a louder stomp, so I guessed it was Dad's heavy feet.

I buried my head in my arms. I thought if I hid then maybe, this once, they would leave me alone.

'Come here, lad.' Daddy grabbed me by the hair and pulled me down the stairs. I tried really hard not to, but a squeal escaped me and Daddy yanked harder. I had to bite my lip to stop myself from crying out. I moved my legs as fast as I could; I was scared that if I fell over, he would pull all my hair out of my head.

'Here he is. The star of the show.' Mummy was waiting for me in the living room. Her smile was all twisted. She was sitting on the sofa with her legs tucked underneath her. She leaned forward when I went into the room like she was going to tell me a big secret.

'Social services want to take you into care.' She said the word *care* like it was a horrible nasty taste on her tongue. 'Do you know what they do to little boys in care? Little boys just like you?'

I shook my head. My heart was beating so hard my chest hurt.

'They rape them.'

I didn't know that word, but it sounded really bad. What was she saying? Daddy knew I didn't understand and leant into my face. His breath smelled like beer and fags.

He whispered, 'They make you kiss their cocks, then they stick them inside you.'

I knew that word. It's what Daddy calls his willy when he wants Mummy to make him happy. I didn't want a cock in me. Where do they put it? My body shook all over, and I couldn't make it stop.

I cried.

'It's okay. We have a plan,' said Mum, looking at Dad. 'We need to hide you for a while. If they can't find you, they can't take you away.'

I nodded. That sounded like a really good idea.

'He agrees!' Mummy laughed.

Daddy laughed, too. He said, 'Come on then, boy,' and grabbed me by the top of the arm. I trotted behind him as he pulled me into the kitchen.

We went out the back door and into the garden.

When he opened the door to the shed, it's like a billion alarms have gone off in my head. I have always hated the shed. It's full of massive spiders that Daddy said would bite my head off. I'm not sure if he was just trying to scare me, but just in case, I never come in here.

Daddy tried to push me into the dark hole, and I couldn't help fighting back. I tried to push him away so I could get out. My arms were waving around, and Daddy grunted when I whacked him in the stomach.

I couldn't go in there.

I was crying and I was loud, but I didn't care.

I couldn't go in there.

Dad punched me in the face, knocking me sideways. Then he knelt on the stone floor, so his face was right in front of mine. I tried to turn away, but he grabbed my chin to make me look at him. His face was purple, and he was squeezing his teeth together. I wanted to look away, but I was too scared.

'Get the fuck in there,' he whispered. 'Now.' And he shoved me into the shed with his foot. The door slammed shut behind me and I heard the bolt scrape across.

I stepped backwards, and my back touched the wall, which made me freak out.

This is all my fault. I shouldn't have called Speak Up. They did this to me. They must have told that man about me, and now I'm stuck in here.

Forever.

A whole day has passed now, and I just sit and listen to the rain. And hide from the spiders.

Chapter Fourteen

MICHELLE

There's an ominous atmosphere when I enter the Speak Up office the evening after my dinner with Kelsey and Travis. Everyone is keeping their heads down, and the usual camaraderie feels dampened.

I skirt around the rows of desks and head towards Pam's office, but the blinds are down and the door is unusually shut. 'What's going on?' I whisper to Tanya, a young volunteer from Yorkshire. She turns away from her screen and scans the room, her eyes falling on Pam's office.

'Social services are here,' she sighs. 'Puts us all on edge. You know, in case they bring bad news.'

I'm confused; there's always someone from social services calling in. We have to have a close relationship with them, given our line of work. What is it about this time? What's going on?

'But, why is everyone so tetchy?' I ask her.

'She's shut her blinds. Can't be good.' Tanya's phone rings and she waves me away as she answers it.

I hover around Tanya's desk for a few seconds until awkwardness kicks in. I'm thirsty and the kitchen is conveniently located close to Pam's office, so I skirt past slowly, trying to catch a glimpse through the gap in the blinds.

I can just make out the back of a man's head. He's leaning over Pam's desk, pushing something soft and purple across the surface. His upright posture suggests he means business. He's short and has an incredibly shiny bald head.

I step closer to the door and drop the biro I'm holding. As slowly as I dare, I bend to pick it up, straining my ears in the hope their words drift out through the crack in the door.

I just hear one word: 'Teddy.' My blood runs cold.

Is Teddy okay? What is going on? Are they getting him out of there?

I would never admit this out loud, but Teddy has always been my favourite. I'm not sure if it's just when he can be alone or if it's more a deliberate effort but his calls always time with my shifts, so I get to talk to him on a regular basis.

When he calls, he just wants to talk about the things that make him happy: pirates; his friend, Robert; making pictures with the clouds. There's a darkness laced in his words when he speaks of his parents, but he's always so positive. I love that about him.

He's stronger than I ever was.

A shadow looms over me, making my body jerk. 'Lost something?' Lisa. She's frowning, her eyebrows practically touching.

'No,' I gulp. 'I'm just going to grab a coffee. Fancy one?'

She shakes her head, her eyebrows now meeting in the middle of her forehead. She looks nice today in a floral dress and garish beads. I wonder who she's all dressed up for. She usually looks like she's just got out of bed.

'That's Graham from social services,' she barks, jutting her head at the door. 'What's going on? What do you know?'

'N–n–nothing.' The word comes out as a stammer, and I swallow my embarrassment at being caught snooping.

'Look,' Lisa glances at Pam's door again. She looks scared, which feeds the nerves in my stomach. 'You've spent a lot of time with Pam lately, right?'

I shrug. 'I wouldn't say a lot.'

'Oh, you've definitely become her little pet. Just be careful, yeah? Especially when it comes to that one.' She waves her hand towards the office and walks away.

I stand there perplexed, my mouth wide open. I have no idea what just happened. Was Lisa warning me about Pam? Or the man she's talking to? Or maybe she was just talking a load of crap.

Ever since I started here, Lisa has given me a wide berth. When I questioned Pam about it, she just chuckled. Apparently, Lisa isn't particularly friendly with anyone. Pam had said to me,'But then, you are beautiful, Michelle, and a hit here at Speak Up. I wouldn't be surprised if Lisa is just a little *jealous*?'

I laughed it off, but maybe Pam has a point. Lisa clearly doesn't like me getting close to management. Is she trying to scare me out of a job?

I am just about to walk away when Pam's door opens and the man steps out. His eyes widen when he sees me standing outside her office for no apparent reason.

'Pam, visitor,' he says. His voice is razor sharp, professional, deep. A complete contradiction to his mole-like appearance.

'Michelle! What are you doing there?'

'Erm, just seeing if you wanted a drink? Either of you?'

'No, thank you.' Her tone defies her manners. She's really mad and I press my lips together.

'Okay, no problem, I'll just get off then.'

I scuttle back to my desk and watch as Pam leans down to kiss the man from social services on the cheek. He pats her on the hand and walks away at a shocking speed for such short legs.

Pam watches him until he's out of sight, then turns to me. I catch her gaze and look away, my cheeks burning. I must look so nosey, so unprofessional. It's no business of mine what Pam gets up to in the office. I'm sure whatever, or whoever, that man came to talk about is okay. Everything is in hand.

Though there's something in Pam's eyes that puts me on edge. An excitement. A fire. She's up to something and I *really* want to know what it is.

I watch as she turns away and walks back into her office, closing the door behind her.

Chapter Fifteen

TEDDY

I'm so hungry.

Light is starting to come under the door again, meaning it's morning time. I'm glad – daytime means it's warmer. The sun makes the door warm and if I push my body against it, I can get warmer, too.

I'm still scared, but the crying has stopped. It's like my tears have turned off. Sometimes I feel a spider run over my face, but when I touch it, there's nothing there. My mind is tricking me.

I wish I wasn't so cold. My teeth won't stop chattering and my body hurts where my muscles keep going hard. When Daddy first locked me in here, I couldn't stop crying. But soon I got a headache, and my tears ran out, so I stopped. Now I don't know what to do.

I imagine stories in my head to take me away from here. Stories about pirates. I like pirates. They have one leg and patches over their eyes. They're broken but don't care; they still live on the sea and have the best time.

In my story, they have a really big ship and they're sailing over wavey water, making them bounce up and down. Then a massive octopus comes along and wraps its arm around the boat, snapping it in half.

But just then, a wizard shows up and magics a big sword out of thin air and he stabs the octopus, saving the pirates from drowning. He's a hero. And the pirates are so happy, they give him hugs and jewels from their treasure chest.

I wish the wizard would rescue me.

I must tell Michelle about the wizard. She'll say something that will make me laugh. I like laughing with Michelle, it makes me feel stronger. She makes me feel less lonely. I wish Michelle was my mummy.

My tummy rumbles, ruining my thoughts. I look over to the corner again. There's a freezer there. I didn't even know it was in here. My tummy hurts so badly. It feels like my tummy is going inwards instead of outwards. I crawl towards the freezer. I just want to know what's inside. Just a little peek. Mummy and Daddy won't know.

My fingers are really cold, and I'm scared they'll snap when I pull the freezer door open, but they don't. They hurt me though, and I have a little cry, stuffing my hands under my armpits to warm them up a bit.

It doesn't work, so I give up and go back to the freezer with my super icy fingers.

The freezer has a few boxes in it. They're all white from the ice. I swipe my hand across them, trying to imagine what's inside. Pizza? Chicken nuggets? My mouth is watering. There's a bag in here and I dig my hand inside. Bread. Mummy won't notice a slice of bread missing. Right?

The slices are stuck together, but the thought of eating something has got me all excited, so I pull the bag out and whack it on the floor.

The noise is so loud and I wait, holding my breath. Nothing happens. Mummy and Daddy don't come.

I'm so hungry now. The slices break apart and I bite into one. It's cold, and really hard, but my mouth warms it up a bit and it goes down my throat easier.

It tastes amazing.

I've polished off the first slice and take a second before pushing the loaf back into the freezer, praying I've put it back in the same spot. Mummy can't know I am stealing food, or she'll never let me out.

***

The light has disappeared now. The first time it started going away, I thought Daddy would come and get me. But he didn't. When will my punishment stop? They can't keep me in here forever. Or can they?

Maybe the little man with the baldy head will come and get me. I feel hopeful, until I remember he's from social services. I don't want to be raped.

But, I don't want to be in here, either.

I've finished the bread and stashed the bag behind the freezer, hoping Mummy has forgotten it's in here. Butterflies tickle my tummy when I think about what she will do if she finds the bag.

Now I want my bed. My bedroom.

I miss Michelle. She's always nice to me. She tells me to keep my head up and stay strong, because nothing lasts forever. I try to remember her words when my tears start to fall down again.

I should have let Michelle come and help me. I should have been brave.

If Michelle knew I was in here, she would save me. I know she would. She would never lock a kid in a shed. She would give me food and drink, and she would let me shower and use the toilet.

I stamp my foot.

There's a scraping sound at the door and I lunge to the back of the shed, hiding behind my hands. The door opens and someone shines a torch inside. It's too bright, so I squeeze my eyes shut to stop it from hurting my eyeballs.

'It's okay. I've got you now,' says a voice I don't know. I peek from behind my fingers. A man is looking down at me. He's small and has zero hair. He's the man who was at the door!

He squats down and holds his hand out to me. 'Come with me. It's time you left this place.' I have two choices: ignore the man and stay here in this horrible shed, or go with him wherever he might take me.

I reach out and take his hand.

He leads me through the back door, into the house. Someone else runs out the front, slamming the door behind them. Are Mummy and Daddy still here? It's weirdly quiet. The house is always quiet when they're out, but there is something weird going on. Something feels different in here. It's like the air is heavy.

'Look that way,' the mole-man says, pointing at the wall. He doesn't want me to look in the living room. But, I do. I can't help it – my eyes just go that way.

Mummy is sitting in the armchair in the corner of the room. She's all slumped into the cushions, like she's asleep but really, really deep. Her skin is a funny colour, and she's got something tied around her arm.

Daddy is lying on his side in the middle of the room. There's foamy sick in front of his face. He looks angry, but he's still.

Are they dead?

'Come on, kiddo, keep walking.' The man puts his hand on my shoulder and gently pushes me out of the room. I hadn't realised I had stopped to look.

Then, I realise what's happened. The bad guys have got me.

Chapter Sixteen

MICHELLE

The next day is my day off from the vets. I was going to spend the day in the bath with some scented candles, but I'm eager to talk to Pam about Teddy, so I decide to spend my free time at Speak Up.

Pam is just her usual chirpy self and shuns my attempts to talk about Teddy. At six o'clock, the office is quiet, Pam is reading through some documents in her office and Lisa is on the phone to the internet provider, judging by the colour of her face it isn't a successful call.

I'm bored and frustrated. The rain has just started falling outside and I don't fancy walking home in the inevitable downpour. I pull on my jacket, ready to head home to my comfortable bed and some low-budget horror film on Netflix.

'Fancy a lift home?' Pam approaches my desk as I'm heading for the door. She has her handbag thrown over her shoulder and a fur-lined hat on her head. She looks incredibly cosy.

I glance out of the window. Rain is now hammering against the glass. The world beyond is invisible through the torrential downpour. There's no way I'm walking home in that. Especially when the heated seats in Pam's car are on offer.

'Sure. Thanks.' I zip up my coat and match Pam's stride to the main door out of the office. Just as we start walking down the stairs, the door at the bottom swings open and two police officers enter.

They're polar opposites of each other. The first to enter is a man who towers above me. He brings with him a strong scent of cheap aftershave, making my nose shrivel. His colleague is barely five foot tall and she has a grim, determined look on her face that immediately makes me feel nervous.

'Pamela Greene?' the gigantic man asks us.

'That's me.' Pam sounds amused. I'm bloody terrified. Police never bring good news.

'Can we have a quick word?' I look at Pam for her reaction, but she doesn't acknowledge me, so I follow them upstairs into the main office. Lisa is the only other staff member left in the room and she cranes her neck to listen, but keeps her eyes on her screen to hide it. I snigger to myself. She's going to be so pissed off that I got a front-row seat.

'Ms Greene. We believe a Teddy Owen has been in touch with you regarding his welfare.'

My heart sinks. This is it. My thoughts jump to the worst conclusion: Teddy is dead. I sit down on the nearest chair; I don't think my legs can hold me up. Pam stands rigidly. This isn't the first time she's gotten bad news in here, and she doesn't appear phased.

'That's right. Would you like a copy of his case file?'

'That would be very helpful, Ms Greene. Thank you.'

Pam calls over to Lisa and asks her to copy all notes and call recordings onto a portable drive. Lisa catches my eye pointedly as she opens her drawer to retrieve a memory stick.

'Is Teddy okay?' Pam asks. My heart is in my mouth. But, the police officer just waves her hand, wafting away Pam's question. Whatever has happened to Teddy, it's confidential.

'Please, is Teddy okay?' I beg. 'Is he alive?'

'I'm not at liberty to say at this point.'

What the fuck? I *need* to know if he's okay, but as soon as I open my mouth to ask again, the officer raises a hand to shut me up. Pam rests her hand on my shoulder, warning me against annoying this officer of the law. We need to work *with* them, not against them.

Lisa strolls over and hands the female officer the memory stick containing Teddy's notes. She hovers, hoping to participate in the conversation, but the police officers say their goodbyes and take off.

We watch them leave in silence before Pam turns to Lisa.

'Thank you, Lisa. I will see you tomorrow. Don't stay too late now,' Pam says, ushering me to the exit. I dare not look at Lisa as I walk past her. I can feel her glaring at me. I want to reach out to her and persuade her I know nothing. I'm not privy to whatever is going on here.

Pam knows something; I know she does.

We walk down the stairs and splash through the rain to her car in contemplative silence.

Pam slips the car into reverse and backs out of her parking space. We head off down the high street in the opposite direction of my house.

'What do you know about Teddy? Why are the police here?' I ask her. Pam's expression didn't change once during her conversation with the police. If I'm honest, her reaction – or lack thereof – made me feel uncomfortable. No one can be that emotionally removed.

Pam indicates left and pulls in front of a Land Rover that beeps as it just misses Pam's rear bumper. Something soft rolls out from under the seat and taps my ankles. I glance down. It's the purple bag Graham handed to Pam in her office yesterday.

'If there is one thing I have learned about the police over the years, it's that they have strict procedures. Everything has an order. We just have to take a step back and not get in their way.'

She's fobbing me off and I'm fuming.

'Just tell me what you know!' I'm well aware of how rude I'm being. Pam doesn't owe me anything, but a little reassurance would be nice. I just need to know if Teddy is okay.

'Calm down, Michelle,' Pam snaps. 'Believe it or not, I know what I'm doing.'

Chastised, I keep silent. I push my lips together to wipe off any hint of a pout.

After a few minutes, Pam breaks the silence, her voice softer now. 'Sorry I snapped. It's been a difficult few days.'

'I get it. I'll shut up. I'm just a novice.' I didn't mean that to sound as petulant as it came out. It's the truth. I *am* a novice.

'Michelle, you've surpassed everyone's expectations, including mine. You're not a novice.'

Her words wash over me, but all I can think about is the bag now resting against my ankle.

The dashboard beeps just as Pam turns into the petrol station. 'I timed that well.' Pam giggles her girl-like laugh.

A couple of minutes later, she's filling the car under the shelter of the fuel station, the wind whipping her coat around her. I watch as she shoves the nozzle back into its holder and runs into the tiny shop, where people are queuing to pay for their fuel and shopping.

My fingers twitch and I glance down at Graham's bag on the floor.

Fuck it.

I scoop it onto my lap and pull the zip open.

Throwing a glance over the bonnet, I see Pam is third in the queue. I have a little time yet.

The bag is like a make-up bag, with designated loops for brushes and pouches for eyeshadow and blush. Only, I don't think this bag has ever been used for its intended purpose.

Tucked into each loop is a syringe. There are five in here, all sitting in an organised row. I almost drop the bag in shock. Then, I pull the inner zip open and peer inside. A bag containing a dirty-brown powder is tucked in the middle.

What the fuck?

I'm stunned. Pam doesn't do drugs, does she? She seems so well put together. So professional. There's no way she's using. And Graham brought this bag into the office yesterday. Does that make Graham her dealer? No fucking way.

A shadow passes the car and I quickly zip the bag up and push it back to the floor just as Pam opens the door.

'You okay there?' she asks me, her brows furrowed.

'Yeah, I dropped my phone. I think it slipped under my chair.'

Pam nods and gets in her seat. She doesn't bother to see if I have my phone and my legs begin to wobble with relief.

She pulls out of the petrol station, chatting away about the woman who was in the queue in front of her. But, I can't focus on her words. I just nod along and pray we're home soon.

A few minutes later, I drag my attention back to the present and realise I don't recognise the road we're on. Pam has driven us out of town.

Trees line the road and fly past us at a worrying speed. It's a far cry from the rows of terraced houses that surround me on my usual commute home. Alarm bells ring loudly in my head. 'Where are we?' I ask her.

'Just taking the scenic route.' Pam's jaw is set hard, her lips pressed together into two thin lines. She's gripping the steering wheel so hard her knuckles are white. 'We need to have a little chat.'

I gulp. 'Actually, I'd just like to go home. Kelsey's expecting me. She'll worry.'

'Oh, come on, Michelle. You already told me earlier she's staying at her new boyfriend's tonight.'

Shit.

'I want to go home, Pam.' Pam ignores my pleas and presses her foot down harder on the accelerator. The car is speeding down the puddle-strewn road; headlights shoot past us from the opposite direction. The multitude of potholes make the car bounce around dangerously.

'Tell me the truth, Michelle. Did you look in that bag just now?'

My silence screams the truth.

'Did you look in the pouch?' Pam asks me. Her voice is terrifyingly monotone.

I figure, seeing as Pam knows what I did, I might as well face it head-on. My fear has peaked. There's nowhere else to go from here. But, I could learn the truth about Teddy.

'Why do you have heroin, Pam?'

Pam yanks the steering wheel downwards, pulling the car to the left. She slams on the brakes, causing the back tyres to skid and scream. My head is inches from hitting the dashboard.

As I catch my breath, I clutch my heart and my eyes dart around, looking for someone to call out to for help. We've turned into a side road; it's a small dirt track that I imagine leads to a farm. A puddle spans the entire width of the track in front of us.

Blood rushes to my head, deafening me. I shake my head to gather my thoughts and reach out to grab the door handle. Alarm bells sound between my ears when I hear the doors click. Pam has locked me in.

I turn to Pam. She's staring at me with tears in her eyes.

'Michelle. We need to talk. I need you to understand.' She doesn't sound scary anymore. Just sad, and a little scared herself.

Her change in tone is more terrifying than anything else that's happened tonight. I feel her confession is going to be huge. Life-changing.

Pam puffs out the air in her lungs and grabs the steering wheel, stretching her arms straight. 'The drugs aren't mine, obviously.' She forces a chuckle. 'What you need to understand, Michelle, is that I am willing to go to any lengths to help my children. And I am sure you feel the same.'

Of course! If I had the chance to stop their pain, I would do anything. Absolutely anything.

'Well, Teddy needed extra lengths.' She turns to me, her face hidden under shadow. All I can see is her glistening eyes.

Realisation punches me in the stomach. I recoil back into the passenger door.

'Did you kill them? Teddy's parents?'

Pam's nod is slow and deliberate. I can see the cogs working in her brain behind her eyes.

'Teddy needed help. We both know that. Graham couldn't get in to see if he was alive. The logical step was to remove the barrier.' Her voice starts out calm, but becomes more hysterical as the words come out. 'You must understand that, Michelle. You, of all people, must appreciate what it's like to live with these kinds of people. They don't deserve children.'

'They didn't deserve to die, though!' I cry out.

'Is that really what you think?' Pam screams. 'They were nasty, harmful people. They contributed absolutely nothing to society. They were a menace to their neighbours, and poor Teddy is scarred for life. He will never fully recover from what they did to him. Graham found him locked in a tiny shed. Did you know that? No food, no warmth, not even a pot to piss in. So, tell me, Michelle, do they really deserve to live? Or should they rot in hell?'

I bite my lower lip and stare into the rain.

'Or answer this: does Teddy deserve to die instead? Because that's where he was headed, and you know it. I had to do something, Michelle. I couldn't just let that little boy die.'

I don't know what to say.

Out of the corner of my eye, I see Pam wipe her face. I turn to face her, and I'm horrified to see tears pouring down her cheeks.

'I see your point. I really do,' I mumble. 'But, what I cannot understand is *how*. How could you physically do that? Pam, you took their lives away.' My blood runs cold, freezing me into place.

Pam sighs. 'When you respect the *why*, the *how* is easy. Someone has to look after these children. Everyone knows that the system is flawed. It takes courage to make a change.' She takes a deep breath, steadying her voice. 'I love each and every child that calls into Speak Up. That's why I do it. Keeping that in mind makes it easy.' She leans across me and pulls a tissue out of the box stashed in her glove compartment. She blows her nose noisily. 'Plus, these idiots make it so easy. Wave a bag of heroin in their face and they practically kill themselves.'

Something jostles for my attention in the pit of my stomach. I watch as rain slides down the window. 'Where is Teddy now, then? You can't just kill his parents and pack him off with social services. Talk about red flags.'

'That's Graham's domain. He's worked for social services for years. Like I have said, we don't do this willy-nilly. It's all thought out in meticulous detail. Graham knows exactly what reports to file; which ones need falsifying. Then, he ensures each child is placed with loving parents. It's a delicate operation, but one we have mastered through decades of thought and practice.'

Each child. Plural. I shake my head. 'How many children have you *helped* like this, Pam?'

She sighs and closes her eyes. 'I don't know anymore.'

'Fuck.'

I lean my head back on the headrest and press my fingertips into my eyes. I feel like I've had so much information thrown at me in the last few minutes, I might never catch up.

'Michelle ... When you were younger, your parents treated you appallingly. They died. Have you ever considered where you'd be if they hadn't?'

Of course, I have. I've been over my history countless times. Whenever there is a quiet moment in my head, it's immediately filled with pain and horror from my childhood. Their abuse ruined my life. Had they lived, maybe I wouldn't have.

Pam continues, 'My guess is you wouldn't be where you are today. Helping people. Doing a job you love. Being a great friend to me. And Kelsey. I've seen it all before. You would most probably be so damaged that you'd be stumbling from day to day, completely missing the point of life. All joy sapped away.' She presses a hand on my knee. 'Or, you might even be dead.'

Her words sting. That is exactly how I was living before Speak Up gave me a fresh look at my life. Before Pam picked me up off the ground. I was a drunk, shit at work, and a hurtful friend to Kelsey, who has nothing but love for me.

I groan.

'I feel so tired,' I whisper. I feel like I could sleep for days.

'Just tell me you understand where I'm coming from with all of this. I need to know you're on board.'

'So I don't go to the police?'

'Yes.' She touches my arm. 'And – so you can help me fight this war.'

Chapter Seventeen

MICHELLE

I turn over and stare at the glowing digits on my alarm clock. 03:04. I'm so desperately tired, but sleep is yet to seize me.

Thoughts keep whirling around my head. I try to block them out so sleep can settle, but the more perverse side of me wants to mull it all over. Pam kills people. People who hurt children.

Pam kills people.

I'm swarmed by memories of yesterday evening. Pam's words keep swirling around my head like a fly that just won't piss off. I'm sweating, yet when I push my duvet away, I freeze. So, I toss and turn trying to find a position I can relax into.

It's useless.

I reach under my bed and feel around. To my relief, my fingers clasp the cold neck of a bottle. Hurrah. My emergency supply of vodka. I don't know what kind of emergency I had envisioned when I bought this, but I can guarantee it wasn't this.

My past concerns suddenly seem absurd. My past is just that – the past; things that are gone. So, why did I need to self-medicate for so long? What was the point? Surely a friend turning out to be a murderer is a better excuse to drink?

I hold the bottle against my chest. It's cold and a delicious shiver runs through my body. I untwist the cap.

My thoughts of Pam keep flip-flopping. Pam is a murderer, but she murders for the welfare of the children I want to help. The children who desperately need to get out, before they wind up dead themselves.

Pam is a murderer.

Pam is a vigilante.

Like Batman? I snigger into the darkness, breathing in the alcohol fumes. Even just the smell of the vodka has made me feel giddy, and the tiredness has turned me silly.

Batman was hot though, so he was allowed to cause chaos in the name of protection. Plus, he's fictional. Pam is very much real, as are her actions.

I touch the bottle to my lips.

On the drive back home, Pam told me they found Teddy locked in the garden shed, covered in piss and cobwebs. His skin was blue from the cold. He was going to die there.

Pam saved Teddy's life. That's undeniable. Every child that calls Speak Up is on the path to devastation, whether it's death, pain, or a life of misery. Pam stops that. She's better than Batman. Our bad guys are disgustingly real, and they don't don a cheeky grin and a vibrant costume.

I screw the lid back on the bottle and place it on my bedside table. Drinking will not help with this. I need a rational mind.

I need sleep.

The pillow encases the back of my head as I snuggle back down. I pull the duvet up to my chin and my body feels heavy. My eyelids slowly close and sleep finally finds me.

***

The sound of Kelsey squealing interrupts my dreams, and I'm forced back into consciousness. It's 10:27 and a rare Saturday that we're both off work. What is she squealing about?

My bedroom door bursts open and Kelsey walks in clutching an enormous bunch of flowers in shades of white and yellow. They're beautiful.

'Ooh, they're nice.' I try to drum up some enthusiasm. I don't want to shit on Kelsey's happiness. 'What did Travis do wrong this time?' I mean it in jest, but Kelsey scowls at me.

'As if Travis would do anything so cliché,' she retorts. 'But no. They're for you! Why didn't you tell me you were seeing someone? We can double date.'

Right now, amid my scattered emotions, the thought of double dating makes me want to vomit, but curiosity prevents me from scorning Kelsey. I take the flowers she's handing to me.

I read the note attached to the paper wrapping.

Michelle. When can I take you out for dinner? Aiden XX

My eyes widen and I grip the note tighter. Does Aiden know about Pam? Is he going to try to sweet-talk me into keeping quiet?

'What's wrong?' Kelsey asks. She's pursing her lips like she always does when she's worried.

'I'm fine.' I force a smile. 'It's just a shock, that's all. It's not every day I get flowers.'

Kelsey laughs. 'Well, it's about time. You're a catch.' I resist rolling my eyes.

'You're going out for dinner with this Aiden guy, right?'

I nod. I need to talk to him to find out exactly what's going on. I need to sort through all the noise in my head before it explodes right off my shoulders.

Kelsey leaves my room singing "Sexual Healing" at the top of her voice, whilst swaying and dragging her hands over her body. I think she's trying to be sensual. I laugh. Despite everything, Kelsey is a breath of fresh air. I wish I had seen that years ago, instead of pushing against it.

***

I decide the best course of action is to spend the day ignoring my problems. I banish my phone to my room so I can focus on just enjoying Kelsey's company. Like the old days. Before the drink got me.

Curled up on the sofa, we watch episode after episode of *Grey's Anatomy*, debating who's the hottest doctor (Owen Hunt, obviously).

At six in the evening, there's a knock on the door.

'Ooh, that'll be the pizza,' I say, jumping up.

I'm cold now that I've left the comfort of the sofa, so I jog to the front door. When I push the door open, I'm shocked to find Travis on the doorstep.

He has a sheepish look on his face. 'Sorry for intruding. I was working nearby and just wanted to say hello to Kelsey. Is she in?'

I step aside and let him in, shutting the freezing temperatures outside behind him. 'Go straight through. She's in there.'

I don't even finish my sentence and he's in the living room, greeting Kelsey with a lingering kiss. They're so cute together. I turn away in case I'm intruding. Should I leave the room? What's the protocol here?

Thankfully, Kelsey pulls away.

'What are you doing here? I thought you were working.'

'I am. I was nearby and thought I'd take a break.'

'Nearby? Oh my God, what's happened?'

I hadn't connected the dots until Kelsey said that. If Travis is working nearby, then something horrible must have happened near our house.

'A few days ago, two people overdosed a few streets over. They've left behind an absolute mess. It's all over the news – change the channel.'

I quietly take a seat on the armchair by the television, my hands clasped together as Kelsey grabs the remote.

She is agonisingly slow at finding the news channel, and I am just about to rip the remote out of her hand when the familiar red banner appears on the screen.

We're faced with an image of a small shed. The ticker along the bottom states: POLICE HUNTING FOR BODY OF SMALL BOY AFTER PARENTS DIE OF OVERDOSE.

The newsreader looks glum and is using her most melancholic reading voice: 'The whereabouts of seven-year-old Theodore are still unknown.'

She hands over to the sports news reporter with astonishing ease.

Theodore.

Teddy.

I leap out of my chair. I can't listen to this anymore.

Where is Teddy?

I need to speak to Pam.

Now.

Chapter Eighteen

MICHELLE

My taxi pulls up outside Pam's gate. 'I'll drop you here, love,' the driver tells me. He's tapping away at his next fare on his phone, and waiting for Pam's gates to open is obviously too much effort for him.

I don't have the energy to argue with him, so I hop out and throw a twenty-pound note at him. I exit the car, bracing myself against the cold. The driveway feels much longer when you're on foot.

I finally reach the door and ring the doorbell. An ominous bing-bong calls out from inside the house. No answer.

'Come on,' I mumble into the neck of my coat, trying in vain to find some warmth.

My taxi has driven off and Pam's house is in the middle of nowhere. I don't know what to do. I spin around a few times trying to decide my next move, and breathe a sigh of relief when headlights approach the house.

The car pulls up in front of the row of three garages and the driver's door pushes open. 'Michelle. Is everything okay, darling?' Pam calls out in the dark. 'You look terrible. I was worried I would never see you again.'

Pam bustles over to me, clutching an umbrella to her side, and opens the door and motions for me to go in first. Pam pulls off her coat and takes it into the cloakroom by the door. She comes back with her arm out to take mine, but I pull my jacket tight around my body. My arms wrap around my torso like armour and Pam just nods at me, concern written all over her face.

Now I am here, I don't know where to start.

'Come into the living room. Graham, will you light a fire for us?'

I spin around. I never heard Graham enter. He's like a little Gollum creeping around in the shadows. Without a word, he heads into the living room, presumably to light the fire as instructed.

He's much shorter than Pam and is wearing a black shirt and chinos. He is a complete contrast to Pam, who is wearing the palest pink trouser suit.

Pam sees me shiver and hooks her arm in mine. 'We need to warm you up.' I don't tell her it's the adrenaline making me shake, not the cold.

'We'll just put the kettle on,' Pam calls out to the living room and gestures to me to follow her. Graham pops his head out of the living room door and offers the smallest nod. I watch him watch us walk away. My feet trudge along the hall as if made of lead.

'What's wrong? What are you doing here?' Pam whispers.

'"What's wrong?" What do you think is wrong?' I didn't realise how angry our last conversation had left me. And lost. Now Pam is in front of me, I could claw her eyes out. 'You're a murderer.'

'Oh, don't be so crass. There's more to it than that, and you know it. Those people deserve to die and don't pretend you don't agree with me,' Pam spits. She turns and fills the kettle. How dare she be mad at me? I'm just saying it how it is.

Her motives might be black and white in her head, but in mine they're gloomy shades of grey.

'Tell me where Teddy is.'

Pam opens the drawer and pulls out a teaspoon.

'He's been placed with a lovely foster family in the Cotswolds.'

I scoff. 'Don't lie to me, Pam. It's all over the news. Teddy has vanished and I want to know where the *fuck* he is!' I slam my palm down on the worktop, making Pam jump.

'Everything okay in here, ladies?' Graham is standing in the doorway, holding his ash-covered hands out in front of him. His gaze reaches mine and my blood runs cold. His eyes are black and tiny, like little pebbles. There isn't a hint of warmth in them.

'Actually, no,' says Pam. 'I think you need to explain to us where Teddy is.'

I practically crick my neck, whipping my head to look back at Pam, then Graham, and back again. There's an uncomfortable silence between Graham and Pam, and I don't know what's more terrifying – Pam's loud rambunctiousness with an appetite for murder; or this silent ninja, who I feel has even bigger secrets stashed away. Both are giving looks that could kill.

Pam turns to me. 'I have already told you, Michelle; Graham is my contact at social services. He helps me rehome the children I help. Did you really think he just waltzes into work with a child in his arms and tells them what we did? Do you really think it's that simple? Use your brain, Michelle.'

'And you're okay with all of this?' My voice is way louder than intended and Graham squints at me, his bushy eyebrows connecting over his piercing dark eyes.

'If you're referring to Pam's sheer heroism, then yes.' He walks over to the tap and washes his hands. The water runs black down the plughole. 'So, you're Michelle. Pam has told me about you. She tells me you're special.'

Pam is nodding at me emphatically. I don't respond. "Special" how? What is he going on about?

Graham shifts to face Pam and folds his arms. 'Tell me what is going on here.'

Pam blushes. 'I just want to put Michelle's mind at ease. You told me Teddy has been taken into care, but Michelle here has heard through the grapevine that the police cannot locate him.'

'He's in care.' Graham speaks slowly as he pulls a towel from a hook. He dries his hands at an agonisingly slow pace as we wait for further explanation. He turns to face me and I squirm under his gaze. 'Michelle, do you know how hard it is to place these children somewhere safe? Do you know how careful I have to be to make sure a pattern doesn't emerge? Am I okay with it? Certainly. I think we have demonstrated the lengths we'd go to for these children. And Teddy is no exception.'

Pam nods gently and holds her hand out to Graham. 'I am truly appreciative of that.'

My eyes flit between the two of them. They both share a look of sincerity, but whereas Pam's contains sadness, Graham's is cold. Pam works with compassion. He means business.

I'm still not satisfied.

'But where the fuck is he, then?' I yell. I'm done with Pam's arse-licking and I'm craving a stiff drink. And some damn answers.

Graham presses his fingers together before heading over to a massive wine rack wall that separates the kitchen from the dining area. He pulls out a bottle of red wine, then fumbles around for a bottle opener in the top drawer next to the rack.

Pam abandons the half-made tea and dutifully pulls three wine glasses down from a cupboard behind her. She places them on the counter for Graham to fill with the beautiful crimson liquid.

Their actions take an exasperatingly long time, but the promise of wine is too tempting, and I wait patiently, my heart hammering in my chest.

'As you already know, Teddy is with a family in the Cotswolds.' He takes a sip of his drink, leaving a red stain on his top lip. 'Tracey and Mark Thompson have been trying for a baby for years, but sadly haven't been able to conceive. They cannot afford IVF, and they're unable to adopt because Mark has a criminal record. Fraud.' He casts his eyes downwards. He looks sad. 'Do you know how heartbreaking it is to be told you can never be a biological parent? It rips you apart.'

I turn away, embarrassed by Graham's apparent pain.

'So, I helped them. Off the record. I understand your concern, but I've given Teddy a chance at true happiness. He deserves the best parents, and I really think Tracey and Mark will give him the most incredible life. I hate to say it, but social services won't be able to help him. We simply do not have the resources. The poor boy will be passed around for years and will never know a true home. I think he deserves better than that. Don't you?'

I don't know what to say, so I help myself to another glass of wine, emptying the bottle. Deep down, I know he's right. When the system is so broken that kids are being killed, it makes sense to fight against it. There's too much at risk.

It's all just so messed up. This is too big for me to handle.

I groan and place my palms on the counter, head bent down. My legs ache. Why are we standing? I need to sit down. I need to sit down *now*. I spin around, searching; my legs are wobbling. Pam leaps into action and pulls a stool towards me. Gratefully, I sit down and take a deep breath.

'Thank you, Graham. I am grateful for your help as always,' Pam says, then turns to me. 'I know it's a lot to take in, darling,' she says, placing her hands on my shoulders, her face inches from mine. She smells like breath mints and wine. 'Think back to your childhood. Think of how your parents treated you and how that made you feel. We can stop that from happening to so many more children, Michelle.'

We. The word feels huge.

Pam glances at Graham and he nods. She turns back to me. 'You joined Speak Up to help children. Now this is your chance to truly help, Michelle. I haven't got the benefit of youth like you. Help us save more children like Teddy.'

'You want me to kill people?'

'I want you to rid this country of evil.'

I scoff. 'That sounds very dramatic, Pam.'

Pam shrugs her shoulders. 'But it's the truth. The truth *is* dramatic.'

I think back to when I was six years old. I'd been in my room for days, eating tins of sausages with my fingers, the sharp metal nipping at my skin. Mum called me downstairs, and hope fired my heart. I was so excited to be surrounded by something other than my bedroom walls and I prayed I could have something to eat. Mum was waiting for me at the bottom of the stairs. She had her angry face on, and I had to fight the urge to run back upstairs.

'Having fun?' she asked me. I shook my head. 'I heard you laughing up there.' I glanced upstairs, trying to figure out what was going on.

I was so sure that I hadn't been laughing. When was the last time I laughed? Was I going crazy?

Before I had a chance to think of a reply, Mum pushed her thumb into my mouth and pinned my tongue down. I coughed, and she gripped harder. My arms were flailing. I wanted her to go. I wanted her to just leave me alone. She was grinning at me, enjoying herself, and I just sat there, blinking, taking it. Terror flowed through every cell in my body when Mum pushed her thumb into the back of my throat. She had me pinned to the stairs. I couldn't scream. I couldn't even cry.

I went limp and just took it, praying it'd be over soon.

The sound of her laugh rips through me, and I shake myself back to the present.

I bite my lip, then turn to Pam. 'I can't kill someone.'

'Baby steps, remember?'

I nod, my eyes fixated on hers.

Pam's laugh tinkles around me, a stark contrast to my mother's sadistic guffaws. 'And full training will be provided by yours truly, of course.'

I take a deep gulp of my wine. Pam and Graham are watching me. Pam's lips are pressed together, her eyes full of concern. Graham is smiling at me, revealing his yellow teeth between his thin lips. He doesn't blink, not once.

'Fine. I'll give it some thought.'

Chapter Nineteen

MICHELLE

I stare at myself in the mirror. Who is this person staring back at me with eyes so dark and red-rimmed? My hair is frizzy and strands of grey cut through the dark brown. But, worst of all, if you look carefully enough, the depths of my eyes contain a darkness inherited from my twisted parents. An abyss I'm digging further into.

Can I kill someone to protect a child?

I have no doubt that I would have killed my mum if I had the chance. If only my tiny hands were as strong as my conviction.

Victims of domestic abuse tend to stay with their abuser because they feel love for them. There was no love in me. Disgust? Yes. Fear? Absolutely. But no love. When you're a victim of abuse, the concept of love becomes so fucked up that you confuse it with fear. With hate.

It's a blur of emotion that breaks you and leads you down a path of self-destruction.

As I left Pam's, I told her I would sleep on it before making a decision. She grabbed my arm as I was getting into my taxi and said, 'Michelle. You need to be sure. This isn't something you can just dip your toe into.' Then she hugged me and whispered in my ear, 'I'll stand by your side whatever you do. Please stand by mine, too.' A sob caught in my throat.

I've slept on it for three nights. I called in sick at the vets and have avoided going into Speak Up so I can have some breathing space. Though, ironically, the smell of my bedroom suggests a serious lack of air in here. It smells like meat.

There is a gentle knock on my door. 'You okay in there?' Kelsey calls out. Her sixth sense has told her I've sunk so low that I'm to be avoided. She's right to do so. Coming into my room would be like poking the bear. I would snap her pretty little head off if I saw her, and I really don't want to be nasty when we're getting on so well.

I don't respond. No, I'm really not okay. Stupid question. I roll over in my bed and wait until Kelsey's footsteps head back across the landing, making the floorboards creak as she departs.

I know what I want to do next. I'm just struggling to face it head-on. It's like looking at an eclipse. Look too closely and you're damaged for life, but throwing it a glance proves too tempting.

I can understand Pam's point of view. Damn, part of me even thinks it's admirable; but, it's all just too dark. Too immoral. It's frightening.

One thing I know for sure though, I will not be turning her in to the police.

I throw my duvet back and stroll into the bathroom, careful to check that Kelsey will not pounce on me with her incessant questioning. I can hear her downstairs in the kitchen, singing that tune from *Frozen*. Badly.

I grab my toothbrush and load it up with Kelsey's expensive charcoal toothpaste.

A million questions spiral around my mind. How does Pam do the killings? She can't drug everyone, surely? It would be too obvious. And how many lives has she taken already? My questions terrify me. My imagination is teasing my nerves.

I spit the toothpaste into the sink and rinse my toothbrush, pushing all thoughts of Pam's extra-curricular activities out of my mind. The front door slams as Kelsey heads to work and my shoulders relax. I don't want to go back to my cesspit room. I crave sunlight and fresh air.

In a desperate bid to stay distracted, I find the balls to text Aiden to see if he's free to meet. I need to talk to someone who isn't Pam to see what information I can glean on the whole situation.

He replies right away. *I can take the afternoon off for you. You eaten? Xxx*

No. What you thinking? Xxx

Taxi will pick you up in ten minutes. Xxx

I drop my phone on my bed. Holy shit. I had better hurry.

I love having the house to myself. Blasting Slipknot as loud as my speakers go, fires me up to face the world. I pull on some black skinny jeans and a low-cut top. My boobs look good in the deep V-neck.

I push all thoughts of Pam to the side. I need to divert my attention to stop myself sinking to terrifying depths, and Aiden is the perfect distraction. It's like dancing in the periphery of hell.

I don't find many guys attractive. It's like my brain bypasses appearances, so I always assumed that part of me was switched off. But, Aiden is a breath of fresh air. I get flutters between my legs when I think of him. I bite my lower lip in anticipation of seeing his biceps bulge through his sleeves, his scruffy hair flop over his eyes, and imagining his huge hands clasped around my arse. Okay, maybe I need a cold shower.

It's a long drive to the outskirts of the business district. It's an uncharacteristically glorious day, and I watch as adults flit around trying to cram as much personal time as they can into their one-hour lunch breaks. Some brave souls have dared to wear short sleeves, though I swear I can see their goosebumps from here.

When the taxi drops me off on the outskirts of town, Aiden is waiting at the door to a converted telephone exchange building with a huge smile on his face. The sun is beaming down on him, highlighting the green flecks in his eyes. I want to enjoy him, but doubts flitter across my mind. Does he know what Pam's up to? She assured me he doesn't, but I'm not sure what to believe anymore. So much of our friendship has been built on lies.

I shake my head, pushing my questions aside. There's only one way to get answers; I need to properly talk to him.

'Hello, stranger. I thought you were ghosting me.' He pulls me in for a hug and I breathe in his sandalwood scent. All thoughts of Pam drift away. I'm lost in him.

'Sorry, had a rough couple of days,' I say, as Aiden leads me up a set of stairs. I'm surprised to find the corridor at the top only has one door. Does his flat cover the entire floor? It must be huge.

At Aiden's command, I push the door open and gasp. His flat is one massive room, segregated into areas with exposed metal pillars and half-height walls. The kitchen sits at the other end of the room, modern and glistening as the sun pours in through the full-length windows.

Next to the kitchen is a dining table large enough to seat eight. Then the left-hand wall is dominated by a luxurious navy blue sofa, which is faced by what must be a sixty-five-inch TV mounted on the wall. I spin around, taking it all in. Tucked away in the corner to my right is a massive bed. It's surrounded by luxurious, thick curtains that sweep across the space, separating it from the rest of the room.

'Wow,' I gasp. I've never felt a room so airy and spacious. I feel a ludicrous urge to run around in circles, squealing.

'You like?' Aiden laughs, leading me over to the kitchen.

'I love!' I linger after him, taking in the expensive furniture and perfect design. Pam really knows how to look after her son.

A wooden board lies on the kitchen work surface. It's laden with cold meats and cheeses. A loaf of freshly baked bread sits next to it.

'Did you bake that yourself?'

'Did I fuck.' Aiden laughs. 'Opening packets and making it look nice on a chopping board is about the best I can do.'

'Well, it looks amazing.' I've been living on Pringles and olives for the last few days and my stomach grumbles in anticipation. Aiden slowly turns his head around to look at me. He raises his eyebrow at my belly gurgle, and I feel myself blush.

'We'd better eat before that alien breaks free.' He nudges me with his shoulder, and I laugh. Scooping up the board, Aiden takes me over to the sofa and places the food on the coffee table. I throw myself into the softest cushion I have ever felt.

We eat our lunch as Aiden regales me with stories from his youth. He strikes me as a cheeky little boy with a love of winding people up and causing mischief. He mentions Pam frequently in his stories, but his dad is ominously missing. I'm intrigued and eager to keep the conversation off Pam – for now.

'Tell me more about your dad,' I ask him. His face creases up and I immediately regret asking. 'Sorry, you don't have to do that. That was a stupid thing to say.'

He brushes my concern aside with a wave of his arm. 'It's fine. It's ancient history.'

'Must have been tough for you. I imagine a heart attack doesn't give you much time to prepare.'

Aiden sighs and sinks back into the sofa. He takes a deep breath, eyes closed. 'Fuck it. I've got nothing to hide ... He killed himself.' His explanation is so brusque that I consider the conversation closed. I reach out to touch his hand, but he pulls away. 'I don't tell many people that. It doesn't need discussing, so I just tell people he had a heart attack. Stops any awkward questions.'

Awkward? I have never felt so awkward in my entire life. I am such an idiot to go delving into his personal life.

Sensing he needs some space, I pick up the board containing the remnants of lunch and take it over to the kitchen. I find the dishwasher, which is disguised as a cupboard, and I load it up.

The guilt makes me clench my teeth. Why am I so damn nosey?

As I close the dishwasher, I feel Aiden gently press up behind me. He whispers into my ear, giving me goosebumps. 'Sorry, I didn't mean to embarrass you. I just don't talk about Dad that much. He was a bit of a tool.'

I spin around and lay my hands on his shoulders. Aiden has a curious mix of affection and hatred on his face. From his proximity, I assume the former emotion is for me. But, then why does he hate his dad? I suppose killing yourself is a difficult sin to forgive.

'I get it. I don't like talking about my parents, either,' I whisper. His hand brushes mine and I flex my fingers to hold it, but he's already moved away.

'We've got plenty of baggage between the two of us, eh?'

I start to laugh, but before the sound can escape, he comes close again and presses his lips on mine.

A shiver runs up my spine. He's so gentle I can barely feel his lips against mine. Just as I am sinking into his affection, he pulls away and looks at me.

We gaze into each other's eyes for what feels like a lifetime. Then Aiden pulls me in towards him so that my body is pressed against his. His mouth greets mine with a vigour and passion that weakens my knees. A moan escapes my lips.

All thoughts of Pam have escaped me. There's only this moment. Right now. Here.

Chapter Twenty

TEDDY

My new bedroom is nice. I have a big bed with a drawer underneath and there are a few clothes in there. Some of them have holes in them and there's a massive pink stain on the pyjamas, but I don't mind. They look nice on me and one top has a pirate ship on it. That's my favourite one. There's also a little bookshelf in the corner, with lots of books on it. Some have folded corners and scribble marks. There's a doll lying behind the door that stares at me when I'm lying in bed. I gave her a kick to turn her around so she can't see me anymore.

The best thing is, I'm allowed to sit in the living room whenever I like. The lady showed me how to use the TV remote, but there were too many buttons, and I'm still not sure. So, I turn it on with the red button and watch whatever comes on. It's usually the news, but right now I'm watching a pretty lady show some people around a house in a country called Australia. It looks nice there. Everyone is smiling.

The front door opens and the man with the squinty eyes walks in. 'It's me,' he calls out. 'Glory, you here?'

The lady, Glory, comes out of the kitchen, wiping her hands on a tea towel.

'Here. Any news?'

She sounds nervous. Maybe even scared. My eyes dance between them both as they talk. It's like I'm not even in the room.

Glory is really nice to me, but I keep catching her watching me with tears in her eyes. It made me feel weird, so now I just leave the room whenever she walks in.

'Yeah. He'll get picked up on Saturday. Same time as the last one,' says the man. This time, he looks at me. I turn away; his eyes scare me.

'Saturday? Jesus, that's ages away. You know I'm not comfortable keeping them here that long.'

'Like the cash though, eh?' the man shoots back at her. 'Didn't it get your girl in rehab last year? Not that it did any good.' He laughs.

They stand staring at each other for a little while before Glory says, 'Okay. We'll be ready.'

We? Does she mean me? Ready for what? Where am I going now? I want to stay here. I like the books and I get to use the TV remote.

Since I got here, I've thought about my mummy and daddy all the time. I know they're dead and that means they are gone forever, and I really miss them. A bit, anyway.

They were the only people I ever knew. I didn't know the world would be so big and strange. Everything is just new out there and I don't like it. Not one bit.

The man nods at Glory, then turns to me. He kneels down really close, like he has a secret he wants to whisper to me.

'You being a good boy, yeah?'

I nod.

'You being nice and quiet for Glory?' He pulls his phone out of his pocket.

I nod.

'Well done. You'll be leaving here soon, okay?' He looks at the phone and smiles.

'Where am I going?' I whisper.

He winks at me, but it isn't a nice wink. My body shakes. 'Somewhere far away from here.'

I look for Glory, but she's gone into the kitchen. I think I can hear her crying.

I don't want to go far away from here. I want to go home.

Chapter Twenty-One

MICHELLE

I didn't intend to sleep over. Who sleeps with a guy on a first date? I'm such a slag. But I'm a little bit proud of myself.

We sat on the sofa until the early morning hours. Talking, drinking, kissing. By the time we noticed how late it was, it made no sense to get a taxi home. Aiden slept on the sofa, and I slept in the bed. I now smirk at the memory on the way to work.

'Aiden,' I loudly whispered across the open space of his apartment.

'Yeah?' he whispered back. 'You okay?'

'No. I'm cold.'

'Do you want another blanket?'

'No. I want you.' Aiden's laughter cut into the darkness; seconds later, he bounced into bed next to me. I find solace in that we didn't have sex. I'm classier than that, plus we were a little too drunk. But, we kissed and cuddled, and I fell into a deep, beautiful sleep with his arms wrapped around me.

I felt safe.

***

Maggie isn't in to interrogate me on my fake illness when I arrive at work, which adds to the joyful feeling in my heart. Though, my mood dips somewhat when I see my first client waiting for me.

'Good morning, Pam,' I say to her and bend down to take Felix's head in my hands. 'Hi, boy!'

'Good morning to you, too. You seem spritely today.'

I turn away so Pam can't see my red cheeks. I'm not ready to face her. Her presence invites big feelings, and I just want to float on my cloud for a little longer.

I take Felix's lead and Pam walks back over to the door. She pokes her head out to see who's around. Satisfied that the practice is empty – bar Sharon filing her nails at the front desk – she closes the door quietly and turns to face me.

'I wanted to see how you're getting on.'

'You mean, you want to know what I've decided? My life-changing decision whether or not to kill people?'

Pam cocks her head to the side, her perfect curls dropping to her right shoulder. 'Well, yes; though I prefer to think of it as saving vulnerable children.'

Pam still sounds like Pam. Looks like Pam. Acts like Pam. Except now, I know her darkest secrets and she is so exposed to me. I can see her rawness. I see her truth.

And I can feel mine, edging its way up inside of me. And it's terrifying. Through the shockwaves, I can't help but feel something akin to respect. Pam is determined to help these children even if she's putting herself at risk.

I admire that. Though I quash the admiration down. I'm not ready to face it yet.

'I just want to know how you started all this. Did you just wake up one day and think, *I know how to help these kids, I'll just go and stick a needle in the parents*?' I pull Felix into the low sink, and he begrudgingly gets in for a hose down.

'If I tell you, it must not leave this room. You cannot tell Aiden you know. I know how close you two are.' Shit, does she know I stayed at his last night? I only left his apartment an hour ago. He can't have told her already, for Christ's sake. I feel a little icky.

'Aiden tells me he plans on asking you out on a date,' she smirks, stalling.

I blow out the breath I've been deliberately holding. Oh thank God, she knows nothing. Fraternising with Pam's son when I am dealing with her confession feels shameful. I have no self-control.

Felix shakes water all over me, bringing me back to the present.

My curiosity gets the better of me. I want her to get back to her ominous proposal. I want to know the origin of all of this. Maybe if I can understand where this started, I'll have the whole picture and I can make some sense of it all.

'I won't tell him.'

Pam sighs. 'You know how much I love my son. And one day, when you have children, you'll understand that love makes you do things you never imagined you'd be capable of doing. It's a love that can drive you crazy.'

I squirt Felix with a deodorising shampoo and work it into his fur with my fingertips. He groans and pushes his back into my hands.

'When Aiden told me that his father was touching him, I just saw red.'

I whip my head around to look at Pam. She's avoiding my gaze, her fingers twiddling the zip on her coat.

'Aiden's father was my first kill, Michelle, and I do not regret it. What he did to my son was unforgivable. The justice system simply could not provide the justice he deserved. He deserved the ultimate penalty. Aiden deserved that, too.'

'How did you kill him?' I can't believe I'm asking. Do I want to know the answer?

Pam waves her hands with a nonchalance that sends chills through my entire body, then says, 'I drugged him up and slit his wrists.'

I cough and swallow the bile that is crawling up the back of my throat. I turn the water off and let Felix shake off before throwing a towel over him.

I'm shaking. I can't breathe.

Felix jumps out of the sink and starts zooming around, oblivious to the tension in the room.

'Michelle.' Pam is right behind me; her floral perfume chokes my sense of smell. 'You must see why I had to do it. That repulsive bastard touched my son in places a child should never, ever be touched. He took so much from him. I had to take his life, Michelle. I just had to. It was the least I could do.'

To my horror, I realise Pam is sobbing into her sleeve. She looks pitiful. Tiny and weak. She feeds on her heroism, and I have turned it into something nasty. I can see her world shattering around her as she relives the ultimate pain caused by someone who was supposed to love her. Her integrity is lying in pieces on the floor.

I wrap my arms around her, pulling her into my soggy apron. Felix trots over and places a paw on Pam's leg. She continues to sob into one hand and pats Felix with the other.

'I understand,' I whisper. 'I really do.'

We cry together, releasing the pain we've been through. Both victims. Pam the fighter. Pam does what she does, because there are so many more victims out there. She just wants to put a stop to it. I can see that. I can feel that.

All I wanted as a child was to feel safe. I didn't want masses of Christmas presents or trips to Alton Towers, just safety. Pam is providing that to these children, and, if I'm honest, to me too.

When our tears subside, Pam pulls away and looks at me. 'Look, if you don't want to help, I completely understand; but please, you can't tell anyone about all of this. It would put so many lives in danger.'

Tears are slipping down my cheeks. Aiden was thirteen when Pam killed his dad. How many years was he subjected to such disgusting abuse? How did Aiden turn out so gentle and sweet? He's so ... well ... normal. Better than normal. And that's thanks to Pam.

'You have my word, Pam. Your secret is safe with me.'

Pam sobs.

'And, Pam?'

She turns to face me. Her makeup is smudged and I can see the bags under her eyes. She hasn't slept in days. She dabs at her face with a floral handkerchief.

'I want to help you.'

'You do?' She drops her handkerchief to the floor and claps her hands with delight. Felix grabs the handkerchief and takes it to the corner of the room for a good chew.

'Yes. We can't let people get away with this.'

Pam claps her hands together again. Her cheeks are ruddy and glistening from tears. 'Would you like to join me on my next case? Learn the ropes?'

'Yes.' I nod with a confidence I'm struggling to summon. 'Do you inject them every time?'

'Oh no, sometimes that just won't work. But it's a good place to start.'

I'm equal parts horrified and curious. This feels like some sort of fucked up job induction. Still, I'm almost looking forward to seeing how this goes.

Chapter Twenty-Two

MICHELLE

The last week has dragged, and now it's ten o'clock on Thursday night when Pam pulls up outside my house. Thankfully, Kelsey is at Travis' tonight, so I don't have to try and avoid her nosey questions. I leave the house with the weight of what's going to happen sinking into my shoulders.

'How are you doing?' Pam asks when I shut the door of the Fiat Punto hire car behind me. She looks weird in a black parka, no make-up, and her hair pulled back into a tight bun.

I don't answer her. I don't think there are any words that can sum up how I'm feeling. What is the word for terrified, stunned, sickened, and excited all rolled into one?

Pam drives up to the main road and takes a left towards the motorway. Our target, Kate, lives two hours away, so Pam has ample time to fill me in on the plan.

'There are three essential rules you must never forget. One, we must not be seen.' I nod, staring out the windscreen into the blackness. That's a bloody obvious rule. A chill creeps up my spine and Pam continues. 'Two, wear gloves at all times, and tie your hair up. Three, you watch me; that's all you have to do. This is training – a confidence builder. At no point do you get involved.'

'Okay.' My voice sounds weak, and I cough to toughen it up a bit. 'Okay,' I repeat a little louder. Yeah, that didn't work.

'And, Michelle. If you need to leave, leave quickly and quietly. Come straight back to the car and wait for me.'

'Won't the police trace the car back to you?'

Pam grins. 'No, they'll trace it back to a Diane Herne who lives at a non-existent address in Devon.'

This really isn't Pam's first time. I try to relax into the experience.

'What are we going to use to ... you know ... kill her with?' I ask her. 'Drug overdose?'

'No. Kate isn't a drug addict. So, that means we do not have an obvious cause of death to lean back on. I think we can both agree that we need this to pack a punch and be over quickly. Just watch and learn.'

I gulp. 'What if she overpowers you?' Can Pam overpower someone fighting for their life? Does she have some sort of superpowers I'm not aware of?

Pam throws me a knowing glance. 'You don't need to worry about that,' she chuckles.

I grunt with frustration. Pam is deliberately dancing around the edges of the plan. Probably in case I bottle it. It's pissing me off.

I keep dragging my mind back to why we're doing this. I'm on the edge of my seat, part of me eager to jump out of the car and run.

I know that this Kate woman made her child drink bleach. Pam won't tell me who the child is. She says it'll distract me from the task at hand and make me emotional, which can lead to mistakes.

Pam continues. 'Graham has already taken Kate's daughter into care. He collected her from the house earlier today. Kate was devastated apparently, but it's hard to sympathise when you've heard her little girl sob over the phone. Graham is meeting her new family tomorrow, and he's confident all will work out well.'

I need to address the elephant in the room. 'So, why are we doing this? If her daughter is already gone?'

'Because the woman is vermin, Michelle. And disgusting vermin always find a way to thrive. It'll only be a matter of time before she finds someone else to play with.' She pulls into the right-hand lane, narrowly missing a white transit van. 'I've seen it more times than I can count. A child is taken away and the parent gets bored. Months later, they're pregnant with their next toy.'

I listen to Pam's laboured breathing, and I wait for her to calm down before I ask my next burning question.

'Does she not have any other relatives she can go to?'

'In this case, no. She has an uncle, but he's in prison for stabbing someone with a broken bottle, and quite frankly, even if she had family, that doesn't mean she's any safer. There's no knowing if that family member will keep the child away from their abuser. We often find that they're back in the hands of the abuser within weeks, and you can probably imagine what lies ahead of them.'

We're off the motorway now and winding through residential streets. I watch the streetlights whizz by in a blur.

'She's five, Michelle. At that age, children are resilient. She will adapt quickly, and Graham will check in on her regularly.'

We sit in silence, our thoughts ringing loudly in our ears.

Eventually, Pam pulls the rental car into a side road and parks up next to the curb. She turns to me. 'We'll go on foot from here, in case the engine wakes up a neighbour. It's about half a mile away in that direction.'

We give it a minute, then we get out of the car with our heads down. Pam motions for me to follow her down the street.

We don't see a soul on our travels. Everyone is tucked away behind closed curtains and locked doors. We hear music blare out from one house and I turn my head away, just in case they look outside and see two murderers walk past.

A cat jumps out of a nearby bush, and I almost shit myself. It's a scrawny little thing. Her ribs jut out painfully and her collar dangles loosely. I have to resist scooping her up and saving her.

Pam's steps slow down as she eyes up the numbers on the houses. Silently, she slips into the ginnel next to a house and I follow suit. She pulls me into the pitch-black brick tunnel. 'We'll enter through the back. I have a key.'

'How the fuck did you get a key?' I whisper to her, retreating back.

'Graham.' I can almost hear the shrug in her voice. 'He picked one up when he took our girl.'

The garden is full of debris. Sitting by the back door are a broken chair, a mouldy dartboard, and a rubbish bag spilling its contents, torn to shreds by tiny, sharp claws.

Pam slips the key into the back door and nudges it open. I jump back when it creaks. My heart is in my mouth.

We stop at the threshold of the kitchen. Dirty dishes lie across every surface with various shades of mould breeding on them. It stinks. Musty and grim, and weirdly, something sweet. I screw up my face in a vain attempt to block out the stench. Beyond the kitchen, what I assume is the living room is in complete darkness.

'How do you know she's in?' My whisper barely penetrates the space between us, but Pam presses her finger to her lips and shakes her head. She points to the ceiling, presses her palms together and lays her head on them, mimicking sleep.

I nod.

She motions for me to follow her.

We edge our way into the living room, picking our way over the discarded food packets and cigarette butts. We take the stairs slowly, easing our weight onto each, learning which ones creak. Pam is impressively nimble, showcasing her vast experience. I'm horrified at the thought of all the lives she's taken, but I can't lie; I'm also soothed by her capability.

We round the corner at the top of the stairs. Three doors lay across the corridor. One is open and reveals a small, grotty bathroom. The other two doors are shut. Pam holds her palm out to me, gesturing me to stop. She slips into the bathroom and comes back out holding a towel, which she is folding into a neat rectangle.

We continue our path along the corridor.

A flickering light streams out from the gap under the door at the far end and heavy snoring fills our ears. Kate must have fallen asleep watching TV.

Feeling more confident that our footsteps won't wake her up, we proceed with less hesitancy. The snoring continues.

Pam enters the bedroom first.

Kate is lying in her bed like she doesn't have a care in the world; like her little girl hasn't been taken away from her. Her vast form is sprawled out, almost covering the entire double bed. She has a mask over her face. It makes a soothing, whooshing sound as it forces air into Kate's nostrils. There is a distinct smell of flatulence and dirt. We creep over to the side of the bed and look down at her.

She grunts and shifts position, making me gasp and throw my hand against my mouth. Pam throws me a sharp look, an eyebrow raised.

I raise my hand in apology.

Pam was right. If this woman puts up a fight, she won't get far. She is just a couple of pounds away from being forklifted out of here.

A strange calm washes over me as we stand and watch Kate sleep. QVC plays on the TV, advertising four-figure jewellery that Pam would no doubt describe as cheap and tacky. It stinks of cigarette smoke and rotten meat in here.

Pam nods to herself and with shocking speed swipes the mask down to Kate's chest and whips the folded towel over her face. A small, sad smile plays on Pam's lips.

Kate's snores stop immediately and her eyes snap open. Her gaze lands on Pam and she looks puzzled, which is quickly replaced by desperation as realisation kicks in. Her panic reverberates through my entire body.

She tries to drag her heavy arms out from under the duvet, but Pam launches herself onto the bed with surprising agility, pinning Kate down.

The towel has shifted upwards so all I can see is Kate's chin. I watch the rolls wobble, grateful I can no longer see the terror in her eyes. And that she can no longer see me.

She tries to sit up, but her sheer size plus Pam pushing against her, means her abs aren't able to complete the action.

It's taking too long. Shouldn't she be dead by now?

My mind keeps telling me to run, but it can't seem to communicate with my feet, which remain rooted to the spot.

Finally, Kate weakens and slows down her fight to live.

'Now, now, Kate. Time to sleep.' Pam's voice is filled with disgust. She's staring down at the crusty towel, her chest rising and falling slowly with her calm breath. She looks serious, like she's just completed a tricky business deal.

Kate is lying still now, but Pam continues to push down on her face for good measure. She leans over and whispers into Kate's ear. 'I know what you've been up to, Kate. Did pouring bleach down your little girl's throat give you some wicked satisfaction? Eh?'

Pam has finally let go, satisfied that Kate's life has slipped away, her soul claimed by hell.

'Becks will be safe now, you nasty bitch,' Pam sneers.

The penny drops. Becks. Becks Peters? I know her. I've spoken to her at Speak Up. She's a gorgeous little thing. She has a thing for birds and wants to keep all the birds in the sky in her bedroom.

This woman was her mum?

The room is spinning. My lungs feel constricted as I take everything in. The events of the evening have whacked me in the chest. I want to cry. I want to scream.

Becks Peters lived in this filth? With this piece-of-shit mother?

'I hope she rots in here,' I spit out.

Kate's eyes are locked onto the ceiling; red veins frame her pupils and they're bulging out of their sockets.

Despite the drama, the shock, I'm glad she's gone. Her punishment was deserved.

Pam seems to read my thoughts and takes my hand in hers. She gives it a little squeeze.

We take our leave swiftly. Pam shoves the towel in her handbag as we leave, exiting the house the way we came in.

The streets feel darker on the way back to the car. I'm shaking violently. I can't seem to relax my convulsing muscles.

The rental car is within sight when vomit hits the roof of my mouth and projectiles into the drain. My stomach vacates the small amount of food I could handle for dinner and the bile burns the back of my throat.

I'm spitting saliva when Pam takes me by the elbow and opens the passenger door for me. I take a seat and she slams the car door shut before striding around the front of the car to take the driver's seat.

We're halfway home when Pam finally drums up the confidence to speak to me. 'The first one is always the hardest. I promise it'll get easier.'

I'm resting my forehead on the cold window. We just killed someone. I'm wondering when someone will find her. What state will her body be in? The house already stinks. I dread to think what her corpse will add to the place.

'Michelle, talk to me. Are you okay?'

I let the question drift between us. *Am I okay?* The act itself will forever exist as a memory to avoid, but the consequences of what Pam did resonate with me so strongly. Kate can't hurt Becks again. She can't hurt children again.

I feel cleansed somehow. Knowing that's one less call to Speak Up makes my heart sing. One less child who must endure years of abuse.

'You know what?' I turn to face Pam, and she glances at me before diverting her attention back to the road. 'I'm more than okay. I'm fucking fantastic.'

Chapter Twenty-Three

MICHELLE

I slept at Pam's last night. We didn't get home from Kate's until the early hours of the morning, and the thought of being alone scared me. My thoughts keep jumping all over the place, and I'm worried I'll end up in a place of crushing guilt.

I don't know if it was having Pam's calming presence nearby or the adrenaline wearing off, but the second I crawled into one of Pam's spare beds I immediately fell asleep.

It's now nine o'clock and Pam is wandering in, holding a tray laden with coffee and thick-cut toast.

I devour two slices of toast, one with jam and one with butter. Pam sits on the end of the bed, watching me eat, sipping her cup of Earl Grey tea.

'Did you sleep okay?' she asks me, as I lick butter off my fingers.

'I slept like a baby.' I grin. 'Thanks for letting me stay.'

'It's an absolute pleasure. You can stay any time. How are you feeling? You look well.' She takes a tiny sip of her drink, her little finger sticking out as she lifts the teacup.

I perch the tray on the bedside table and tuck my knees under my chin, wrapping my arms around my shins. 'Far better than I thought I would; though I can't stop thinking about Becks.'

'She'll never have to go back there. No one will hurt her ever again. And Kate got what she deserved.'

'I know.' I chew the inside of my cheek. 'I feel like I should regret what we did, but I just can't. It all just feels right – we did what we had to do. But, I'm scared now. I'm scared about getting caught.'

Pam reaches out and touches my hand. 'You just know what needs to be done. That's a quality you should be proud of. It takes courage to make a change on this planet. And we won't get caught, Michelle. We take precautions, and Graham has vast experience cleaning up any loose ends with the police and social services. How do you think I have been doing this for so long?'

I nod slowly. I don't know Graham one bit, and it feels like a massive risk putting my life in his hands. I need to know more about him.

'How did you and Graham meet?'

'We met at school.' She beams at me. I'm surprised. Graham looks at least two years older than Pam.

'Graham was a rather shy boy in the year below me. I guess I took him under my wing and we developed a strange, loose friendship. Then, over the years, we got closer. Once I started Speak Up, our friendship was well and truly cemented.'

'Have you two slept together?' I grin.

Pam giggles and slaps the bed. 'A lady never reveals her lovers, Michelle.'

'So, you have then!' I just can't imagine it. Pam is so glamorous, and Graham is so, well – toad-like.

'Oh, Michelle.'

'How did all *this* start, then? I mean, who broached the subject first?'

'He did.' Pam stares wistfully over my shoulder. 'He hated going to work at social services every day and not being able to provide adequate help. He told me he needed the children to experience a life they deserve, and they would only get that if their parents got hit by a bus or something. Well, I offered to provide the "something". Graham admitted to me that he'd been falsifying reports for a few years prior to our arrangement, so it wasn't a big jump. Then, it all just clicked into place.

'We started off slowly at first. Picked our targets carefully. It took me six months to pluck up the courage to take out my first target.'

Pam stands to collect my breakfast tray.

My thoughts return to Kate and Becks. 'I think I want to do it again,' I admit. 'I want to learn more. When is your next job?'

Pam chuckles. 'We can't get them all. It takes months of meticulous planning. We can't just barrel in there and take out all the abusive parents. Plus, if we do it too often, we will be sure to draw attention to ourselves.'

I blush. I didn't mean to sound so flippant. Obviously, there must be a lot of work to do. But, I want to learn. I want to be involved. 'But, you'll let me help?'

'I don't see why not. You have admirable enthusiasm, but you need to move slowly on this. Saying that, I think we're going to do great things together.' Pam beams at me before heading over to the door. 'I'll let you know when I need you again.' Just as she leaves the room, she calls out. 'Oh, and Aiden is on his way over.'

I smile and throw the duvet back. My heart is thumping and cliché butterflies dance in my stomach. I showered last night, but I'm paranoid that the stench of Kate's house lingers in my hair so I head into the en suite to scrub myself again.

I stand in the shower feeling the hot water wash over my trembling body, I don't know if it's adrenaline or nerves. Doubts trickle from my mind and burrow into my heart. What is happening to me?

Am I messed up? What kind of person kills people and thinks it's okay? A murderer, that's who. Pam.

In my mind, taking the lives of these people is so justified that I don't feel like I have a choice. Fewer abusers on this planet mean fewer abused children, and fewer abusers going forward. We all know people who are mistreated as children are far more likely to become abusers themselves.

By taking lives, I'm easing so much suffering. That can't be a terrible thing. Right? This isn't about tit for tat, because there will never be any balance. Remove one person and you change a child's life; a child who goes on to make a positive change for future generations. It's a no-brainer.

My mother caused me so much pain. I spent my entire life feeling alone and miserable, and now I feel like I'm waking up. It's as if my soul has re-entered my body.

When she died, the abuse stopped. I may have struggled to cope, but at least I lived to tell the tale. I lived to follow my calling and this feels like the path I was destined to take.

I turn the shower off and step out, wrapping myself in a towel. Maybe if Kelsey moves Travis in, I could move in here. It's so homely and warm. Even the towels feel more expensive than anything I own.

I could be Robin to Pam's Batman.

I head downstairs wearing the clothes Pam has leant me. She promised to leave something comfortable on my bed while I showered and, quite frankly, I'm pissed off. The dress I'm wearing is a rose-red. I'm more inclined to wear black and shades of grey, so I feel massively exposed. Plus, it's tight around my breasts. Don't get me wrong, they look great, but Pam's kitchen isn't really the place for sexy attire. And to top things off, she took away my clothes to be washed. *Fair enough*, I remind myself – they must be riddled with evidence.

Aiden heads out of the living room as I step off the bottom stair. He stops and stares, his mouth open moronically. Slowly, the corners of his mouth lift and the light behind his eyes dances playfully.

'Looking good, Michelle,' he says, throwing me a wolf whistle.

I roll my eyes so far back I think I can see my brain. 'Don't. I feel ridiculous.'

'Oh, you shouldn't. Trust me.' He licks his lips and holds out a hand. I take it and we head into the kitchen.

'You know this is your mum's dress, right?'

'Oh, thanks for ruining my naughty thoughts,' he groans, running his hands through his hair. I laugh at his discomfort.

He looks adorable in dark blue jeans and a smart yet casual green jumper. He's dressed smarter than the last few times I've seen him, and it suits him. Then again, I reckon he'd suit a bin bag.

'So, what brings you here?' he asks me. I was going to ask him the same question, but this is his mum's house. Why shouldn't he be here? We're not all from broken homes.

'I did some work with Pam last night and we finished later than expected.'

Aiden doesn't respond, and I wonder how much he knows. Does he know what we got up to last night? Does Pam reveal her secrets to her little boy? I highly doubt it. She wouldn't risk her precious relationship with her only child.

'Where's your mum?' I ask, changing the subject. I thought Pam would be in here fussing over something, but she's nowhere to be seen.

'She just had to pop out. Though I think she's just disappeared off to give us some alone time.' He raises both eyebrows at me and there's a cheeky glint in his eyes.

'Yeah?' I give him what I hope is a reciprocal saucy smile.

'Oh, yeah. She's pretty eager for us to get together.' I cringe. Pam has joked with me about us hooking up, but I didn't know she'd been talking to Aiden about us, too. How many people are in this relationship? I don't fancy a threesome situation. Things are complicated enough as it is.

'You not working today?' Aiden asks. He's standing super close to me. He smells delicious. I'm getting hints of coconut hair wax and menthol shaving foam.

I shake my head. 'I've dropped some hours at the vets to spend more time at Speak Up.'

'And you're happy with that?'

'I wouldn't have done it otherwise. Why do you ask?'

'Well, I know how pushy my mum can be. I didn't want you to be pressured into something you're not one hundred percent happy with.'

Truthfully, I have doubts about losing some hours at the vets. If Kelsey and Travis decide to step their relationship up a notch and move in together, I'll be homeless. I need to be proactive and save for a deposit for a new place. I don't like how the uncertainty bubbles in my stomach when I think about where things are heading. I just hope Travis is afraid of commitment or something and I can keep living there.

I shake that thought away. Ultimately, I just want Kelsey to be happy.

'I can make my own mind up, thank you,' I snap. I know I'm being tetchy, but I don't like him insinuating that I'm a pushover. If Pam is pushing me, then I'm worried about the direction I'm headed.

No. I definitely know my own mind.

Aiden shrugs and turns to the fridge and grabs the apple juice. He pours two glasses and hands one to me. Our hands touch briefly, and I have to fight the urge to grab him by the waist of his jeans and pull him into me. I want to absorb him. I want to feel his weight on top of me.

He is looking directly into my eyes with one eyebrow raised, like he can read my dirty thoughts. I turn away and hop onto the work surface to drink my juice sitting down.

'What do you do, Aiden?' I ask him. 'I mean, what do you do for work?' It's a topic I have avoided so far. I was worried he'd say he lives off Pam's money and the cringe factor was too huge, but now I'm intrigued. He's certainly dressed smarter today. Has he just come from the office?

'I work in transport. I have my own company. Mainly distributing from Crawley.'

'Yeah? Sounds interesting.' It really doesn't.

'Try not to sound too sincere.' Aiden laughs. 'You're right though, it can be boring. But, it pays the bills and creates jobs, so I'm not complaining.'

'What do you transport?'

'All kinds of things,' he says, turning to refill his glass. Is he avoiding answering? I don't press him. I wouldn't want to talk about my latest activities either. That's definitely a secret I will take to the grave.

Aiden takes a last gulp of juice and places his empty glass in the sink. He has a swagger that screams bad boy, but a gentleness that yells sincerity. It's an intoxicating mix. How does this man function so easily with his abusive history? It's a testament to Pam's parenting and his incredible ability to rise above it all. He's inspirational.

I watch him as he tells me about a gig he went to a few months ago where the singer jumped into the crowd, only to completely misjudge his launch. 'He smashed his back straight into the barrier in front of the crowd. We all thought it was part of the show and we fucking cheered! The poor bastard was carted off on a stretcher.' He is throwing his arms around enthusiastically and his smile doesn't once leave his face. It's so fucking endearing and my laughter echoes through the enormous room.

'You have a beautiful smile,' he tells me, running his hands up my thighs. Electricity shoots up my spine and I cannot resist anymore. I stretch out my legs and pull him closer to me. I wrap my legs around his waist as he watches my dress ride up my thighs and I press my palms onto his cheeks, dragging my fingertips into his hair. We smile at each other, then kiss.

The kiss begins slow and tender, but the taste of each other spurs a passion inside of us, and I pull him in closer.

I'm panting, breathing in his musky scent.

'Let's go upstairs,' he whispers and pulls me off the worktop, my legs wrapped tightly around him. He rushes me into the hallway, then to the bottom of the stairs. I'm giggling! I don't think I have laughed so much in my entire life!

'Oh, my goodness! Have I interrupted something?' Pam exclaims from the front door. Her smile belies her mortification as she hides her eyes behind her fingers.

Aiden drops me to the floor and I pull the hem of my dress back down.

I wish I was wearing underwear.

Chapter Twenty-Four

TEDDY

The floor is freezing. It was okay when we were moving, but now it's getting cold again. I miss the rumbling sound of the van driving over the road. Everything is so quiet now. I can't even hear the birds singing. I imagine them tucked away in their nests like everybody is tucked up in their cosy beds.

The man who was driving has been gone for ages. He has a ring of grey hair around the back of his head and there's a crinkle in the back of his neck. It looked like a sad face looking back at me during the drive. I like that one better than the angry face looking forward.

I tuck my knees up to my chest and breathe into my hands. A shiver starts at my toes and finishes at my head, leaving my head feeling all fizzy. I wish I had a blanket. The coat Glory gave me is nice, but it's too short and the sleeves move up my arms when I hug my knees. I squeeze myself tighter anyway.

Finally, I can hear someone singing. Their voice is getting louder as they get closer. I really want to shout out to them. Maybe this person could help me. But, then it might be the man and he made me promise to be quiet. He said he'd kill me if I make a single sound and I don't want to die. So I squeeze my lips shut.

I keep super quiet. The man's singing sounds all blurry, and Mummy and Daddy taught me that a blurry voice normally means you're feeling moody. Nasty.

The back door swings open, and the man looks down at me. He's smiling. I am so glad I didn't call out. Everything is okay.

'All right, champ?' He's never called me that before. He leans against the van door to steady himself. 'Thought you might be hungry.'

He throws a brown bag at me. It smells amazing, and the bag is still warm with grease stains. It burns my cold hands. I look at the food, then I look at the man. Is this really for me?

'Go on then, you ungrateful twat.' I don't need telling twice and I rip the bag open, spilling the chips and burger onto the van floor. I set about cleaning up the mess as quickly as I can.

I push the cheeseburger into my mouth and swallow, forgetting to chew. When was the last time I had something to eat? It's a cheesy, oozy mess and the bun has little seeds on it. I think the red sauce is called ketchup. It tastes like heaven and my eyes fill with tears.

The man wobbles again and grabs the door frame to stop himself from falling backwards. 'Go easy now, kiddo. You don't need to shove it in so fast. You'll give yourself the shits.'

I don't go easy. The chips are long, salty, and hot, and I push four into my mouth at a time. This is the best food I have ever tasted. I close my eyes and let myself forget I'm sitting in a van for one second.

The pretending doesn't last long. Once the food is gone, the man grabs the bag and throws it onto the road behind him. Then he slams the door shut and goes back to singing his song about being a champion. It's a song I recognise from home. Daddy used to sing it when he played on his pretend guitar, strumming at the air and jumping across the living room. It's a happy memory and tears sting my eyeballs as I think about it.

We're moving again, but the van feels shakier this time. I think it's because the man is drunk. He farts and it really stinks. It's like rotten meat and the beer Daddy used to drink before he ... The man chuckles at himself and farts wet bubbles again. It makes me gag. Stuffing the food into my mouth and the wobbly van have made me feel really sick. Now his fart smell makes the food shoot straight back out of my mouth.

I'm sick everywhere.

'What the fuck?!' The man screams at me. He turns to look at me and jerks the steering wheel. I'm thrown into the side of the van and crush my arm. More vomit pours out of me, splashing my face.

The van slams to a stop, and I crash into the chairs at the front. I hear the man stomp around the side, then he yanks the back door open and pushes his way inside. I cry out as he grabs me by the ankle and drags me outside. My sick smell merges with the fart smell and I finish emptying my dinner into the dirt. Trees lean over me like gigantic monsters. It's so dark out here.

'You dirty little shit!' the man yells at me. 'Take your dirty fucking clothes off and clean up this mess before I slice you open.'

I'm too shocked to move, and he slaps me around the face. I grab my wet cheek and I cry.

'Crying won't get you anywhere, little dickhead. Take your clothes off.'

Slowly I strip off. It's so cold I shiver all over, and my skin stings. I throw my clothes into the ditch at the side of the road and now I'm standing in just my dirty pants. I swallow down the burning liquid that keeps threatening to come back up and I squeeze my eyes shut. Please, just let this all go away.

The man shines the torch on his phone into the back of the van. 'For fuck's sake,' he mumbles. He leans over and reaches for a roll of big blue tissue and hands it to me.

'Clean this up. And be quick, we're on a deadline.'

I take the tissue off him and pull some off the roll. Then I get to work pushing the lumps of tummy-burger onto the ground outside. It doesn't take long and we're soon rumbling down the road again.

Everything I had in the whole world now lies in the ditch next to the road.

It's just me, in this van, in my pants. In the cold.

The man is quiet now. Sometimes, he swears under his breath.

I wish it didn't smell so bad in here. I wish I knew where we were going.

One thing I do know, though ... where the man dropped his phone.

I squeeze it tight. I'm not going to let it go.

Chapter Twenty-Five

MICHELLE

'How's things?'

I jump, almost spilling my coffee. Lisa is looming over my shoulder. The spotlight beams down on her wide head, making her stature look intimidating.

It's an unseasonably warm day, and I enjoyed the stroll from the vets to Speak Up this evening. Images of Aiden kept flitting across my mind, keeping me company as I crunched my way over the fallen leaves. But, why do I get the feeling Lisa is about to ruin my joy?

'Erm, good?' What does she want? She clearly has an agenda; I can tell by the way she's eyeing me up. Besides, she never talks to me unless she absolutely has to, usually a rota issue or a big problem with a child. I'm hoping for the former. 'How are you?' I give her a big cheesy smile in the hope she goes easy on me.

She doesn't reciprocate. 'You're getting cosy with Pam, aren't you? You've been holed up in her office together all week.'

I just look at her, unsure how to answer that. 'We're just good friends,' I mutter eventually.

'What are you getting up to? Together.'

'Sorry, Lisa, but what has this got to do with you?' Why am I poking the beast? Do I have some sort of death wish or something? When she finds out Pam has offered me a full-time paid job, she's going to lose her shit. So far, Lisa is the only one on the payroll. Everyone else volunteers. Maybe she thinks I am coming for her job.

It's Lisa's job to manage the timetables of all the volunteers, so she's always busy. I don't envy her, really. When people donate their time, they're really flaky with their promises and she constantly needs to call around. I'd rather be on the phone helping the kids directly.

I would never take her job but there's no way I am breaking the news of my employment to her. That's Pam's job.

'You want to watch yourself with Pam. She's not the fairy godmother she pretends to be.' She taps her temple. 'I know stuff about her that'd make your toes curl.' With that bombshell, she turns and walks away.

What the fuck does she mean by that? Does she know about Pam's after-hours activities? I watch as she lurches her bulk across the room back to her desk, throwing me a look over her shoulder as she sits down. She can't know. If Lisa knew, the police would know, too. There's no doubt about that.

All I can think about is finding our next assignment.

I can't help it. The second I pick up the phone, I'm thinking about giving the child a chance at happiness that no one else can give them. My taste for vengeance is well and truly whet.

As Pam keeps reminding me, we can't jump in on every case. As the brains behind the operation, Graham makes the final call on all assignments. We can't just charge in gung-ho and start taking all the fuckers out. We'd be sure to screw it up. Plus, Graham needs to find a family in advance who will take the child, otherwise things will get too complicated too quickly, and the entire project will be at risk.

Of course, not every child needs to be saved. We get several calls from children who don't like their perfectly nice parents. One child calls every time her parents say "no" to her. I don't mind. It's nice to be reminded that some children's biggest problem is not being allowed a new sparkly pink pencil case.

Pam isn't in this evening and the office feels empty without her presence, despite being occupied by ten other volunteers. She's wining and dining a prospective financial backer. Pam is loaded, but she's savvy enough to take a handout if it's offered. It's amazing what local businesses will hand over in exchange for getting their logos on the Speak Up website.

My phone rings.

'Hello, Speak Up. Michelle speaking. How can I help?'

Silence.

I press the earpiece against my ear. I can hear someone breathing on the line. The breaths are short and panicky.

'I'm here when you're ready to talk.' During orientation, we're told the best course of action is to provide space for the child. Even children like to fill silences. It's human nature.

The silence goes on for what feels like forever. I'm just opening my mouth to speak, when a tiny voice pipes up.

'Michelle, it's Teddy.'

I bring my hand up to my face, pushing the headphone harder to my ear so I can hear better.

'Teddy. How are you?' My voice wobbles. I really miss talking to this little guy. His whimper tears at my heart and I lean forward to listen more carefully.

'What's going on, Teddy?' I ask him.

'I want to go home.' He's sobbing. 'When can I go home?'

I open my mouth to speak, but I don't know what to say and I end up just mumbling something nonsensical at him. I need more info. What's going on here? Where are his new parents?

The line goes dead.

I've spoken to Teddy many times since I joined here, and I know what horrors he's experienced, but he has never sounded this ... sad. I feel desperate to reach out to him and give him the biggest hug.

Teddy's words go round and round in my head. He wants to go home? To his piece-of-shit parents? Are things that bad? Or is he just having a wobble? His life has completely flipped upside down; it can only be expected that the little guy is craving his old life. It's all he knows. Even if it was vile.

I get up and go to the loo. I need space away from my desk to let my heartbeat settle.

Both Pam and Graham have vouched that Teddy is now living in an incredible new home in the Cotswolds. I trust Pam, I really do. But then, why does he sound so miserable? What's going on?

When I get back to my desk, I glance at the clock. I'm shattered, and it's only ten to ten. Ten minutes until I can call Pam. I don't want to do it now with Lisa's beady eyes on me.

I open the browser on my computer and type "missing boy, Theodore Goodwin" into the search bar. I click on the top link. An image of a team of forensic officers appears on my screen. They're digging up the garden at Teddy's family home. I know they're way off the mark, but my stomach turns all the same.

It's a very real outcome for many of the children who call in here, and it was a real possibility for Teddy..

I scroll down and re-read the report. It is believed that prior to their death, Teddy's parents locked him in the garden shed. He was in there for days, as evidenced by the bodily fluids and excrement found in there.

A sob catches in my throat. The truth hits hard. Graham found Teddy in the shed. He rescued our little lad.

I am so grateful for that.

I can't do this anymore. I need air. I quickly close down everything on my computer for the night, grab my bag and jacket, and jog downstairs onto the street.

Being late on a Monday night, it's fairly quiet outside. A man is looking in the estate agent's window, perusing the "to let" board. A homeless man is tucking himself into a doorway with his dog by his side. He's always there. I have given his dog the odd treat, but maybe I should get him a blanket or something.

I try to call Pam, but she doesn't pick up. After two more attempts, I give up and leave her a message.

'Pam? I need to talk to you. Can you give me a call as soon as you get this?'

I don't want to give too much away. Pam has lectured me on not leaving breadcrumbs. You can never be too careful.

The walk home feels slow when the temperature drops like this. The ridiculous thing is, I have a driving licence. I just don't want to pay out for a car –they're expensive beasts. Though now I've curbed my need for booze every day, perhaps I could afford a little runaround.

I check my phone. Nothing.

To divert my mind from going crazy, I ponder my car options as I hurry through the park. I want something small; it's been years since I drove, and I'll need to work up my confidence. I quite like the look of them Suzuki Swifts. They look badass.

What was that? I spin around, trying to find the source of the noise. I'm sure I heard a twig snap behind me. Maybe it was an animal. But, there's nothing – or no one – there.

The hairs are standing up on the back of my neck. I sense something, someone watching me, and I pick up my speed.

Footsteps hit the concrete behind me. I break into a run. The footsteps get faster, matching my pace.

I twist my neck to see who's chasing me. My breathing is laboured and my abs ache from the panic.

I only see the rock.

Then I feel nothing but my life slipping away.

CHAPTER TWENTY-SIX

MICHELLE

Jesus Christ, that hurts.

My head is pounding like I've spent the evening drowning myself in an expensive merlot. It wouldn't be the first time.

But no, I didn't drink last night. Did I? I'm sure I didn't. I try to turn my confusion into memories of last night, but I can't drum up any images. Everything is just ... black.

I shift in my bed. It feels weird. It smells clean and the sheets are scratchy. This isn't my bed.

Then it all comes flooding back to me. The park. The footsteps. The sensation of my skull caving in.

My eyes refuse to open on their own, so I prise them open with my fingers. The tubes in my hand make it tricky. I manage to crack them open a millimetre, but the light is abominably bright in here. I squeeze my eyes shut again to regather myself before peering behind my fingers.

Then my ears kick into action, and I can hear multiple people pottering around outside the sky-blue curtain that encircles my bed. The staff are bitching about someone called Mavis who has made a shit round of teas. By the colourful language they're using, I'm guessing Mavis isn't around to defend herself.

There are strange beeps and buzzing noises and when someone walks past, my curtain blows towards me. I pull my thin blanket up to my chin.

Then a gap appears in the curtain and a pretty, young lady in a nurses uniform pops her head through.

She spies me awake and smiles. 'Hello, sleepyhead. I'm Priya. I need to check your blood pressure. Is that okay?' She comes in wheeling a machine and without waiting for an answer, wraps the cuff around my arm. 'You've taken quite a bump to the head there. Still, the abrasion was mostly superficial and Dr Stephens has patched you up nicely.'

'How did I get here?' I'm mortified to feel a lump in my throat and hear my voice waver. Am I going to cry?

'You haven't spoken to anyone yet? Oh, well – you were incredibly lucky, hun.'

I bristle. I hate being called "hun", especially when it comes from someone younger than me.

'Some young man found you in Stately Park last night. You were conscious when the ambulance brought you in, but you were in a bit of a state. We patched you up and kept you in for monitoring.'

'What time is it now?'

'Two o'clock. You missed lunch, but I set aside some shepherd's pie if you want it now?'

'I need to go.'

Priya's smile morphs into a grimace; apparently she's offended by my lack of desire for shepherd's pie.

'You can't go until the doctor has discharged you. Just get some rest. You had a nasty fall.'

'But, I didn't fall. Someone hit me.' I reach up to touch the top of my head where the rock slammed into my skull. I feel stitches, but thankfully the damage feels minimal.

'Hit you? No, hun; you fell. The man who brought you in said you fell.'

'Who brought me in?' I bark.

'Oh! I don't know hun, my shift only started a few minutes ago. I'll go and find out. We'll need to call the police. They'll need to talk to you.'

'No! It's okay. I'm just being paranoid.' I don't want to talk to the police. I want to stay as far away from the police as I can. They might smell Kate's murder on my skin.

'But, if someone assaulted you ... '

'No. I think you were right the first time. Yeah, I remember now. I slipped on ice and down I went. I'm a clumsy idiot.'

The nurse looks at me with an eyebrow raised and I look away, too scared to catch her eye in case she tells me off for lying. We both know it isn't cold enough for ice.

Her mouth bobs open, but she looks in no mood to fight.

A beep sounds on her machine, and she tucks her stethoscope into her ample cleavage. 'Your stats are fine. Who shall I call to collect you? When you're discharged.'

I glance around and discover my phone on the little table next to me. I reel off Pam's number and the nurse leaves. Her eyebrows are tightly knitted together, and she doesn't bother to try to hide her scowl. She is so pissed off. She knows she's being lied to. Never mind; I've got bigger problems.

Nerves trickle through me. I check my belongings and I find that I still have my phone, my bank card, and £5.62 tucked into my jacket pocket, so whoever hit me wasn't trying to rob me. Or were they? Maybe they decided my ancient phone and pocket change weren't worth it? But then, they'd already whacked me. Why not take what they can?

I can't shake the feeling that this is related to Speak Up. Or more specifically, related to what I got up to with Pam the other night.

Does someone know what Pam is doing? But then, why attack *me*? I've only been on one job, and I didn't even do anything. Maybe it was a warning meant for Pam. Or am I being naïve? Maybe someone meant to hurt me. Do I have an enemy?

The room is spinning, so I tuck myself further down into my bed. I just need to chill for a minute. Stressing out about it will not change anything.

My thoughts drift to Teddy. Pam didn't return my call. A quick check on my phone shows me that the Teddy investigation hasn't made any progress. I am in limbo.

I must have dozed off, because the next thing I know I hear Pam's voice ring out in my ear.

'Pam, why are you shouting?'

Pam smiles at me, her teeth so perfectly straight and white. 'I'm not, my darling. I didn't say a word. You must have been dreaming.'

I sit up and rub my head.

'You have been in the wars, haven't you?' Her blood-red coat covers her beige, slim-cut suit, and she has painted her lips the same shade of red. Her hair is pulled back into a ponytail so tight it slants her eyes upwards. She looks sinister, almost creepy.

I don't want to talk about me. I can wait. First, I need answers.

'Teddy called last night.' I try to get out of bed, but Pam gently pushes me back down. 'Pam, we need to find him. He sounded miserable. There's something going on, I know it.'

'Michelle, Teddy is fine.'

I wait for her to go on, but she just stands up and inspects the controls on my bed. 'I'd like a robotic bed,' she says. 'I wonder how much they cost. You know, for a good one.'

'Pam, please. Teddy!'

'Oh, for goodness' sake. Calm down and look.' Pam unclasps her handbag and fishes out her phone. After a few taps on the screen, she turns it to face me.

Teddy is looking up at me through the screen. He's smiling, his blue eyes dancing as if he's been in fits of laughter. He's clutching a packet of ready salted crisps, and crumbs are sprinkled over his lips and his left cheek. He's gorgeous. Happy.

'They took this yesterday. Teddy's new parents sent it to Graham, who sent it to me.'

'But, he sounded so sad.'

'No one is saying this is easy on the children. Their previous lives might have been terrible, but we have torn them apart, and they need time to heal. Even the most abused child can miss their family until they establish their new norm. It takes time, but I promise you, Teddy will be okay.'

We lock eyes. I'm lost in thought about Teddy. Is he really okay? What Pam is saying makes perfect sense. Of course, Teddy will have tough times. But, he didn't just sound sad – he sounded traumatised. Like, the version of Teddy I knew from before. When his parents were still around.

But, they're gone. And Teddy is okay.

'Okay. Thanks, Pam,' I say, though doubts still linger.

Pam clasps her hands together. 'Good. Now we've got that sorted, let's get you back to mine. What did you trip over? Looks like quite the bump to your head.'

I push the covers back and take my clothes that Pam has placed on the end of the bed.

'I didn't trip, Pam. Someone hit me.'

'Excuse me?'

'I was being followed, and when I turned around to see who it was, they whacked me around the head.'

'But, who would do that to you?'

I shrug. 'No idea. I was hoping you would know.'

'Me? How would I know? If you are referring to our little project ... ' She bites her bottom lip, taking a chunk out of her lipstick. 'Have you told someone, Michelle?'

'Of course I haven't!' I'm aghast. Does Pam think I'm casually telling people we're murdering people?

'Then *this* has nothing to do with me. I can assure you; our little operation is kept awfully close to mine and Graham's chests. You're the only one I have ever told about my little secret, and that's the way it will stay. As far as I'm concerned, you're safe,' she says.

'I should go back to mine,' I say. I'm not sure how I feel about Pam right now. This whole situation has made me paranoid, and I want to be alone.

'Oh, don't be silly. You'll be far more comfortable at mine.'

'I need clothes and things, Pam. It's okay, I ... '

'We can collect some en route,' she snaps. I look at her, my brows creased. I don't have the strength to argue, and I pull my top over my head.

***

Seeing Pam in my tiny two-bed terraced house is weird. Don't get me wrong, it's a very *nice* two-bed terraced house, but her presence fills it. It's like her personality is just too much for our little space.

I motion for Pam to stay in the hall while I track down Kelsey. She's going to fly off the handle when she sees me all patched up and I want to talk to her alone.

When I enter the living room, Kelsey and Travis are snuggled up on the sofa. They must both have a rare day off together.

When Kelsey sees me she squeals so loud, I think she's perforated my ear drums. 'Mich! I've missed you so damn much!' She drags me in for a tight hug which I reciprocate with fervour. I hadn't realised how much I had missed her, too.

'How's things?' she asks me. Travis gives me a little wave from the sofa.

'Erm, okay, I guess.' My hand inadvertently touches the spot where the rock collided with my head, drawing Kelsey's attention.

'Oh my God, what happened to you?' She grips my arms and turns me around to scrutinise the stitches on the top of my head.

I gently push her away. 'I fell. Don't look so worried, I'm fine.' I laugh, but it sounds forced.

'What is going on with you?' she whispers. 'You've been weird for weeks and something just doesn't feel right about this.' She wafts her hand in front of my face. 'Things were just starting to get good between us again, and then you go and push me away.'

'Oh, come on. I thought you were pleased I was getting out more. You get more time with your boyfriend now.'

'Oh, don't be like that.'

'Like what? Kels, I didn't mean it to sound bitchy. It's the truth. I am genuinely happy for you! Can you try and do the same for me?'

'I'll be happy for you when you're not coming home with stitches in your head.'

'I told you – it was an accident.'

Kelsey doesn't look convinced and turns to Travis for support. He just stares at me, taking it all in.

Pam breaks the silence by stepping into the room and Kelsey steps back in shock when she sees her.

'Go and pack your bag, Michelle. We should be off,' Pam tells me.

Kelsey squeezes my hand. 'I just know there's something going on with you. I know you, remember?'

I can't be bothered with this, being pulled in two directions. I'm not a fucking pet.

'Kelsey, you're only bothered because you can't control me anymore. I can make up my own mind.'

She drops my hand. I don't know why I said that. Kelsey has been nothing but amazing to me. Last night's events have me all fired up.

'I'm going to stay at Pam's. Give you two some space.'

To my surprise, Travis stands up. He breaks the tension between me and Kelsey by holding his hand out to Pam. 'Pamela, nice to meet you again.'

A smile twitches on Pam's lips. 'Why, hello. What a pleasant surprise. How are you keeping?'

They shake hands limply.

'Very well. Putting your Good Samaritan Award to good use?'

Pam laughs her tinkly laugh. I watch as her eyes shift into focus and realisation sweeps across her face. She's just realised they must have met at some sort of awards ceremony. Her smile twitches into one more forced. The light behind her eyes evaporates.

'It's always nice to be recognised for our good work.'

We need to get out of here. You could cut the tension with a knife. I race upstairs to grab some clothes from my room. Kelsey follows.

'So, that's the famous Pam, is it?'

'I wouldn't say she's famous. Look, you know Pam has been really good to me. She's dug me out of a massive hole and given me opportunities I needed to live my life again. I've been too sad for too long, and I'm finally happy. I thought you wanted that for me?'

Kelsey watches me grab a couple of scruffy bras from my top drawer and sighs. 'You're right. I guess this is all just ... different. But, different doesn't necessarily mean *bad*.'

'Exactly.'

'I just miss you,' she whispers.

'I miss you, too. I'll visit more, I promise.'

I finish packing and head back downstairs. I find Pam and Travis sitting on opposite sides of the living room in silence. Pam is perched on the edge of the armchair, trying not to let her expensive suit touch our fading brown cushions. They both look pissed off.

'Ready?' Pam asks me. I nod. 'Let's go then.'

I turn to Travis, but he looks away, so I turn to Kelsey, who still looks concerned. She gives me a brief hug and I leave.

Chapter Twenty-Seven

MICHELLE

I'm snuggled up on Pam's sofa clutching a hot chocolate when Aiden walks in. He's looking suave in straight-cut dark denim jeans and a crisp white shirt. He's clutching a bouquet of deep red roses.

'Hello, beautiful. Mum tells me you need some company,' he says with a wide grin. His tanned skin contrasts with his white shirt and his forearms look muscular.

I want to kiss him. Instead, I take the flowers and gush over their scent. The flowers are huge, the petals delicate, and colour vibrant. I feel a sense of joy push deep into my stomach.

'Thank you so much, they're stunning,' I say, placing the flowers on the coffee table. 'I'm surprised she called you, after what she walked in on last time.' I blush at the memory of Pam seeing me with my legs wrapped around her son's waist, my arse cheeks poking out the bottom of my (her) dress.

'Oh, please. Mum couldn't wait to tell me about the damsel in distress.' He sits on the end of the sofa, places my feet on his lap, and strokes my shin. 'She seems to think a sweet girl like you will help keep me in line.'

'In line? Are you a naughty boy, then?'

'Wouldn't you like to know?' He throws me a wink. I like that he's naughty, but what secrets is he hiding? One day, when I've got more energy, I'll prise them out of him.

'You not working today?'

'Yeah, I am. But, I'm the boss.' He shrugs. 'Normal rules don't apply to me, so I thought I'd take a quick break to see how you are.'

A thrill runs through me. Breaking the rules sounds right up my street.

Aiden huffs at the tray on the coffee table laden with juice and snacks. 'Take me back to when I was a kid. She was always bringing me trays of food. I swear she secretly wanted a cute fat kid!'

I laugh. 'She's just a really good mum. You're lucky to have her.'

'Oh, don't I know it.'

Speak of the devil – Pam walks in holding a beer. 'Aiden, I thought I heard you.' She tries to hand him the bottle, but he holds his palms up to her.

'No thanks, Mum. I really can't stop. Despite what Michelle thinks, I do have a job to get to.'

I nudge his thigh with my foot, and he gives it a gentle squeeze. Pam practically pees herself watching our affection. She must really want to set her boy up.

'That's a shame,' she simpers pathetically.

'Sorry, Mum. I just wanted to check in on Little Miss Bump here.' He turns to me. 'You okay, yeah? Mum told me someone did this to you. Did you see who did it?'

'No, it was dark, and it all happened too quickly. To be honest with you, I feel like a massive idiot. Who walks through the park in the dark, on their own?'

'You shouldn't blame yourself, darling,' Pam pipes up. 'Anyone should be able to walk wherever and whenever they like without being assaulted.'

'Yeah, but you and I both know the world is a shitty place,' I say.

We sit in contemplative silence. Aiden breaks my train of thought by leaning over and kissing me on the cheek. The tenderness takes me by such surprise that I bring my fingers to where he kissed me.

'I'll see you soon, okay? How about I take you out when you're feeling better?'

'I'd like that.'

Pam slips out of the room, taking my flowers with her. Aiden leans in and cups my face in his hands. I pucker my lips, ready to be kissed.

'Tell me if you remember anything about the guy who did this.'

I look at him quizzically, my lips dropping open. He continues, 'Because I swear to you, I will kill him.'

Without another word, he gets up and leaves. I hear the front door slam behind him and moments later, his motorbike roars into action as he heads down the driveway.

I'm such an idiot. I bloody puckered up for him, and he refused. He must have noticed my faux pas; I cringe. Groaning, I pull the blanket over my head. I feel hot with shame.

I try to console myself. Did he notice? He seemed so wrapped up in killing my attacker that maybe he didn't see me making a complete fool of myself. Besides, he wants to kill the guy who did this to me. That's pretty romantic.

'You okay under there?' Pam giggles. I pull the blanket down. She's standing in the middle of the room with a pink notebook tucked under her arm. 'Are you well enough to talk about our next target? I thought it might take your mind off things. Unless you've got other things you'd like to mull over?' Her grin makes me cringe all over again. No, I definitely do not want to reflect on my stupidity.

I ignore her jab. 'Yes. Come and sit down.' Maybe I should sound less enthusiastic about our next target, but taking my mind off Aiden is very appealing right now.

'Righty then. Graham called. The next child is called Michael, and is all set to be taken into care.' Pam reads from her notes. The notebook is full of her curly handwriting. I wonder if it contains every case she's ever worked on. The police would have a field day if they got hold of that.

'You write everything down?' I ask her. 'In that?'

'Well, I have to write it somewhere; there's a lot of detail to remember. And this is harder to find than a computer, impossible to hack, and easy to destroy in a hurry.'

I can't argue with that.

She continues. 'Michael is a little younger than those we usually help – he's only two, bless him. Almost three.'

'What happened to Michael? I mean, what have his parents done to him?' It's a messed up question, but I need to know. I need justification.

Pam looks at me and purses her lips. She looks sad for me. 'His mum died last year of leukaemia and his dad, Lesley, blamed Michael. He took to beating him as punishment. Graham has already made contact with the father. He's agreed to give him up, no questions asked.'

'It's that easy?'

'Oh, no – money has been promised. You can see how much this man loves his only child,' Pam says darkly.

I'm revolted. The man is willingly giving up his son, for a bit of cash.

'Of course, a little blackmail goes a long way. Lesley didn't fancy a visit from the police.'

I tut. Everything is just so messed up.

'How did you find out about him? He's too young to call into Speak Up.'

'They don't all have connections to my charity. This one was called into the local social services. Graham has a handful of people helping him, and they put in the call.'

How many people are involved in this operation? More people means more hands on deck to get this right, I suppose. More people who could potentially slip up though, too.

'Michael lives in Kent, so it's a bit of a drive. I suggest we get a hotel, make a night of it.'

My stomach flips. Turning murder into a holiday isn't exactly what I would call a restful break.

'What's the plan?' I tuck my legs up and rest my chin on my knees.

'Lesley is a recovering alcoholic. He doesn't do drugs; he doesn't even drink caffeine. He is also over six feet tall and a keen weightlifter, so we need to find a way to overpower this action man.' Pam chuckles at her little joke. 'That said, I think we should let a knife do all the work. A man with the tendency for such violence towards a child always has enemies. Enemies the police can point a finger at.'

A few weeks ago, I would have been shocked, disgusted even. But, things have changed. *I've* changed.

'Can I do it?' I ask. The question spills out of my mouth before I even know it's there. I touch my cheek in shock, but now that it's out in the open, it feels right.

'By all means.' Pam smiles at me, snapping her notebook shut.

CHAPTER TWENTY-EIGHT

MICHELLE

Graham has had a private investigator follow Michael's dad for the last three weeks. This PI guy has discovered that Lesley's routine is wonderfully predictable.

Three times a week, Lesley goes to a boxing club in the middle of Tunbridge Wells. He has an agreement with the manager that he gets to work out after closing time in exchange for free haircuts at the barbershop he owns.

Thanks to the PI, we know that after he leaves the gym, he locks up then heads to the pub near his house in Poundsbridge for an orange juice or two. Lesley hasn't once called social services to ask after Michael. He hasn't even changed his routine. It seems working out is far more important than getting his son back.

We're now sitting outside the gym in our rental van, rubbing our hands together to keep warm. If all goes to plan, we have ten minutes before Lesley emerges. We can see him in the window, lifting weights that must weigh more than an actual grown human.

'Aiden has been talking about you,' says Pam in the darkness.

'Yeah?' I turn to look out the window, trying to keep an air of nonchalance.

'He says he's taking you out to The Apollo Kitchen. I've been there, it's lovely.'

'Oh really? I don't know much about it.' I've already Googled the restaurant and the menu, and I know where I'd like to sit and I know exactly what I'm ordering. And I've planned my outfit. Yeah, I've thought about it a lot.

'Michelle, at the risk of sounding too overprotective, do you actually like him? I love you too, don't get me wrong; but, I have to ask. I just don't want to see him get hurt.'

Oh, here we go. The whole "you better not hurt my boy" routine.

I puff out all of the air in my lungs and turn to face Pam. 'I like him, okay? And I have no intention of hurting him.' Honestly, who *intends* to hurt someone? I clutch the knife in my pocket and shudder at my hypocrisy.

Pam's gaze holds mine in the moonlight. She squints at me, mulling things over, then relaxes her shoulders. 'Good. I thought as much. I just had to say something. To kill time, you know?'

I chuckle. 'Whatever.'

The light spilling out of the gym windows suddenly goes out. Moments later, the door opens, and the Hulk walks out. Only this Hulk isn't green, and his name is Lesley.

We watch as he inserts the key into the door and locks up. He pulls down the shutters and snaps the padlock shut. That's my cue.

'Ready?' Pam asks me.

'Pam, I was born ready.' I just wish my words didn't contradict my confidence.

I slip out of the van, leaving behind the sound of Pam's tinkly laugh. I give her a confident nod through the window before pulling my cap down low and heading over to Lesley.

'Hiya!' I call out. 'You got a light?' He turns to look at me. His bulk is way bigger up close. He must be doing more than lifting some heavy weights in that gym. My thoughts turn to Michael, this colossal man's punching bag. I resist the urge to kick him square in the balls.

'No, sorry, love; I don't smoke. It's bad for you, you know.' He smiles and I internally recoil at the teeth-to-gum ratio. I count three teeth. How does this guy eat? I imagine he lives on protein shakes and a cocktail of muscle-building drugs.

'No worries. Where you headed to?' I bite my lower lip, hoping I'm passing as seductive.

He smiles at me. I notice his head is caved in at the side and his ears are gnarly. He's an ugly fucker.

'Pub. Fancy a drink?'

I pretend to consider it. 'Oh, go on then. Good-looking guy like you? How could I resist?'

I follow him into the alleyway down the side of the gym that leads to where his car is parked. There are no lights down here and the path is narrow. His bulk blocks out most of the streetlight from the road as he walks ahead of me. I slide the knife out of my pocket and press the button to release the eight-inch blade.

I grit my teeth. I need to get this right. If Lesley doesn't die, it's game over for me. If I don't catch him off guard, he could easily overpower me. Stabbing him in the back is not enough. I go over Pam's instructions, cementing them into my brain.

Be quick. Leave no evidence. Don't get hurt. It's like a mantra rolling around in my head.

'Lesley!' I call out. Lesley stops dead and pulls his shoulders back to stand up straight. His height makes me cower back and I have a grit my teeth to stay strong.

The moron takes ages for the penny to drop. 'Wait, how do you know my name?' He slowly turns to face me.

I thrust the knife into his stomach and yank it back. I take a step back and watch him clutch his gut. 'Your son, Michael, told me. I also know you're a piece of shit.' Blood is turning his white vest crimson. It's spreading at an alarming pace and drips from his hands as he bends over. He's looking straight into my eyes and he's furious.

'You little bitch,' he gurgles.

He falls to his knees and hunches forward. Blood is beginning to pool around him. His skin is shockingly white, even in the darkness.

It's not enough. I clutch the knife in two hands and slam it down, forcing it into the top of his back. A rage overcomes me, and I repeat the motion over and over until I lose count. I only stop when his body goes completely limp and drops to the ground with a disgusting squelch.

I'm sweating and I wipe my brow with my glove. My arms ache. I step away from this lump and resist the urge to spit on him. The number one rule Pam gave me was not to leave anything behind, and DNA feels like a massive breach of that rule.

'Rot in hell, you piece of shit!'

CHAPTER TWENTY-NINE

TEDDY

I wince as I pull the soft scab off the side of my eye where the man hit me. Being sick in his van once is bad, but being sick twice deserves a punch. Every time I pull the scab off, I see his twisted face just before he swings for me. I keep picking at it, though. I like that it stings and I enjoy how the blood trickles down the side of my face. It helps me forget the cold. But then it gets itchy, and I hate that.

He drags me out of the van now. I shiver in the car park and try to cover myself up. I wish I hadn't thrown up all over my clothes.

The man hops into the back and I hear him rummaging around, swearing under his breath. 'It fucking stinks in here ... Where is it?'

I think I might be sick again. If he finds his phone, he will definitely find out I used it.

'Aha, here it is!' The man steps out of the van looking pleased with himself and stuffs his phone in his back pocket. 'It always slips out of my pocket when I'm driving; you'd think I'd learn, wouldn't you?' He sounds friendly – he's not mad anymore.

My shoulders relax and I look around. Where are we?

The man waves at me and I follow him along the wall of a massive building. The windows have bars on them and the glass is broken in some of them. The drains smell real bad.

The man taps on a door and I hear a lock slide back. We step into the dark inside.

'Mooney, long time no see. How are you doing, bud?'

Another man. I can't really see him, but he sounds nice. He struggles to say the letter "s" just like my dad did. Tears prickle my eyes.

'All good,' the van driver tells him. 'The boss here?'

I hear something move, so I think the other man pointed somewhere.

We walk down a hall, my eyes starting to get used to the dark. There are lots of doors, all of them shut, but we walk down to the open door right at the end of the corridor. Light flickers on the other side. It reminds me of a TV and excitement tickles me. I'd love to watch TV.

We walk into the room and I have to stop myself from crying out.

There must be over ten children in here. All are sitting on the floor, cross-legged. In total silence, watching TV. I have never been around so many children and I don't know where to look first.

They're all looking at me now, and I remember that I'm just wearing pants. I look for the man, but he's talking to someone else now. Their heads are close together and I think they're having an important conversation so I shouldn't interrupt.

I look around the room again and a girl with bright red hair gives me a little wave. I wave back. She taps the floor next to her. Does she mean I should sit there?

I look over at the man again, but he's moving away so I trot over to the girl and sit on the floor next to her.

'Don't worry, they'll get you some clothes,' she whispers to me out of the side of her mouth. 'I'm Juno.'

'Teddy,' I tell her, pulling my knees to my chest. Everyone has gone back to watching the TV where Homer is strangling Bart. Someone laughs, but I don't think that's funny. Not funny at all.

'Shh,' comes a deep voice from the back. 'Who the fuck was that?' It's the man the van driver was talking to. He's hiding in the shadows, but I know from the sound of his voice that he's the boss.

I twist my head away from the TV so I can focus on what the men are saying.

'Two more nights and we'll shift this lot.'

'Two? I thought last night was the last night?'

'I know, but I have another one being brought over from Ireland and I want to wait until she's here.'

'This is our biggest load yet. Sure you'll get them out of here all right?'

'That's not your concern, Mooney. Chill out.'

Mooney grunts. He doesn't sound very happy. 'Fine. I just can't wait to get off babysitting duties, that's all.'

'Oh, shut up, will you? Always fucking moaning, aren't you?'

'Not at all, boss. I'm glad I can help you. You know that.' His voice has turned all soft and floaty.

He's sucking up. That's what Mummy used to say I was doing when I tried to be nice but didn't really mean it. She didn't like it when I sucked up. It made her mad. Thankfully, this man doesn't seem to mind.

'Not long now.'

Not long until what? What's going to happen next?

Chapter Thirty

MICHELLE

Killing Lesley came disgustingly easy. It was like I'd rolled all the pain I have felt in my life into one enormous ball of violence. The release proved cathartic, and I've been riding the high ever since.

I've been staying at Pam's since we got back from Kent a few days ago. When I'm not cosying up in the lavish living room watching American trash shows with Pam, I'm at Speak Up, taking more calls than ever. My thirst for helping these children is rife.

Speaking of thirsty, Aiden is taking me out tonight and I'm sipping merlot while I get ready. Gone are the days when I would gulp wine back like my life depended on it. My life is enriched with purpose now and wine can be enjoyed. It's a drink, and no longer my lifeline.

Pam took me shopping yesterday, and I bought the most sophisticated black dress I could afford. Pam kept trying to convince me to let her pay for it, but it felt so wrong to let her buy the dress her son was going to take off me.

The dress is a beauty, though. It has a lovely snug fit, giving me the perfect hourglass shape. The built-in bra pushes my boobs up, giving me ample cleavage. And, as Pam pointed out, my nice legs are usually hidden away in my ripped jeans. Getting them out feels slutty – in a good way.

'Aiden is waiting downstairs,' Pam tells me, coming to sit on my bed and clutching her glass from the bottle we're sharing. 'You look truly stunning, darling.'

I finish applying my lipstick and turn to face Pam. Her face is full of so much love and kindness, and I have the sudden urge to reach out and hug her. I have blossomed into someone I didn't see coming, and I only have Pam to thank for that. She's like the mother I never had, and if things work out with Aiden and me, then she would make the best mother-in-law. I blush at the thought.

Pam stands, presses her palms on my arms, and blinks at me. 'I never expected any of this,' she whispers. There's a wobble in her voice and I pray she can keep it together. If she cries, I'll cry, and I spent ages on my makeup.

'I feel like we were drawn together for a reason. This was all meant to be.'

I feel the same. Meeting Pam has been the best thing to have ever happened to me. She's completely flipped my life upside down; a life I wasn't even grateful for a few months ago.

'Thanks, Pam,' is all I can whisper. She nods, her eyebrows knitted together.

'You'll have a wonderful night. Aiden will treat you right. But, at the risk of sounding like your mother,' she says, 'go easy on the wine tonight. We all know alcohol has a tendency to loosen one's lips, and Aiden has a marvellous knack for worming his way in.'

What does she mean by that? Does she really think I will tell him I watched a man bleed to death in the gutter? Sounds like the quickest way to end a date, if you ask me.

'Don't worry. I've already imposed a three-glass limit. I don't want to make a tit of myself.'

Pam beams at me. 'That's good. I told Graham you'd be a good girl.'

I turn away and bite my bottom lip, my good mood suddenly gone. What the fuck does Graham have to do with my date with Aiden? He's got his claws all over this house. I'll be damned if he gets involved in my love life.

I have only spoken properly with Graham once, but he's absolutely everywhere. Pam talks about him all the time. I can smell his musty scent lingering in the kitchen after I roll out of bed in the morning. He dictates what we do and how we do it. I feel exposed, so I need to dig deeper into this mysterious ruler.

Pam tries to appease me. 'He's just worried about our project. He took some convincing to let you in, as I'm sure you can imagine. It's only natural for him to worry.'

I guess she's right, but I'm still pissed. I certainly wouldn't want to let anyone else in on our secret. Prison really wouldn't agree with me.

'One last thing before you go,' says Pam, standing up. She's clutching a small navy blue box. When she opens it, I gasp. Inside is a simple amethyst, my birthstone, encircled in a ring of diamonds. It hangs from the most delicate chain. Pam takes it out and motions for me to push my hair back, so that she can put it around my neck.

'Oh, Pam. I can't accept that.' I'm scared I'll break it. I've never had anything so nice before, and surely something that beautiful would just look weird on me.

'Don't be silly. It'll go lovely with your new dress.' She scoops it around my neck and deftly does up the clasp. 'You deserve it, Michelle. You have been my greatest friend.'

'It's beautiful!' I exclaim. The diamonds flash as they catch the light. It really is gorgeous. 'Thank you, Pam.'

'It's no bother at all. Now, have a wonderful date. Make sure he treats you right.'

'Oh, please – we both know you have raised a prince.'

***

Aiden is standing at the bottom of the stairs. He holds a hand out to me and takes mine tenderly. For a split second, I think he is going to kiss the top of my hand like an eighteenth-century gentleman and I cringe. Thankfully, he doesn't take it that far.

Instead, he kisses me on the cheek and pushes his body against mine. He runs a hand through my hair. 'You look incredible,' he breathes into my ear, sending shockwaves through my body.

'You scrub up well yourself,' I tease. Aiden always looks good. It doesn't matter if he's gone for the grunge look, or the sophisticated businessman look. Tonight, he looks particularly sexy in a black shirt and dark grey chinos. He's pushed his thick brown hair back and he's wearing the biggest smile. I want him to just take me back to his and fuck me, but I also want to at least *appear* ladylike.

***

The restaurant is much bigger than the impression I got from the website. The ceilings are high, and the lighting glistens above us, twinkling down on the stereotypical blue and white furnishings. This place oozes expensiveness and I immediately feel out of place. I bow my head and Aiden takes my hand as the waiter leads us to our table, and I'm grateful for his chivalry.

We sit in the corner of the room, far from the hubbub and bright lights of the bar, and Aiden moves his chair so that he's sat next to me, rather than across the table. It's a simple gesture, but one that excites me all the same.

The menu is pages long and the Greek words are intimidating, so I decide to keep it simple by ordering gyros. Aiden opts to be more adventurous and orders something I can't even pronounce. My stomach rumbles and I pray the food comes out quickly. I've only eaten a crumpet today, and that was hours ago.

I have never been in a public setting with Aiden before, and I sense he's thinking the same thing as an awkward silence descends on the table. I look around. There's a hen party causing a ruckus by the bar. A couple reveal the age of their relationship by their lack of interaction. And to my left is a man sitting alone, happily tucking into a salad while pouring over his Kindle.

Aiden's cough brings me back to my date.

'Do you think that man's been stood up?' He gestures at the man eating alone.

'Well, if he was, I don't think he's bothered. I reckon he prefers the company of a good book.'

Aiden chuckles. 'Then he's an idiot. Last I checked, a book can't satisfy you in quite the same way a woman can.'

I press my lips together and laugh under my breath. 'Yeah? When was the last time you read a book?'

'Never. Too busy thinking about women.'

I'm laughing now. Aiden grins at me over his drink. He winks.

I push my leg against his under the table, and he raises an eyebrow. It's getting hot in here.

'Mum was right about you. You're just perfect.' His voice is musky and deep, he's leaning into me, and I get a waft of his aftershave.

'I've never heard Mum speak so highly of someone. You two have a real connection.'

I lean back in frustration. I really don't want to talk about Pam right now. Not while I'm feeling so hot under the collar.

A waitress arrives with our food and places it carefully on the table without asking who had ordered what. My pitta, piled high with pork, onions, and tomatoes, looks divine.

'You've never told me about your parents.' Aiden's remark catches me off guard and I cough. I take a sip of wine to steady myself. 'I know you had a really shitty past, but I don't know anything about them. You know, as people.'

'What do you want to know?'

'What did they do for a living?'

I grimace. Aiden and Pam have everything going for them. They have such a stellar work ethic and I worry that they might sometimes forget that others can lack that ambition. Or that some people like to sit on their arses and do nothing.

'Well, Mum did nothing but sit around claiming benefits she wasn't entitled to. And Dad was some sort of factory worker. He worked hard. Or, at least he was out of the house all the time, so I assumed he was at work.' My eyebrows crease together. It has just occurred to me that maybe he wasn't at work; maybe he just didn't want to come home.

Aiden mistakes my confusion for sadness. 'There must be a good memory buried away in there somewhere? Friends? School? I want to know more about you.'

I shake my head and swallow my mouthful of food. My gyros are tasting more and more bitter as the conversation goes on.

'My parents had a really cool car.' The revelation shocks me. They really did have a cool car. They had a bog-standard Ford Cortina like most people did back then, but Dad hand-painted it – in a bid to escape Mum at the weekend, no doubt. It was lime green with purple flames on the bonnet. In hindsight it was ridiculously garish, but when I was a little girl, it was the coolest car in the world.

I can't believe I had forgotten it. It's like my brain has wiped all good memories and only retained the bad.

'What car was it?'

'A Ford Cortina. You probably don't even know what that is. I bet you had a Rolls Royce growing up,' I tease.

Aiden casts his eyes downwards, cutting my laugh short.

'Sorry. That was shitty of me,' I say to him. I guess mocking someone's upbringing is cruel whether they're rich or poor. 'I know your childhood wasn't easy, you know, with your dad dying ... ' I desperately want to ask him about his dad, but I can't reveal to him that I know about the abuse. I don't want to ruin the evening.

'Oh, it's not that,' Aiden says, reassuring me by cupping my hand in his. 'I have a horrible memory of a Ford Cortina that I don't think I'll ever forget.'

'Want to share?'

He takes a large gulp of his wine and leans in so he's inches from my face. 'If I tell you, you must keep this to yourself. Don't tell a soul.'

'You can trust me.'

He looks deep into my eyes. The pause feels like forever.

He nods and places his wineglass on the table. 'When I was about ten, Mum clipped our car – an Audi, not a Rolls Royce – into the back of a Ford Cortina by accident. Next thing I know, the car had smashed into a tree.'

My blood runs cold. 'Holy shit. Was everyone okay?'

'Yeah. Mum said everyone lived. Fuck knows how, though. Must have been a hell of a bang.'

'What did Pam do after it happened?'

'She panicked and just kept going.'

'Fuuuck.' The word comes out long and exaggerated.

'I know. I'll never forget the car as we flew past it. The people in it didn't stand a chance. The front had completely crumpled, and the bonnet was thrown back over the roof. It was a weird-looking car. Green with purple flames painted on it.'

Chapter Thirty-One

MICHELLE

'Michelle, stop!' Aiden calls out to me as I flee the restaurant. The gyros in my stomach threaten to regurgitate all over the other patrons, and I grip my mouth as I run outside.

Aiden is stalled by the waiter demanding he pay the bill, which gives me time to run down the road, my heels clicking on the pavement. I flag down an approaching taxi, and I launch myself into the back seat.

***

Twenty minutes later, I throw open Pam's front door. Pam is walking out of the kitchen clutching a steaming mug and a packet of Hobnobs. Her eyebrows raise to the heavens when I come barrelling through the door.

'You killed them.' My chest feels tight, and my breath is short. I hear the taxi pulling off down the drive. Pam is frowning at me, rooted to the spot in her confusion.

'Michelle. Are you okay? You look terrible. Where's Aiden?' She places her drink and biscuits on the side table and comes over to me, pressing her hands on the tops of my arms.

'You killed them!' I can't stop myself from yelling.

'Who?'

'My parents.'

Pam steps backwards and puts her fingers to her lips. Her eyes are wide open and she makes a squelchy noise in the back of her throat. Her expression screams the truth.

'Did you know who I was? Did you know who I was when you came to me in the vets?'

'Michelle, please, it was an accident.' She steps back farther. Her face is so white it's almost translucent. 'I didn't set out to kill them. They were driving all over the road and the weather was appalling. One minute, they were a good distance in front of me, and the next they'd slammed on their brakes. I didn't have a chance to respond.'

She inches towards me, but I step back. I cannot let this woman touch me. Her words are tumbling out of her mouth at an almost indecipherable speed. 'I saw them spin off the road, but I had Aiden in the car and I panicked! We were on our own and I couldn't go to prison, Michelle. I couldn't let them take my boy away.'

'But, it was all right for me to go into care?'

'I didn't know you existed!' Pam turns away from me, her arms flailing. 'Not until later, anyway.'

'So, you did know about me before we met?'

Pam nods, slowly. Why is she being shady? I just want the truth! She takes a seat on the bottom stair and rests her forehead in her hands. I want to shake her – shake the truth out of her.

'Look, Michelle, did you ever wonder what led me here? Why I do what I do?'

What has Pam's penchant for killing people got to do with me? Did she enjoy smashing into my parents? Did it give her a taste? I slam my fists against the wall. I wait for Pam to continue, my mind whirling. A guttural groan escapes me.

'Your parents' death was all over the news, with it being a ... you know ... a hit-and-run incident.'

When I saw that they had a little girl, I just lost my mind. You have to understand, I wanted to scream my guilt from the rooftops. But, I had just lost Aiden's dad. I couldn't lose Aiden, too.'

'Lost him? You *killed* him, Pam. What is wrong with you? Take some damn responsibility!'

'Yes!' Pam screams. 'I killed him and I have no regret about that. Not for one second. Then, when the news announced that the people killed were child abusers, I stopped regretting that, too. I was *glad* they were gone.'

She looks at me, and the fire in her eyes makes me turn away. 'You're a wonderful young lady, Michelle, and it's no thanks to them.'

'So, what – I should be grateful to you?'

She watches me, her chest heaving. When she speaks again her voice is softer, pleading. 'How do you think Becks should feel? And Michael? There's a reason you got involved and that reason applies to you, too.'

A sob escapes me and I drop to the floor. This is all too much. I hated my parents, but to think they died so tragically because of this woman standing right in front of me. My mentor. My only family now.

'Why didn't you tell me all this before?'

'How could I, Michelle? I wanted to help you so much and I was so scared you'd push me away.' Tears are falling down Pam's cheeks, leaving streaks through her foundation. I'm ashamed to realise I'm crying, too.

'So, you knew who I was when you came into the vets that day?'

Pam nods. 'I've been keeping an eye on you all these years. I needed to know that you were safe. When I saw you moving in with Kelsey, I was so pleased. You and she were stronger together. Protected.

'But, then I saw you leaving work one day and you looked so lost. So sad. It broke my heart. You were losing weight; your eyes were sunken. I had to do something. I had to find a way to get you the help you desperately needed. And I'm so glad I did.'

'Who else knew? Was your little boyfriend in on it, too?'

She sighs. 'Graham was my access to you. He kept me updated on where you were placed and how you were doing. I have a lot to be thankful for. Graham really looked after you.'

'You call this being looked after?' I cry. All energy has left me. I want to curl into a ball and sleep.

'You have no idea how good you had it, in comparison to other children.'

Her tone takes me aback. How dare she get angry at me? I'm the victim in all of this.

'So, after you left my parents to die a slow, painful death, you what? Set up Speak Up to find more prey?'

'No, I established Speak Up to help children like you. You and Aiden inspired me. My *prey*, as you call them, are a happy by-product.'

Goosebumps tingle my skin and my feet ache from running in high heels. The clock in the kitchen ticks loudly, reminding me that the world continues to spin.

The roar of Aiden's motorbike gets louder as he races up the drive. We listen, neither of us moving a muscle.

Moments later, Aiden bursts through the door. His hair is standing on end where he's whipped off his helmet. His eyes open wide when he spies me crumpled on the floor, then they practically pop out of his head when he sees his mum's mascara-smeared face.

'What the hell is going on?' He croaks, fear laced into each word. He crosses the room to Pam.

'Mum? What's going on?' He doesn't look at me. 'Mum, you're crying.' He tries to wrap an arm around her shoulders, but she shrugs him off.

At last, Aiden turns to look at me. 'What have you done to her?'

I want to yell at him for blaming me, but deep down I can't blame him for protecting his mother. It's what he does. I swallow my anger.

'Please, please don't get mad at her,' Pam says. Her body looks old and frail, as she slumps onto the bottom stair. 'Michelle has just had some bad news, that's all.' Her eyes are pleading with mine. She wants me to keep this to myself; but, doesn't he deserve to know the truth?

Surely Aiden should know who – and what – his precious mother really is.

'What bad news?' He looks from me back to Pam, and back to me again.

We remain in a stalemate. The atmosphere in the room weighs heavy on my shoulders.

'The car your mum ran off the road that night?' The words come out before I even realise they're there. 'It was my parents.'

Aiden stares at me. He's now sitting next to Pam on the stairs with his arm around her, but I notice his grip loosen as the gravity of my words hits him.

'But, your parents are dead?'

'Exactly.'

I let him put the pieces together in silence. His mouth bobs open a few times and his eyes flick between me and Pam.

'You killed Michelle's parents?' He finally lets go of his mum and she sinks into the floor, a puddle of misery. She doesn't need to respond. Her face says it all.

We sit in silence, letting the events of the last hour sink in. Pam stays where she is on the floor. Her crying has subsided, but her sobs break out now and then, cutting into the silence.

Aiden runs his hands through his hair. 'Jesus Christ. I need time to think.' And to my horror, he turns away and walks out the door.

***

Despite my reservations, I sleep at Pam's. Going to Kelsey's would invite a lot of questions that I just cannot answer. Besides, Travis might be there, and hanging out with a detective right now would not be a good move.

I heard Pam come upstairs as I was putting on my pyjamas. She stopped outside my door, and I squeezed my eyes shut, praying she wouldn't come in. I pictured her pressing her knuckles against the door, but she didn't knock.

Now I lie in bed, unable to get comfortable. My muscles keep tensing and I have a whopping headache.

I can't stop thinking about my parents.

The night they died, I was home alone. I was six. They had gone out to meet some friends and I microwaved myself a macaroni cheese before going to bed. It was super dark out when the police hammered on the door. The terror I felt in that moment beat anything I had ever felt. I was home alone and someone was beating on the door.

I was hiding behind the laundry basket when a lady's voice called through the letterbox. It was the police.

I don't remember much after that. Lots of people talked at me, or gave my hand a little squeeze. Then, I was taken away.

I didn't feel sad, I know that. Maybe numb. Lost. Not sad. Going into care was the best thing that ever happened to me. The scars left by my parents were too deep; there wasn't anything anyone could do to reopen those wounds.

But, did they deserve to die? Like that?

I toss over in my bed and pull my pillow over my eyes.

It was an accident. I know that. Does it make any difference whether it was caused by my parents, or by Pam?

In the grand scheme of things, no it doesn't. But, it sure does affect my feelings towards Pam.

I trusted Pam with so much. We have been through so damn much together and I feel a love for her like no other. She's been like a mother to me.

But, she took my real mother away.

Just like I took Lesley away from Michael. Just like Pam took Kate away from Becks. And little Teddy, sent off to the Cotswolds. And I have no doubt in my mind that it was the right thing to do.

I sigh and turn over, relishing the cold sheets against my hot skin.

There's a tap on the door.

'Go away, Pam,' I mutter into my pillow. Why the hell is she knocking on my door at this time? It's just gone 2am – hardly the time for a chat.

I hear the handle turn and whip my head around. 'Not now, Pam!'

The door opens. 'It's me,' Aiden's voice whispers through the darkness. 'Can I get in?'

I pull open my duvet and tap on the bed. Aiden eases the door closed behind him. He hops into bed fully clothed and pulls me close to him. He's deliciously cold and I tremble against his chest.

'Are you okay?' he asks me. His breath tickles my neck.

'I'm just confused. What about you?' One thing I can be sure about is that Aiden deserves none of this. We're both caught in the same crossfire.

He strokes my bare shoulder with the back of his fingers. 'I'm just so sorry you had to go through that.'

I nod and snuggle in deeper.

'I want to hate Pam, I really do; but there's a little voice in my head yelling at me to be grateful for what she did.'

There's a pause before Aiden speaks.

'I understand. Yeah, it's really shitty what she did and that she kept it a secret for so damn long.' He breathes in through his teeth. 'But, what was the alternative? Give herself up? You would have gone into care anyway, only without Graham looking out for you.'

'You know about that?'

'Yeah, I went to see him.'

I bristle. Once again, Graham is in the midst of my business.

'And I would've gone into care, too,' he continues.

He's right. If my parents hadn't died that night, the abuse would have continued for many more years, and I wouldn't have met Kelsey.

If Pam had confessed, no one could win. Speak Up wouldn't exist, either.

Big realisations make me sleepy.

'Shall we park all this for tonight? Maybe some sleep will give us some clarity?'

'Sleep? I've got a better idea.' He pulls me even closer, and I wrap my leg around his waist, pulling him into me. He kisses me with an intensity I have never felt before.

He pushes me onto my back and pins me down, and I give into him. The walls I have surrounded myself with are officially down. I'm lost in him.

All thoughts of Pam and my parents float away.

CHAPTER THIRTY-TWO

MICHELLE

When I wake up the next day, the clouds have lifted, and only a vague haze remains. My bed feels incredibly soft and warm.

After my parents died, I blamed myself. I thought everything was my fault – the abuse, the abandonment, and their deaths. I could never shake the blame and now I wonder if my recent actions with Kate and Lesley are really me searching for atonement.

If Pam hadn't run Dad's car off the road, I honestly think I would currently be crouched down in a corner of a shoddy house, injecting dirty heroin into my veins. I had seen my parents do it enough times. Until I left my family home, I thought heroin was just something people did; a medicine to remove misery.

Now, I protect other children from that fate.

I woke up this morning and my shock of last night was overcast by a tentative gratitude for Pam. She saved me. My whole life has been messed up. Only Pam has provided me with happiness, and a future.

What she did was so damn wrong, but I can't deny that I am glad my parents are dead. They were pure poison. How can I blame Pam for ridding me of that pain?

I scooch over, but the other side of the bed has long lost Aiden's warmth and the chill forces me to get up. He's only been gone for half an hour, but I miss him already.

I blush at my memories of last night. I can still see Aiden pulling his top off, revealing his glorious abs in the moonlight. He glanced down at me and licked his lips before whipping off my shorts with a shocking deftness. Then, he kissed me in places that don't normally see the light of day.

I spend a long time in the shower, reliving last night's joy, before heading downstairs to look for Pam. We need to talk.

She's not in, so I assume she's gone to make things up with Aiden or headed into Speak Up. The kitchen is immaculate, so I skip breakfast in case I leave a crumb on the sparkling worktop. Then, I head down to the bus stop to catch a ride to the Speak Up office.

After the shitshow last night, I need to put some good back into the world.

The office is quiet today. Most of our volunteers either work or study during the day and volunteer in the evening, so daytimes always operate with a skeleton staff. There's no sign of Pam.

I head over to my desk, and I spy Lisa in Pam's office, standing with her back to me. She's alone and the cheeky bitch is rummaging through Pam's filing cabinet.

Leaning against my desk, I stand and watch her with my arms crossed. I wait.

Finally, she turns around and sees me watching her. Her face drains of colour and I raise my eyebrows at her. She better have a good excuse.

She bows her head and scurries out, empty-handed.

'I was just looking for a new wall calendar,' she mumbles as she passes me. 'We need to get ready for the new year.'

'Yeah? I thought you kept them in the stationery cupboard?'

Lisa scratches her head and avoids my gaze. 'I know, I just couldn't find one and thought maybe Pam had misplaced them.'

My heart is hammering in my chest. Is Lisa on to us? I can tell she's lying – her neck is flushed red and her eyes flit everywhere except onto me. We pause, each trying to decide our next move. She looks scared. I'm worried I do, too.

Seconds pass before Lisa scurries back to her desk and flops into her chair, where she pretends to be super focused on her screens. What is she up to?

My phone rings, dragging my attention from Lisa's antics and throwing me into work mode.

The calls that come in over the next few hours are bland. One hoax call really pisses me off, but I push it aside when I get a call from a girl named Mila.

We haven't received a call from Mila before, but before she even speaks, I know her tragedy is bigger than any I have ever dealt with. She is having difficulty breathing. Her high-pitched cries are tragic.

'The baby won't breathe,' she pants.

The hairs on the back of my neck stand up. 'Okay, Mila. Can you give me more information? Where are you?' I try to keep the urgency out of my voice. I don't want to scare her away.

'My baby brother, Dylan. Daddy put a pillow on his face to make him comfy and now Daddy's gone and the baby won't breathe. What do I do?'

A raging heat courses through my veins. I pinch my arm with my nails, drawing blood. I want to scream, swear, and cry, but I can't. I can't help Mila if I have a breakdown.

'Where do you live, Mila? I'll call an ambulance for you.' I close my eyes and pray she doesn't clam up. *Don't hang up*, I pray.

To my relief, Mila reels off her address without a thought. She lives just the other side of the canal, two minutes away. Without thinking, I hang up the phone and run, dialling 999 on my mobile as I go.

I check my jacket pocket for my knife.

***

My chest burns from heaving in the cold air and my vision wobbles as I run. I reach the house in just under four minutes.

Mila's house is small, but tidy. It sits on its own, tucked behind a row of giant conifer trees at the end of a quiet cul-de-sac. I hammer on the door, but there's no response. I'm peering through the window when a man approaches from behind, jangling the house keys in his hand.

'Can I help you?' He's wearing dirty overalls, yet has perfectly coiffed hair and a dazzling smile. Like butter wouldn't fucking melt.

'You live here?'

He doesn't respond. He has the nerve to look confused.

I look him in the eye. 'I'm here for your son.'

'What? Who are you?'

'Take me to him.' Why is this arsehole so jovial? He should be fucking scared. I grip the flip knife in my pocket. I have carried this around since the night I took Lesley down. I refuse to feel vulnerable.

'Tell me who you are, before I call the police.'

'The police are already on their way, you sick bastard. Now take me to Dylan!'

'Dylan?' His entire face turns purple. His hand clenches into a fist around his keys. Fear flits across my mind, but I push it away. I have to focus. I have to protect the children in that house.

'Lady, you're starting to piss me off. Now do one, before I do something I regret.'

'Not until I see your son,' I growl. Time is not on my side. I need to get through to this monster.

He stomps up to me and before I have time to react, he grabs me by the throat and pushes me against the wall. I don't have the breath to cry out for help, and I pray someone walks by, but there isn't a soul around. 'Who the hell do you think you are, you stupid slag?' he murmurs into my face.

His hand grips tighter and my heels lift off the ground. My feet scramble around, trying to catch the ground with my toes.

My hand finds my pocket and I fumble around for the flip knife. The knife pings out with ease and I push it into the man's flesh. He grunts and lets go and I fall on my arse.

The man slips to the ground, clutching his side. His keys clatter as they fall beside him. I step over the pooling blood and scoop them up. I head over to the door, unlock it, and step inside.

'Mila?' I call out. No reply. Oh God, please let her be okay. I scan downstairs and find no toys, no small clothes, no books. There is no trace of children whatsoever, so I run upstairs. The first bedroom is the master bedroom; the bed is made and not a single dirty item of clothing lies on the floor. I try the other bedrooms.

Nothing. Not even a cot, or a rogue small sock. Or a child.

I feel like I'm going to melt. This man doesn't have children. I've got the wrong man.

Or, it was another hoax.

Sirens wail out from the road behind the house. Shit.

I race back outside. The man lies unconscious on the gravel, blood oozing between the stones, creating little morbid islands. He's breathing, but only just.

I run.

Chapter Thirty-Three

MICHELLE

It takes me three attempts to unlock the front door and once I step into the tiny hallway of the silent terraced house on Devonshire Street, I squeeze my eyes shut and drag my hands down my head, scraping blood through my hair. The door slams behind me.

My panting turns to wheezing as panic sets in. I turn my hands over in front of me. Blood streaks across my right palm. It sits underneath my fingernails, still wet. I press down on one nail and blood oozes out from under the nail bed.

I retch and run into the kitchen.

My vomit just about makes it into the sink. It runs down the edge in blobs. Tears stream down my face.

I turn on the tap and thrust my hands under the hot, running water.

The water runs pink, mixing with the splatter of bile.

'What happened to you? Oh my God, are you hurt?' I twist to find Kelsey standing at the kitchen door, her mouth wide open as she stares at the mess in the sink. Her eyes flick to my face.

I stand and stare. I'm frozen to the spot. My mouth hangs open.

Kelsey tears her eyes off my blood-stained top and looks into my eyes. I want to look away, but I don't know where to look. So, I just stare into her deep brown eyes. My whole life flashes before me. Kelsey has been there for me during every shitty step of my life. She has dragged me out of the gutter, given me a home, and found me a job.

I can't do this to her. I can't drag her into my mess.

Kelsey finds her voice first. 'Seriously, what happened?'

She heads over to the sink and holds my hands in hers. She turns them over and tries to rub away the stubborn blood stains.

'Oh, Michelle,' she whispers. Over and over. 'Did someone hurt you?'

A sob erupts from my core, and I collapse onto the floor in a pool of grief. Kelsey drops to the floor with me and cradles my head on her shoulder. She wraps her arms around me and squeezes my waist.

She waits, whilst I cry.

Every piece of pain pours out of me. I have taken hit after hit throughout my whole life, and I have bottled it up for too long. I can't do this anymore. Look at what I have become.

'Come on, sweet. Let's sort this out.'

Kelsey pulls me upright and tugs down the zip on my jacket. She raises an eyebrow at my blood-soaked T-shirt and without a word, slips off my jacket and pulls my shirt over my head.

She hooks open the washing machine with her free hand and throws my T-shirt in.

I have an overwhelming urge to explain. 'Kelsey, please understand. I had no choice. I thought he'd killed the baby. I thought he was going to kill me.'

'Oh, Michelle. What did you do?'

I tell her about the prank call and the innocent man I ... killed. Murdered. I force my voice to remain calm and measured. I need to tell her what I did.

Kelsey just nods along, as if I'm telling her about a bad day at the grooming parlour.

Without a word, she picks up my jacket, slides her hand into the pocket, and pulls out the flip knife.

'What are you doing?' I ask her, pushing myself into the corner of the room.

As she stands up, she pushes the release on the knife and jumps as it flips open. I wince at the memory of the sound from just moments ago. Before I pushed it into that poor man's stomach.

Kelsey drops the knife into the sink and stoops to grab the bleach from the cupboard. She pours the yellow gloop over the knife, coating it, letting it sit.

'What are you doing?'

'Take your jeans off, they'll need a wash, too.'

She means business and I dare not refuse. I kneel up and push down my jeans, slipping out of them. Kelsey takes them from me and throws them into the washing machine along with my jacket. She turns it on to the hottest setting and the machine springs into life, its sole task to remove the evidence of what I have done.

'Kelsey. You don't have to do this.'

'Someone needs to sort you out.'

'It doesn't have to be you. I can sort myself out.'

She throws me a look that screams I can't be trusted. She has a point.

'Why do you do this stuff for me? You're always picking up my shit, no questions asked.'

'Because. I love you.'

She joins me on the floor again and leans against the back door. She sits with her long legs crossed. Her palms rest on her knees. There's a sadness in her. I'm breaking her.

'No, really – why do you keep picking up after me? There's got to be a better reason than just loving me. This … ,' I wave my arm around the kitchen, ' … isn't love. I have always been such a mess and you have cleaned me up time and time again. Then just as I think I'm getting sorted, I do *this.* This can't be just love.'

She gives me a curious look and her eyebrows crease together.

'You really don't remember?'

'Remember what?'

She pauses before shaking her head. 'I don't think that's a conversation for now.'

'No, it's definitely a conversation for now!' I shout. What is with everyone keeping secrets from me? I can't bear any more mysteries.

'I'm calling Travis,' she announces, pushing herself off the floor. 'Go and shower.'

'What? No! You can't call him. Look, I'll face this when I'm ready. I just need time to figure all this out.'

'No, you idiot. I'm not handing you in, am I?' She jerks her head at the washing machine where my clothes are sloshing around, and the bubbles are pink. 'We need his help. *You* need his help.'

I shake my head and pull my knees close to my chest. I shiver, but I don't know whether it's from the cold or terror.

'Please don't call him,' I whimper. 'He won't help me. I know you love him, Kels; but he won't help me.'

'He's on your side. Trust me.'

I do trust her – how can I not? But, there is no way in hell I can trust her detective boyfriend. I can't trust him, and I can't do this to Kelsey. I'm on my own.

I need to grow some balls and turn myself in before I drag anyone else under with me.

I sigh.

'Don't even think about it,' Kelsey tells me.

'What?'

'Turning yourself in.'

Damn. How does she do this?

'What's the alternative? Run? Oh, come on, Kelsey! It's the least I deserve.'

'Talk to Travis.'

Why is she so damn persistent?

'Jesus, Kelsey, you think the light shines out of his arse, don't you? He can't help me. What detective is on the side of the murderer?'

'One who knows the truth, Michelle.'

Truth. That'd be a fine thing. No one around here is capable of the truth. I stare at Kelsey, goading her to tell me, but she just stares back with a blank expression on her face.

Kelsey breaks first. 'Travis knows what you've been sucked into, and he's sympathetic.'

'Sympathetic?'

'Let's just say he knows more about Pam than you do.'

'Tell me.'

Silence. I realise I am standing. When did I get up? My skin itches and I claw nail marks into my arms.

Silence.

'Tell me!' I scream.

'Just trust me on this one. Stay away from Pam and everything will be okay. It won't be long now, and you don't want to get caught in the crossfire.'

Fuck this. Fuck everyone.

I thought the abuse was bad. The depression. Turns out being lied to over and over is a pain that cuts far deeper. So many secrets. It seems everyone has information on me. Except me.

And I'm done with that shit.

As I head upstairs, I hear Kelsey calling out behind me but I ignore her, slamming my bedroom door behind me.

I grab some clothes off the bedroom floor and yank them onto my trembling body.

I don't want to go back into the kitchen for my boots, so I find some grotty trainers I used to jog in (many years ago) and slip them on.

As I leave the room, Kelsey is still pleading with me.

'Please, Michelle, don't go to her. She's bad news.'

I turn around on the stairs and jab my finger into her stomach. 'Look, Kels, I am grateful for everything you have done for me, but you know jack shit about Pam. I'll get what I deserve, but I'll be damned if I let Pam go down, too.'

I continue down the stairs then reach for the doorknob.

'And what about Graham? Are you so sure about him?'

I twist my neck to look at her.

She looks unsure. And scared.

'What do you know about Graham?'

'Mich, he's involved in some sort of child trafficking ring. He's been arrested! You have *got* to stay away from those people. They're vile. And just look at what they're doing to you.'

I leave. I need to warn Pam.

Chapter Thirty-Four

MICHELLE

I'm a mess. My hair tie is clinging on for dear life and tendrils stick to my sweaty forehead. I stink, too. A mix of body odour, blood, and terror.

The Uber driver keeps glancing at me in the mirror. I scowl back, forcing away his polite chat about the weather.

My mind is awash with confusion. Kelsey can't be right; she's just trying to scare me. She has never liked Pam, and given my downfall it's no wonder she's looking for someone to blame.

But, I'm to blame. This is all on me.

I know Pam. Her passion in life is helping children. Her own child was abused, for God's sake. She wouldn't take children away from their abusers, only to throw them into the proverbial fire. She just wouldn't.

I stare out the car window and thoughts spin around in my mind, over and over. I stabbed someone. I fucking stabbed someone. Our mission felt so right before, and now I have let in an infection. It turns out running a knife into a child abuser is a very different sensation than doing the same to a run-of-the-mill jackass.

Can I claim it as self-defence? I mean, he had his hands around my throat. But, how would I explain the knife in my pocket? Why did I just run like that?

Pam will know what to do.

I want to scream and cry. I want to tear my hair out of my skull, clump by clump, just to feel a different kind of pain. My life keeps tipping upside down, and there is no way out this time.

I just need to get to Pam. She'll know ... She just has to know.

'Drive faster,' I tell the driver. He offers a curt nod, but doesn't press his foot any harder on the accelerator. I throw myself back into my seat, rolling my eyes.

When we pull up outside Pam's house, I'm relieved to see her car parked in the drive and I run inside. 'Pam!' I call out. I hear movement upstairs and start to head up there when Pam appears from the dining room.

'Michelle, darling? You look awful. Is everything all right?'

'Oh my God, Pam, I've really fucked up.' I burst into tears and drop my phone and wallet on the side table by the door. Pam reaches out and wraps her arms around me.

'Talk to me.'

My mouth bobs open. Then closed. I don't know how to tell her I killed an innocent man. I've forgotten all the words. Instead, I burst into big baby tears. I groan and writhe into her enclosed arms.

I'm just so sorry. So sorry for killing that man. So sorry for complicating everything. So sorry for distracting Pam when she should have been focussed on what was going on around her. So sorry for bringing Travis into her life.

This is all my fault.

'Oh my gosh, Michelle! Are you hurt?' She motions at my bruised neck, then tugs me into the kitchen and sits me on a stool. She turns to the wine rack and drags out a bottle of whiskey and sets to pouring me a huge glass. I spy Felix wandering around outside, sniffing the grass and rolling in whatever disgusting thing he has tracked down.

I take the drink. 'I don't know where to start,' I mumble.

'Start at the beginning.'

She needs to know everything. If I have learnt anything, it's that keeping things from people only results in bigger problems.

I fill her in on the call from Mila about her so-called brother, Dylan. I tell her how I stabbed the man who I can only guess had been framed with the baby's murder.

'What did you do then? After you stabbed him,' Pam asks me. She has planted her palms on the kitchen worktop and she's staring at the marble between them. Her lips are pressed together making a thin, pale strip.

'I ran away,' I whisper.

'For fuck's sake, Michelle. What do you think you are doing? Why did you even go there?'

'I thought I was helping. I just saw red.'

'We don't get to "see red", Michelle. We have to stay cool and calculated. It's how this whole operation works.' She drags her hands over her face, smudging her mascara. 'Do you realise you've gone and ruined everything? Have you thought about the impact of that, Michelle? You might as well have welcomed the police into Speak Up with your wrists held out for them to cuff. We're done for!'

'I know,' I whimper. 'I just had to tell you before I go to them. I had to warn you.'

'Them?'

'The police.'

'Don't be so silly. You're not going to the police.'

'But, I have to. I can't just stab someone and walk away.'

Pam laughs and the high pitch rings in my ears. 'Like Lesley, you mean?'

'That's different and you know it.'

We stand in stunned silence. Pam is so furious, I'm too afraid to tell her the rest of the news.

'Where did all this happen?' Pam leaves the kitchen and returns holding her phone. I give her the address and she taps away furiously.

'Pam, you shouldn't get involved. You ... '

She raises her hand to shush me and I snap my mouth shut.

Finally, she slams her phone down on the counter and stares at me. 'Graham will sort it. Now we just have to wait,' she says. I'm desperate to ask what's happening, but Pam is pacing the room, mulling everything over.

I finish my whiskey in one large gulp.

'There's more.' My voice comes out as a tiny squeak.

Pam rolls her eyes to the ceiling and holds her hand up, telling me to wait. She turns to the fridge and pulls out a bottle of chardonnay. She pours herself a large glass and drinks half of the contents. She then nods at me, urging me to continue.

'The police think you're involved in some child trafficking ring.'

'What?' she barks.

'Graham has been arrested. I'm sure he'll convince them they've got it wrong.'

'Arrested!' She slams her glass down, snapping the stem on the work surface. 'You could've told me that before I fucking texted him!'

'They're wrong though; they'll figure that out.' I'm stuttering like an idiot. 'He's probably out by now.'

'Of course they're bloody wrong, Michelle. There's no trafficking ring. Talk about crossed wires!' She finishes her wine from the broken glass. 'But, do you really think we need the police poking into our business? Our activities are hardly legal. Graham is a clever man, but I don't doubt he's slipped up somewhere along the line. The number of documents he's faked over the years ... Oh, this is so so bad.'

'What's bad?' Aiden wanders into the room with a nonchalance that stuns me.

'Oh, nothing dear. Nothing to worry about,' says Pam, plastering a fake grin on her face, her eyes dull with fear.

He's been upstairs this whole time?

'Oh, come on – what job have you fucked up on? I didn't think you had another bad guy on the cards right now?'

What? My mouth hangs open. *Does he know?*

'Oh, Aiden, darling. It's nothing.'

'Mum, tell me what's going on.' His tone is calm, yet his demeanour is icy. I haven't seen this side of him before. I can hear my blood pulse past my ears and I want the world to swallow me up.

Pam throws a glance at me, and an awkward silence fills the air. Aiden doesn't take his eyes off her.

'Oh, come on, Mum, tell me – what job have you fucked up on?'

My eyes dance between the two of them. I don't know where to look.

'It's not that. All the jobs I've worked on have been clean. Michelle can vouch for that. Graham himself can vouch for that.'

Aiden's eyes dart between me and his mum. 'So, what's the problem?'

I can't hold it in anymore. 'You know what Pam does? What *we* do?'

'Of course, I know. Mum can't keep her massive trap shut, can she?' He pokes an index finger in Pam's direction and she recoils.

'Aiden has always known, Michelle. I don't keep secrets from him.' Her voice is wobbling. Why is she so scared?

'And you're okay with it?' I ask him.

'Well, yeah. It made sense to me after what I went through with my dad. Surely you, of all people, understand that.'

Aiden's phone rings in his pocket. He takes it out, glances at the screen, and declines the call.

'Aiden, honey, you don't need to worry. Go into work. By the time you're finished for the day, all of this will have blown over.'

'Don't be so stupid. I'm not leaving you until I know what's going on. You're my mum and you look like you're about to keel over. Plus, the woman I am falling for looks like shit. So, will someone please tell me what the hell is going on?'

I run my hand through my hair, my fingers catching on dried blood.

Pam glances at me, and I take a deep breath. 'You don't need to worry about your mum. It was my mistake,' I say, heading over to Aiden. I press my palm against his chest.

I want him to wrap his arms around me, but he doesn't move. He continues to look down at me with his cold eyes. 'I killed someone without going through the right channels. I've made a complete mess of things. But, your mum will be okay. I'll make sure of that.'

How I'll make sure of it, I'm not too sure. I'll have ample opportunity to talk to the police. I'll confess to anything if it means keeping Pam out of prison. And Speak Up operating.

'Who did you kill?'

'Just a guy connected to a child at Speak Up.'

'Who, Michelle?'

'You don't know him. Please, Aiden, just let this go.'

Pam interrupts. 'Once Graham gets out, we can sort something out. There isn't a single problem he can't fix. I'm certain of it.'

'Gets out?' Aiden pushes past me and I trip over my own feet, landing on the floor in front of him. I'm too stunned to move. 'Gets out of where, Mum?'

Pam avoids her son's eyes and murmurs, 'He's been arrested. Just a little misunderstanding.'

Aiden suddenly reaches out and yanks his mum's hair so her neck is bent viciously down to his chest. He leans over her. 'Tell me what happened!'

'That's all I know!' she gasps. He yanks harder. 'But, I'm sure there's nothing to worry about. They just want to talk to him about a child trafficking ring. He's probably just implicated because of his job. He'll soon sort it out.'

'This is a fucking mess!' Aiden screams and slams his mother's head down on the kitchen counter. Her skull hits it with a loud crack and she bounces back before crumpling to the floor. I recoil in revulsion, shuffling on my backside into the cupboards behind me.

Felix barks at the back door, jumping at the glass, foam flying from the sides of his mouth.

I am paralysed. I can't breathe.

Aiden turns to me.

'The police will be here soon.' His tone has completely changed when he looks at me. He's softer; sad. 'We need to leave right now.'

'Leave? No.' I watch as Pam's body twitches violently on the floor. 'What did you do to her?'

'Forget about her. I'll take care of you. None of this is your fault. I told Mum not to involve you, but she was adamant. After last night's little revelation about your parents, now I know why,' he tells me.

How can I trust this guy when I don't know who he is? I shake my head. I can't take my eyes off Pam.

'Aiden, please don't leave me here like this,' Pam gurgles from the floor. Blood drips into her eyes.

Aiden ignores her and grabs my arm tightly. 'Come on, we need to go.' I shake my head and press my back into the cupboard door. I still can't take my eyes off Pam. 'Now, Michelle!'

'Don't go,' Pam whimpers. 'We can sort all of this out.'

Aiden groans and turns to face her. He bows his head and kicks her in the stomach. She grunts as she hits the cupboard behind her. 'You've gone and fucked everything up!' He kicks her again. His arms fly out to the side as he keeps slamming his boot into her.

At one point, Pam opens her eyes and looks at him. There is still love there. Love and terror.

'You're a burden, Mum. You served one purpose, and now you've fucked it. You're *nothing* now. Nothing!'

I throw myself at him and drag him away. 'Stop it! Please!' I scream at him. I cannot believe this is happening. Everything is so broken. 'Who even are you?'

Aiden spins around to face me. 'You know who I am. I'm just Aiden. Your Aiden.'

'No, you're not; you're a stranger. A twisted and nasty piece of work.'

'Says the murderer,' Aiden shrugs. My stomach sinks. He's right. I'm a massive hypocrite.

I feel deflated. I need to keep him occupied while I figure things out. 'Why didn't you tell me you knew about all this?'

'I didn't want you to get involved, Michelle. And I have to admit, falling for you threw me off my game.' He looks pained. 'I tried telling her, but it was too late – you were in too deep. So, I tried scaring you off, but you were like a dog with a bone. You came bouncing back more eager than ever.'

'Scare me off?'

Aiden looks out the window into the trees beyond the house. 'The attack in the park. That was me. But, you have to understand ... '

'You hit me?' I cut him off.

'No! I could never hurt you, Michelle. I paid some scumbag to do it. But, he was supposed to just rough you up a bit. Scare you. Not put you in hospital. The bastard took it too far. And that bastard had to pay.'

'But ... why?' I'm so confused. Hurt. How could Aiden do that to me? In the blink of an eye, he's gone from sweet and kind to an absolute monster.

'I thought you'd connect the dots back to Mum's little project and leave well enough alone. But, it just seemed to fire you up.'

Pam moans gently. Her finger twitches as she tries to grasp at consciousness.

'I need to call an ambulance,' I say.

'No.'

'She'll die if I don't. She might have internal bleeding or something.'

Aiden shrugs.

Chapter Thirty-Five

MICHELLE

'What the fuck is going on with you?' I face this stranger who has morphed in front of my eyes.

Just hours ago, Aiden was a gentle, beautiful, classy man. Now, he's a man who beats his own mother. His mother, who worships him; who would do anything for him. His mother, whose honourable values are so strong, she's willing to do the unthinkable. His mother, who is currently lying on the kitchen floor, dying.

Aiden has the audacity to look confused. 'I'm protecting you, Michelle. Surely you can see that? Pam has got you involved in her mess and now I'm getting you out of it.' He reaches out to hold my hands, but I pull away. I don't want this man touching me. 'Oh, come on. You're choosing her over me?'

'She's dying.'

'So? The game is over for her, anyway. She dies or she goes to prison. She's no good to anyone.'

His indifference stuns me.

'I need to leave,' I tell him. If I can just go, I can call an ambulance.

'Not on your own. I'm coming with you. You've got a massive target on your back. I can get you away.'

'Just stop this, please. I've got to make this right. I don't know what's going on with you, but you can't just leave her here like this. And I can't just run.' My anguish catches in my throat. But, my begging just makes him grin.

'You're cute when you're desperate. Oh, come on. Run off into the sunset with me. It'll be romantic.'

What does he think's going to happen here? Does he seriously think he can just change my mind and we go skipping off into the distance together? Pam moans gently on the floor. She's turned a nasty shade of grey.

She needs help, fast.

My eyes flit between them both. I need to get out of here, and I know there's only one thing I can do.

I blow the air out of my lungs and force my eyes to meet his. I smile and cock my head to the side. 'Where will we go?' I take his hand in mine. My hand makes a jerky movement when our skin touches, but he doesn't seem to notice.

Aiden beams at me. 'That's my girl. I knew you'd come around. We're the same, you and I. We just do what we think is best.'

I want to grab his eyeballs and rip them out of his head. The same? Some of our actions may have looked the same, but our intentions are very, *very* different, and I will not be tarred with the same brush.

I killed for justice – justice for children who needed desperate help. Aiden beat his own mum, for what? Fun?

'We are the same,' I tell him.

'I mean, we've both had parents killed by *that*,' he motions at Pam, looking pleased with the connection he's just made between him and I.

He's not wrong though. We do have that in common.

Maybe that's why he's so messed up. Did his dad instil this level of violence in him?

'Though, your parents went out with a bang. It took some convincing to get her to finish Dad off.'

He tries to tug me into the hallway, but I resist.

'Convincing?'

He hesitates and looks me up and down. 'Yeah, some people just deserve to die. Child abuse isn't the only thing wrong with people. But, it was a good excuse to get Mum's arse into gear.' He chuckles. '*Mummy, Daddy keeps touching me. Down there.*' He grabs his crotch.

My knees buckle and I have to push against the kitchen counter to steady myself.

'He didn't abuse you.'

'Fuck, no. That man was weak. The twat was seeing some other woman, though. A barbie doll. I saw them together from my school bus. I knew if I didn't wipe him out that he'd leave Pam and take all his money with him. We'd have been left with nothing.' He laces his fingers through mine, ignoring my panic. 'So, I got Pam to take him out. And, look how things have turned out. It's because of me that Speak Up exists.' He jabs his thumb to his chest with a disgusting bravado.

'You see? We're the same, Mich. We know what to do in order to change the world, and we go out and do it. Mum knew what to do as well, until the silly cow dropped us in it.'

Pam! I have to keep her in the forefront of my mind. I can't let Aiden sweep me away into despair. I can't make out her chest moving from here. Has she stopped breathing? Oh my God, is she dead?

Aiden senses my panic and places his finger under my chin, turning my head to face him. 'Don't look at her. Look at me.' He kisses me lightly on the lips. 'It's time to go,' he says, pressing his forehead to mine.

If there's one thing Pam has taught me, it's that no one can overpower me anymore. Pam saved my life. I owe her the same.

'I need something from you first,' I whisper into his ear.

I wrap my arms around Aiden's neck and smile. He reciprocates by planting his lips on mine and I kiss him. Our hands are everywhere, touching, groping, squeezing. He moans into my ear, and I pull his head into my neck. He kisses me. I swallow the fear that brings me to the cusp of a scream.

I open one eye just a crack and scan the worktop. The knife block is too far to reach.

I ease him away from me and spin him around to pin him against the worktop. I lick my lips and he grins down at me. Despite his mother's dying body lying beside us, he's turned on. I can feel his erection against my stomach. I bite my bottom lip and instruct him to push his jeans to the floor. He unzips himself.

'Be quick. We don't have long.'

Disgusting. But, I push through.

Aiden closes his eyes as I kiss his chest, heading down.

Bingo.

I reach across and grab the biggest knife.

I press the knife against Aiden's throat.

'Michelle, what are you doing?' His voice has hints of laughter and I push the knife into his skin. I feel the edge catch against his flesh and beads of blood appear beneath the metal.

I have no qualms about taking out another evil bastard.

The silly twat really thought I was going to suck him off next to his dying mum.

'Come on, Michelle. Don't do this.' He sounds whiny. For the first time in his life, the spoilt twat isn't getting what he wants. I resist laughing at him. I need to stay focused. The knife is shaking in my hand as nerves course through me. Aiden glances down at it and smiles at me.

'Scared, Michelle? You wouldn't really hurt little old me, would you?' He grins. An evil so shocking shines through his eyes that I take a step back.

I'm out of his reach now, still pointing the knife at his heart.

'I'm going to make a call,' I say, jabbing the knife in his direction. 'Move a muscle, and I swear to God I will slit your throat.'

Aiden laughs. 'Spoken like a true psycho-bitch. That's so sexy.'

'Wanna see how psycho I can be?' I spit the words at him, but the shake of my hand betrays me.

'Oh, I know what you're capable of. But, you won't hurt me.'

'Of course I will. I know how evil you are.'

'Mich, you won't hurt me, because I know too much.'

Confusion flits between my ears.

'I know about what you and Pam were up to. I know what Graham does for you. I know you killed that man today. I can surely help the police connect the dots, can't I?'

I feel the blood drain from my head and I start to sway. There is no way out of this. We're all going down. If Pam is alive, she's going to prison. There will be no more Speak Up. All those children will be ignored. Forgotten.

This isn't happening. There is nothing left to save. And it's all because of this man.

'What has any of this got to do with you, Aiden? Just walk away, I'll call an ambulance for Pam and all will be fine. You don't want to get involved in any of this.'

'Fine? Graham has been arrested, Michelle. None of us are fine.'

'What's Graham got to do with you?'

Aiden shifts to the side quickly and shoves the knife away from him. I take a step back, the knife skitters across the floor.

'I've got everything to do with that fucking idiot. Who do you think pays that bastard? He goes down and he'll take me with him. We need to leave here, now.'

'You pay him?'

He groans in frustration. What am I not getting here?

'I'm the fucking boss, baby!' He hammers on his chest. 'I told you I work in transport. I just transport kids, that's all. And Graham provides some of my stock.'

'Stock?' I'm barely audible. Sweat trickles down my back. 'Stock.'

'Yep. I send those little shits all over the world. British kids are in demand.'

'What for?'

'Oh, I don't care about the specifics.'

I can't hold back anymore. I run to the sink and spill the contents of my stomach down the drain for the second time today.

'You okay? Had a bit of a shock?' He sounds smug.

Rage overwhelms me and I scream. I lunge forward and thrust the knife at him.

Aiden steps to the side and slaps the knife out of my hand. I watch in terror as it clatters to the ground. He deftly wraps an arm around my waist and turns me away from him. The other arm squeezes my neck.

I dig my fingernails into his hand, desperately trying to pull it away. Panic rips through me.

He hisses into my ear, 'Here's the deal. We're going to walk away from here. We'll go our separate ways. Leave the body here.'

Body? My eyes desperately search for life, but Pam's laboured breathing has stopped.

Pam is dead.

She spent her whole life helping her son and he has fed on it, digested it, and turned it to poison.

My tears flow freely, and I give up fighting Aiden off me.

'Tell a soul about what I just told you, and you're dead.'

'I don't care.'

'What?'

'I don't care!' I scream. My life is over, anyway.

'Oh, really? What about Teddy? Care about him?'

My eyes flit upwards to look into his. All mockery has vanished; he means it.

'You have Teddy?'

'Oh yeah, he's a good kid, very *innocent*.'

'No, please, not Teddy. Leave those kids alone.'

'Then do as I say, or Teddy is dead.'

He slaps me on the arse and leaves. I hear the front door slam behind him and his motorbike roar into life.

My eyes flit around the room, desperately trying to take everything in. What just happened?

I spy Felix pawing at the glass door. His howls penetrate my soul.

Chapter Thirty-Six

MICHELLE

I run into the hall where I dumped my belongings and grab my phone. Face ID isn't working and as my trembling fingers attempt to enter my PIN, I hear a police siren come raging up the driveway. Did Kelsey call them? She she tell them I was here?

I pull the door open and watch as Travis' unmarked BMW comes to a stop right in front of the door. A police car follows suit behind him.

Travis runs over to me, and I hold up my hands, accepting my fate behind bars. I give up.

'Where is she?' Travis yells. I just wobble on the doorstep, my legs threatening to give way. 'Michelle!' he yells again, demanding an answer.

I feel bodies push past me as the police rush into Pam's house. Moments later, someone calls out to Travis. Travis gives me one last glance before stepping into the house.

Then everything becomes a blur. More cars appear. A van. Hordes of people run into Pam's beautiful home.

I await my fate, wringing my hands together.

It feels like a lifetime later when they wheel out a black zipped-up bag. I realise it must contain Pam's body and I sob into my hands. I reach out to her as she passes me on the driveway, but hands pull me away. Pam was like a mother to me. Her methods may have been questionable, but she was a guardian angel who just wanted to help the most vulnerable. And she paid the ultimate price for her passion.

'Sorry, Pam,' I whisper to her as they push her into the back of the van. 'It's all my fault.' This all went so wrong after I got involved.

I bite my lip until I draw blood. I was providing that bastard with *stock*. He treated them like fucking *meat*. Maybe Pam dying is a blessing. Aiden's revelation would have surely killed her, anyway.

I want to crawl into a hole and die.

First, there are lots of questions from the police; so many questions. I can't lie about what happened in that house. I don't have the mental capacity to lie. Besides, trusting my instincts has gotten me here. Now, I can only pray that Travis can help me to appease my sins.

Someone questions me relentlessly, and all I have the strength to muster is, 'It was Aiden.' Then someone else hands me a cup of tea, and Travis on a nearby wall. I tell him everything: how Pam murdered people in order to save the Speak Up children; how Graham helped her; how Aiden beat Pam to a pulp; and how Aiden used the knowledge of Pam's activities to feed a fucking child trafficking ring.

But, I don't tell him about my involvement.

I don't tell him about the man I killed just this morning. They can figure that out for themselves. I need to buy myself some time to just breathe before I'm locked away.

I need to find Teddy first. I have to make sure he's safe. Only then can I face my consequences.

'Michelle, I need you to come to the station to make a formal statement,' Travis tells me. I nod.

I am led to a police car and taken away.

***

Kelsey drives me home from the police station in silence. She's being sickly sweet and kind. Kelsey only sees the good in people, and it's a comfort to know there is still some good left in me – in her eyes, anyway. I sit beside her in utter shock.

Once she's parked the car outside our house, she turns to me. 'We'll figure this out, okay?'

I nod and start to respond, but she gets out of the car before I can form a sentence.

The second we get in the house, Kelsey slips into the kitchen to put the kettle on and I head straight upstairs to shower.

The police haven't yet connected my kill this morning to today's events.

I know I am on borrowed time. Ironically, life before all this was a prison. Now, the prospect of going to prison for murder and helping to feed a trafficking ring is almost comforting.

I deserve prison.

I deserve so much worse than prison, actually.

After my shower, I throw myself onto my old bed. I sink into the mattress and my mind and body are so exhausted that sleep comes quickly.

I dream of Aiden – both the one I know now, and the one I thought I knew. They're played by two different people. The good one is backlit by celestial light, whilst the bad one is shrouded in black. I hate them both.

Each tugs at one of my arms, desperately trying to pull me into their respective lairs. I'm terrified. I know that no matter which one I choose, only bad things will come of it. Someone will always end up getting hurt.

I wake up with a start and sit upright. My arms tingle. I rub my eyes and pull my knees up to my chin. How have the police not pieced it all together yet? Have they found Aiden? Where is Teddy? Please let Teddy be okay. I can't have his blood on my hands, too.

As consciousness firmly digs its claws into me, I realise I can hear voices coming from downstairs. I step carefully out of bed, avoiding the debris that inhabits my floor, and I tiptoe to the top of the stairs to listen. Travis and Kelsey are having a heated conversation.

'Let her sleep, Trav. She's had a massive shock.'

'That's just it. I don't think she's shocked at all.'

'You think she had something to do with the trafficking? With the murders? Michelle is like a sister to me, Travis; I know her better than anyone. She wouldn't hurt anyone.'

'For fuck's sake, Kelsey, do you know how much damage that family has done?'

'Yes, Trav. But, you've already said it: Michelle was caught in their crossfire. She isn't the cause of all this. You can't punish her for something she hasn't done.'

'Even if she wasn't involved in the trafficking case, what about the man she stabbed and left for dead?'

'You promised me Pam would take the fall for that.'

'I can only misdirect. It won't last forever. Pam wasn't even there when the guy was killed Kels, she'll have an alibi.'

Silence.

They know about the man I killed. Holy shit. I no longer know how I feel. Guilty, definitely. Scared, maybe. Hopeful, absolutely not.

I'm disgusted by the amount of damage I've caused. I don't like Kelsey and Travis arguing about me and I refuse to be the dynamite that implodes their relationship. I head downstairs.

As I enter the living room, they both swing around to look at me. They're both standing in the middle of the room, an angry tension surrounding them. Kelsey smiles at me reassuringly, fear playing behind her eyes. Travis is scowling. He looks tired; his usually unspoilt face is unshaven and dark shadows sit under his eyes. He looks like he's aged ten years in the last four hours.

'Hey,' I mumble. 'Any news on Teddy?'

Travis looks at Kelsey before turning his attention to me. 'Have you seen this before?' He holds up a pink notebook emblazoned with gold poppies. Pam's journal. My stomach flips. This is it. Travis has got all the evidence he needs.

Pam's diary was a ticking time bomb. For someone so put together, she was royally stupid to keep that.

'Michelle, this supports everything you have told us,' Travis says. 'This notebook only covers the last couple of years, but we expect to find more.' He holds his hands out towards me and sighs. 'Michelle, you spent so much time with this woman. How did you not know what they were doing?'

I raise my eyes to the heavens. Pam kept me out of it. She kept me safe.

'Pam's sole purpose was to help children. We had that in common. I just wanted to help. I didn't know what was happening behind the scenes.'

The lie slips out before I have a chance to catch it, and I'm glad. There's still hope for Teddy if I am still here. I need to help them find Aiden.

'So, you maintain that you don't think Pam had anything to do with the trafficking?'

'Absolutely not.'

'We're not in the station now. This is off the record.'

'She didn't!'

'So, you didn't know what Graham's involvement was?'

I shake my head. It's the truth. I'm still not entirely sure how all of this pieces together. 'But, I'm guessing he was the connection between Pam and Aiden.'

'Yeah,' Travis says. He sounds so tired; so sad. 'Like you, I believe Pam had good intentions. She didn't know she was working with the man who fed the devil – her own son.'

He sits on the sofa, giving Kelsey's shoulder a squeeze en route.

He continues, 'I have to admit, Graham is a clever man. He's been getting away with this for years. I dread to think what we're going to uncover.'

'How? How did he do all of this?'

'He had a lot of methods. It would depend on the circumstances. When the parents were particularly callous, he would offer them money. Easy. Sometimes he'd tell the parents their child has been taken into care, but file the paperwork to say the child is being cared for by a relative. As far as social services were concerned, the matter was resolved.'

I blow air out through my teeth. Is it really that easy to take a child?

Travis surveys me with his cold police-officer glare.

'You look shocked.'

I laugh. 'Shocked? Travis, there isn't a word for how I am feeling right now. My killer friend is dead, and my child-trafficking boyfriend is on the run for killing her. I'm not shocked, I'm numb. If I felt anything right now, I'd be in a broken-down heap in the corner of the room.'

Travis nods, and Kelsey rushes over to embrace me, but I shrug her off.

'What's going to happen to Graham?' I ask Travis.

'Charged. He's refusing to give up information. He sits there like a fucking hobbit, licking his lips and smiling. I want to just ... '

He doesn't have to say it. I know what he wants. I want to wring Graham's neck, too.

Kelsey pipes up. 'Michelle, Aiden must have told you something. Anything. What did he tell you about his friends? His hobbies? Where he worked?'

I feel all colour drain from my cheeks as I'm flooded with memories of our time together. It felt special. Damn, *I* felt special. What an idiot. One memory niggles at me, though. 'Crawley,' I spit out. 'He once told me he has a warehouse in Crawley where he ships out TVs.'

Travis yanks his mobile out of his pocket, makes a call, and starts barking orders down the line. I pull on my boots.

'Michelle, where are you going?' Kelsey asks.

'Crawley!' I call back, following Travis out of the door.

Chapter Thirty-Seven

MICHELLE

I sit in the passenger seat of Travis' BMW, twiddling my thumbs nervously.

We're hurtling down the M23, a few miles away from the warehouse where we suspect Aiden has been keeping the children. It didn't take much for the police to find the warehouse rented by a company that doesn't exist.

My thoughts drown out the sound of the roaring engine and rumbling road beneath the wheels. I am grateful when Travis breaks my morbid trance. 'I promised Kels I would protect you as much as I can.'

I don't know what to say to that. Travis knows I killed that man. What must he think of me? He sees people perform the most heinous acts every single day. How can he just sit in the car with someone who stabbed a man to death?

'I know. But, you don't have to. I'll handle it.'

'It'll kill Kels to see you go down. You're the only thing she's got.'

'That's not true – she's got you,' I say, my voice barely audible.

'She sure does.'

He deftly manoeuvres around a Vauxhall hogging the fast lane. 'Fucking hate people who drive sixty miles an hour on the motorway.'

'Look, when we have Teddy I'll come clean, I swear. I just have to find Teddy first.'

Travis nods. 'You killed that guy for a kid, didn't you?'

'Yes.'

'Fucking hell, Michelle, your vigilantism is a little close to Pam's. Don't you think?'

'We shared the same values, I guess.'

'That's what worries me. Just how much did you share with that woman?'

I stare out the window, letting the accusation surround me.

'We have your call to 999 recorded. What happened? How did you get it all so damn wrong? The man was a known twat to the police but, Michelle, he didn't even have kids.'

His words confirm what I already knew. They confirm the biggest mistake of my life. They confirm that I am the biggest idiot on the fucking planet.

I tell him about the prank call.

'Jesus, Michelle. What a fucking idiot.'

'I know.'

We're off the motorway now. Rows of warehouses zip past. We follow three marked police cars down a pot-hole-ridden road, my arse frequently bouncing off my seat.

I bump into the door as Travis swings to the left into a car park.

Police cars pull up around us and armed officers jump out and march towards the double doors in formation.

'Stay put. Don't do anything stupid,' Travis tells me as he gets out to join the raid. I sit on my hands, willing myself to do as I'm told.

It lasts all of five seconds.

Fuck this. I hop out of the car and, keeping well behind the group of officers, follow the throng over to the building.

As we approach the building, I strain my head to see past the police officers. The corridor is dark. Fire exit signs provide the only light, and everything is cast in their eerie green glow. It smells like rotting wood, and the air is icy cold. I hold back by the door, eager to know what's going on, but careful not to get in the way.

Goosebumps erupt all over me when officers start yelling. I hear crying. The sweet sound of children crying.

They're alive.

***

I watch as they bring the children outside, each one cowering in the sunlight. Some are crying; some are clutching onto one another for dear life; some are laughing hysterically. They all look too skinny. Too small.

Most cower from their saviours and it breaks my heart. Will these children ever learn to trust again?

The twisted bastards who kept them here have done a runner before we got here. Most probably tipped off by the delightful Aiden.

The car park is now rammed with cars. Water, snacks, and blankets are being passed around to the children who grab at them. Forms are being filled in. The press has got wind of the situation and they're jostling beyond the tape to see who can get the juiciest story.

Fifteen. I count fifteen kids. And that's just this time. God knows how long this has been going on. I would bet money that these children aren't the only ones he's shipped off into his twisted network of perversion. Tears prickle my eyes when I think of the children we cannot save.

I scan the car park again. Fifteen. None of them are Teddy.

The atmosphere then shifts and voices quieten. Everyone stands still and most turn to look at the door.

A paramedic backs out of it, pulling a trolley. A sheet covers a tiny human being lying on top.

Teddy?

I run forward screaming, 'Teddy!' I almost reach him when Travis grabs me by the waist and pulls me back.

'I need to see him!' I beg, but he just shakes his head at me. 'Please, Travis.'

The floodgates open, then. I sob for Teddy. I sob for the mess I have made. I sob for letting Aiden get away.

What have I done?

Chapter Thirty-Eight

TEDDY

Two hours earlier

I am just drifting off to sleep when the shouting starts. We've been sitting in silence for so long that the noise makes my ears ring and my heart beat fast. I sit up straight to see what is happening, but I remember the big man's words: no talking, no messing about, don't even breathe too loud or I'll fucking cut you. I flinch as I remember them, waiting for the man to slap me for sitting up, but there isn't anyone in the room with us. That's really weird. There's always a grown up around somewhere.

It makes me feel horrible. Confused.

A few other children sit up with me now and we all watch the door, waiting for someone to tell us what to do. No one comes. The shouting stops and the room gets so quiet. Quieter than it's ever been before, and worry tickles my tummy.

Most of us are sitting up now. Some brave children are standing and craning their necks to see what is happening in the corridor outside the room.

Eventually someone pipes up, 'I think they've gone.' Her voice shakes like she's excited and scared at the same time. I recognise the voice. It's Juno. Juno has been my friend since I got here. On my first night, she held my hand as I cried myself to sleep and ever since she's been my best friend. She's speaking so quietly now, but her words hit loud and clear. They're gone.

We're all alone.

A few of the younger children start to cry. Someone by the door giggles. Most of us just stand gawping into the darkness.

What do we do now?

Time passes. Most of us have crept towards the door, unsure whether to make the move into the corridor. There is no one here.

If we leave this room and get caught, then they might kill us. But, if they're gone, we will get hungry and we'll die.

I am shaking, and not just because I am cold. Everything feels tingly and weird. My breathing feels difficult.

I glance over at Juno and I can just make out her face through the darkness. She's glowing green from the exit sign above her head. It makes her look creepy. Her tears are shiny on her cheeks and she's pressing her lips together. She catches my eye and takes my hand.

We step into the corridor at the same time. I put one arm up to shield my face, waiting for the blow.

But, it doesn't come.

Nothing happens. They're gone. They're really gone.

Juno drops my hand and walks faster. She's ahead of me now. She's almost at the door.

Then I hear it. The scraping sound of a lock being slid back.

'Juno, get back!' I scream. I lunge forward to grab her, but it's too late. A man stands in the doorway; the sunlight blasting behind him makes him hard to see. He towers over Juno, who crouches to the floor in the corner.

'What the fuck are you doing out here?' the man growls. He kicks down on Juno with his chunky shoe and I hear a nasty crunch sound as her head hits the wall.

She lies still.

I hear everyone around me scatter back into the room. Some are stupid enough to scream. Though none are as stupid as me. I run towards the man. I don't even know what I am doing. I just know that I want to hurt him so bad.

My arms and legs are out of control as I go at him. I whack him a few times and I hear him grunt, but it isn't enough. He stays standing. He's smiling down at me like I've made a joke.

Nothing has ever been less funny.

The man holds a hand out and places it on my forehead, pushing me gently back. He laughs at me and all fight escapes me. I'm too tired. Too small. I give up.

'Easy, tiger. You've got some nerve, haven't you?' he teases me. He bends down to face me properly, still holding my head back.

'Look, kid, tell me where Teddy is and I won't punish you for that little performance.'

He wants me.

I gulp but say nothing, choosing to glare at him instead. I try so hard not to look at Juno to see if she's okay.

The man is clever. He knows and turns to face Juno. He lets go of my head and walks over to the wall where Juno lies in a heap. Blood has splattered the wall where her head hit it. I watch as his hands form into fists.

'I'm Teddy!' I blurt out. I can't have him hurting Juno again. He might kill her. 'Please, leave her alone.'

The man nods, and I breathe a sigh of relief when he walks over to me, leaving Juno alone.

'That right, is it? You better not be lying to me.'

Why would I lie? It would be so much easier to tell him Teddy was someone else. But, I don't know what he'd do to someone else, and I can't do that.

The man looks around at all the other children who have been watching in silence.

'You.' The man points at Becks, a quiet girl who hasn't said very much since she got here. 'What's this boy's name?'

'T— T—,' Tears are dripping off her chin. The man's foot moves and I nod at her, begging her to just say it. 'Teddy.'

He looks down at me and smiles. He looks like a mad man when he smiles.

'Well, then, Teddy-boy – let's go for a drive.'

I want to go back into the room behind me. My prison, where all my friends are hiding. Who is this man? Where is he taking me?

'Come on, boy. Stop dawdling.'

Tears burn the back of my eyeballs as the man takes my hand and pulls me outside.

I breathe in the air. It smells like smoke and dirt, but it feels fresh and clean against my face. The world feels all new and shiny. I can hear cars drive past on the other side of the big hedge and I wonder if I can run faster than this man. Who am I kidding? Maybe I could scream for help? But, if I do that, he might kill me. I just keep following the man.

'This is your lucky day, my boy,' the man says, taking me over to a big motorbike with sparkly wheels. He slams a helmet onto my head, making my neck bend awkwardly. 'I've got an important job for you. You're going to help me win back the girl of my dreams.' I clamber onto the bike and he sits in front of me. I look for somewhere to hold on, but I can't find a handle. 'Don't fuck it up now, kiddo – you're my last chance.'

The engine roars into life and I grip the back of his coat. I have never felt so scared. As we move off, my head whips back and I fight against the weight of the too-big helmet to bring my head back up.

The world flies by so fast. There are so many cars out there. They keep shooting past as the man weaves in and out of the different lanes.

At one point, loads of police cars go past, all blaring out their noisy sirens. I sit up straight, hoping someone would recognise me, but they're gone before they have time to see me.

I think about Juno. I really hope she's okay. Maybe she's back in the big room now where the other kids can look after her.

'Nearly there, kid,' the man tells me, coming off the really busy road.

Nearly where? Where are we going, and what is this man going to do to me when we get there?

Chapter Thirty-Nine

MICHELLE

Teddy has been missing for three whole days.

I have been watching the news avidly. Journalists are camped outside Pam's house. I have watched the police raid her home, picking it apart, turning its former beauty into a pigsty. Pam would have been mortified.

The police are looking for Aiden and have sightings all over the world. One day he's allegedly in Glasgow, and the next in Zurich. I know he isn't far, though. I can feel it in my gut.

He's watching me.

Travis has tried to be supportive, but he's coming around less and less often. I hear him and Kelsey arguing all the time, my name cropping up frequently. I cringe at my guilt and shut my bedroom door, closing out their animosity.

I am sitting here in my room waiting like a fucking idiot. Waiting for the police to do what I have to do. I have to find Teddy. This is on me. I just don't know how.

I just pray they find Teddy soon, so I can put a stop to all of this. Once Teddy is safe, I can hand myself in. Draw a line under this mess.

But until then, I need to give Aiden a reason to keep him alive. That reason is me.

I'm on borrowed time and it is making my skin itch. It's as if the walls are closing in on me as the police are pulling evidence from left, right, and centre.

Travis says they're closing in on a number of people involved. The investigation has moved on from Pam and is more focussed on the network of people involved in taking, hiding, and transporting children across the globe.

They're looking at the bigger picture. Maybe I'm too small a piece for them to notice.

That doesn't stop the guilt from gnawing away at me. I killed in order to feed a trafficking ring. I murdered an innocent man. I stood by as Aiden beat his mum to death.

I am the reason Teddy is with that man.

I used to long to change, but now I know standing still is the safest place to be.

So I wait.

Kelsey is working today, so I venture downstairs for a cup of coffee. As I step off the bottom stair, I stop in my tracks. There's something on the doorstep outside.

The frosted glass blurs my vision; all I can make out is a patch of deep red.

I tread carefully, heading down the hall, dragging my hand along the wall. But, I can see the lock is turned from here and I relax my shoulders.

No one is here. Right?

I secure the chain lock and open the door just an inch, so I can peer out. No one.

At my feet lies a bouquet of gloriously plump red roses. There must be fifty of them, wrapped in delicate pink tissue paper.

My stomach drops to the floor. I know who this is.

I close the door and slide the chain, so I can open the door wide. I jerk out an arm and yank the roses into the house before slamming the door shut and double-checking the latch is locked.

My fingers shake as I slip the little card out of the envelope.

I'VE MISSED YOU, BABE. XXX

I gasp and drop the flowers to the floor.

There's a noise. A tapping noise. Inside my house. My head jolts around, my breath catching in my throat.

Kelsey shouted "goodbye" just over an hour ago. She's not here. Travis won't spend time alone with me since everything kicked off.

Who is in my kitchen?

I tread carefully back along the hallway, desperately wishing I hadn't left my phone upstairs.

I hear the tapping sound again. Whoever it is, they're in the living room.

It can't be him. He wouldn't risk coming here, would he? Although, he's such an arrogant prick – I wouldn't put anything past him.

My hand reaches for the living room door, and I push it open, bracing myself for what is on the other side.

'Alright, babe?' Aiden grins at me. 'How have you been?'

I gasp. 'What are you doing here?' It comes out as a growl. My fear is completely masked by anger and disgust.He's sitting in the armchair in the corner of the room, leaning back with a grin plastered across his face like he hasn't a care in the world.

'I've brought you a little gift. I thought you'd like it, babe.'

He motions at the kitchen door and I glance over. Teddy is standing leaning against the doorframe, a small carton of orange juice in his hand. He doesn't make a sound.

I guess the bruises on his face have taught him to behave.

His eyes are screaming at me. The poor boy has been through so much. He needs out of all this. I don't know how much more that little lad can take. I need to help him.

'Teddy!' I run toward him, arms open wide. Aiden leaps up and steps in front of me, barring my way.

'Now, now, all in good time. We need to talk first.'

'I've got *nothing* to say to you.'

'Oh, but I've got lots to say to you. Remember our little agreement? Keep quiet or the kid gets it? Remember that, Mich?'

He steps around Teddy and runs his hand through his hair, trickling his fingernails down his tiny face. Teddy squeezes his eyes shut.

I grit my teeth.

'I didn't agree to anything. Touch him, and I kill you.'

'It's almost like you want him dead. You never change.'

'Just tell me what you want, Aiden. Why are you here?'

'I'm here for you, silly. And I get what I want. I always do, and I'm not letting you be the exception.'

I can't stop myself from laughing. 'You get what you want? You sound like a spoilt brat.' My laughs come in thick bursts. My life is utterly ridiculous. How have I gotten myself involved with this dickhead?

I continue, 'You've lost everything, you stupid bastard! You've got nothing left and you still come round here acting all fucking superior, like I'm lucky to have you. Like I should just fall into your arms like you're the catch of the fucking century.'

Out of the corner of my eye, I see Teddy's eyes widen. He's looking at my laptop bag sitting in the corner of the room.

Good lad, Teddy.

'You just need a little *persuasion*, babe, that's all. It's funny how you were all interested when I was loaded. I'm not as attractive now that I have lost it all, is that it?'

'It's got nothing to do with money. It's *you*. You're evil. Pure evil.'

'We can talk this through. I know we can. Run with me. I'll help keep you out of prison.'

Teddy leans over towards my bag, which catches Aiden's attention. He sticks out an arm as if to swipe him. Teddy cowers.

'Leave him the hell alone!' I scream, catching Teddy's eye.

'Then come with me! Leave with me now, and he can stay here. Keep up this bollocks, and I'll slit his fucking throat.'

'Like fuck you will!' I scream, spitting on him.

Then I run. I head upstairs, praying he follows.

I can hear his footsteps hammering on the stairs behind me. I slam my bedroom door behind me, but he pushes it back, whacking my heel against the wood. I cry out and fall onto the bed and he launches himself on top of me.

'I'll show you,' he grunts. 'I always get what I want.'

He has one hand pinning mine above my head while his other works at my jeans. I jam my knee up, trying to hit him between the legs, but I don't have enough room to make an impact.

His strength overwhelms me, and my panic shifts to exhaustion.

I scream and he slams his forehead into mine. Everything goes momentarily white.

When I refocus, he's gone.

I gasp, forcing air into my panicked lungs. My wrists hurt where his fingers dug into me.

Teddy!

I gurgle out a cry of relief when I see him standing next to the bed looking at the floor. He's clutching my flip knife that I had tucked into the front of my laptop bag.

Aiden lies groaning on the floor, a slash gouged into his back.

'Come on, Teddy. Let's go.'

He takes my hand and we flee.

Deep in my heart, I know we're free.

Epilogue

MICHELLE

'How are you doing today, Michelle?'

She pokes the end of her biro into her mouth so that it rests on her lower lip. There is a trace of black ink spider-webbing into her pink skin.

I shrug.

'You know, it might be more beneficial for you if you talk to me. It's what I'm here for.' She shrugs and leans back into her leather chair.

I want to talk. I do. I just can't. I'm full to the brim, and the slightest knock will cause everything to come spilling out.

I've come full circle, only my pain is now contained in silence instead of a bottle of merlot.

My counsellor sighs.

'Why don't we start with something small. What did you eat for breakfast?'

I picture my breakfast. Congealed scrambled eggs and warmed bread that tried to pass as toast.

'I didn't eat my breakfast.'

There's a hint of a smile on her lips. She's working her way in. I feel my defences crack open just a little.

We sit for the remaining forty-eight minutes in relative silence. Birdsong drifts through the open window.

Eventually Trish, my therapist, gives up and we watch a seagull fly through the grey sky, calling out to the unknown.

'I'll see you next week,' she says.

I head back to my prison cell.

***

'I was disappointed not to see you last week.' Either Trish is telling the truth, or she is an exceptional liar.

'I was poorly.'

'So I heard. Are you okay now?'

I nod.

'I'm glad to hear that. So, tell me, have you heard from Kelsey?'

My eyes drift up to hers. She has never mentioned Kelsey before. What's with the change of tack? The jolting shift in conversation draws tears to my eyes.

I nod.

Kelsey has been trying to get in touch for weeks, but I push her away. I don't deserve her. She has a good soul, whereas mine is pure poison.

'You should see her. I'm sure she misses you, and it'll help you cope.'

I nod, but I have no intention of seeing her. She doesn't deserve my mess. I don't deserve her light.

A tear drips down my cheek.

God, I hope she's safe.

'Any news of Aiden?' I ask. She tilts her head to the side, surprised by my sudden question. I look at her through desperate eyes. I need to know what's happening.

'They're still looking for him. I assume you've been watching the news?'

I nod.

'Then I'm sure you'll hear as soon as I do. The reporters are all over it.'

That's not true. Since that pretty pop star overdosed and was taken to rehab, the trafficking case has appeared on the news less and less. It's a non-event now.

'How did he get away again?' Trish asks me. She knows this. Everyone knows this. But she's wedged the door open and wants to keep worming her way in.

My mouth engages before my brain, and I start to speak before snapping my mouth shut and shaking my head at her. She fails to hide her frustration this time and furiously taps her pen on the desk.

What does she want me to say? Does she really want me to live through that day again? I have been over and over this with the police. I have no effort left to give. I'm done talking about me. I need to hear about the people I love, but no one tells me anything.

I still see Teddy's face when I lie awake at night. Tears streak his face as the police pin me to their car.

I can still feel his little hand in mine. Clutching. Clutching. Then, gone.

We escaped the bad guy only to run into the arms of the system. To my fate.

I waved to him from the car window. I tried to reassure him, but his tears revealed the truth. He's damaged and I won't be there to help him heal. I'm useless.

Getting arrested for murder wasn't a shock. I knew it was coming.

Murder. Singular.

The police never found evidence of my involvement in Pam's killings. There was no mention of me in her notebook. No evidence of me left with any of the victims. Graham never mentioned me before he hung himself in his prison cell.

And I'll keep all that to myself.

For Teddy.

Everything is for Teddy.

I have to help him.

Trish nods, her eyes squinting at me. 'You know, Teddy keeps asking after you.'

'How is he?'

'He's doing okay. He's safe, in therapy. Like yourself.'

Safe. That boy will never be safe, forever haunted by demons.

'And I hear your friend Lisa is doing well?'

Lisa? My God, I haven't given her a second thought. I heard through the grapevine that Speak Up shrivelled and died when Pam's notebook was released to the press. I felt sorry for the staff, but I knew they would be okay. They are good people, and good things happen to good people.

'Yeah, she's setting up a new charity. There's a big crowdfunding campaign to get it started. It's going well, I hear.'

I nod.

'You must miss your volunteer work. I know you were ... passionate about helping those children.'

I know what she's doing. She's picking at my weak spots in the hope that I crack open. It's not working.

'We only have a few minutes left, Michelle. Are you sure you have nothing you want to talk to me about? Something you want to get off your chest?' Trish places the lid on her pen and closes my file. She sighs. 'Stop punishing yourself; you've been punished enough. You don't need to make it worse for yourself.'

I'll never get what I deserve.

I never got my full punishment.

Murder.

Just one.

Fake Mila's dad. Harry Reynolds. Age thirty-four. No children.

Apparently, the hoax call came in from his friend he owed money to. His friend thought he'd get a visit from the police, who'd scare him into paying up.

Instead, he got the hot-headed knife-wielding nutjob. He got me. And he lost his life.

I'll take my punishment with my hands held high in surrender.

Only once I have killed Aiden, will I be vindicated.

Trish brings me back to the room with a cough.

'That's all we have time for. But, please, if you take any advice – please see Kelsey. It will do you some good to connect with the outside world. You've got to stay strong.'

She's right.

***

Kelsey greets me with a tight squeeze. I watch the guard by the door. His eyes are on us and I push Kelsey away before he has to intervene. I don't want to make his job harder today.

'God, I've missed you so much,' she tells me as she takes her chair on the other side of the table.

My heart swells as I look at her and a sob catches in my throat. I have missed her, too. She was the sunshine in my life and since waving goodbye to her in the courtroom I've been cold and alone.

'I miss you, too,' I whisper, refusing to cry. Failing miserably.

She chats about the vets. She's jovial, but there's a strain to her mouth that belies her breezy attitude.

'How's Mags?' She bristles at the pet name for my former boss, making me chuckle, a sound that sounds alien to me. 'Did she give you a hard time?'

'Let's just say she took some convincing.'

'Cow. She never liked me.'

'Oh, come on. I introduced you to her and now you're banged up for murder. You can hardly blame her for being wary of me.'

'Wary,' I chuckle. 'I bet she was foaming at the mouth.'

Kelsey laughs. 'Actually, she had fire pouring out of her ears, too. Even Felix doesn't like the bitch. And that soppy idiot loves everyone.'

Oh, Felix. When I heard Kelsey adopted him my heart leapt with joy. He's in a good home. He's loved.

'And how's Travis?' Travis came to visit me not long after my sentencing. He wanted to explain why he turned me in for Harry Reynolds' death, but I waved it off. I would have thought less of him if he *hadn't* turned me in. We're all acting on our own individual morals. It feels good to know that his are set straight.

Kelsey shifts in her seat, her eyes flitting everywhere but on me. 'We broke up.'

'What?' It comes out louder than I expect, and a guard behind me shushes me.

'There was just too much ... tension between us. It was never going to work.'

My mouth gapes open. 'Kelsey, you can't break up with him. Please! I'll put this right. I'll talk to him.'

Kelsey raises a hand. 'It's really okay. He works too much, anyway; I barely saw him. I need a guy who I can cuddle up with on a Saturday night and not have to fret about every day. An accountant. Or an architect.'

Bollocks to that. Kelsey deserves happiness and Travis is the only thing that has brought her happiness since ... forever.

I start to talk, but Kelsey holds up her hand, cutting me off.

'I mean it, Michelle. Keep your nose out of this one.'

What choice do I have? It's not like there's much I can do from in here. And I can't defy Kelsey again. She's been my rock. My hero. She's more than I ever deserved.

Which reminds me.

'Kelsey, you said there's something I don't remember. Before all this happened. The reason why you were so willing to help me for all this time.'

She sighs uncomfortably. She thought I had forgotten.

'Not now, Michelle.'

'Oh, come on. I can't bear any more secrets. Please.'

She eyes me up, biting the inside of her cheek.

'Do you remember Lee and Cassie? They took care of us for a bit.'

'Vaguely. Was he the creepy one?' I must have been about ten years old when we were placed with them. I had been split from Kelsey for over a year before our fates temporarily drew us back together. 'Wait, didn't he die?'

Kelsey nods.

'That's right, he fell down the stairs.'

'Oh yeah.' I remember Cassie coming home from working the night shift at Tesco and screaming. The commotion made us run out of the bedroom where we were watching Sharkey and George. Lee was crumpled at the bottom of the stairs. Dead.

'I was there. You were there.' The memory makes me shudder. Where had I repressed that for all these years? Lee was all right. Aloof, but let us get away with whatever we wanted.

'Michelle, that man was raping me.'

Her words almost knock me backwards. Raping her? I don't know how to respond.

Pieces of my childhood start to fit back together. The blur gains clarity at disgusting speed.

No.

I wake up in the middle of the night. I need the toilet. Only when I walk across the landing, I am distracted by the lamp in Kelsey's room – it's on. I poke my head in to see if she's okay. But, she's not there. All I see is Lee's hairy backside, pumping into Kelsey's bed.

'You saw him. You put a stop to it. You saved me.'

I push myself back in my chair, shaking my head at her. 'No, I didn't.' But, as the words leave my mouth another flashback forces itself into my mind.

Holy shit.

I was frozen. I couldn't move.

When he just appeared right next to me on the landing, I jumped and lashed out. My tiny hands shoved him. He tripped over his own feet and disappeared over the bannister. I heard the thump and crack as he hit his head on the wooden telephone table.

Then I crawled into bed with Kelsey and we slept.

'You saved me, Mich. And I saved you.'

I don't know what to say. I've killed before?

'Look at me, Michelle.' I force my eyes to meet hers. 'What you did that day was the right thing to do. You think I was the only child he was raping? You're a good soul. I have never doubted that for a second.'

I push away the tears and lean onto the table. How could I just forget?

Kelsey touches my hands, but yanks it back when the guard yells at her to back off.

'Now you know. You know everything. You know why I will do anything for you. You hear me? *Anything*.'

What is she getting at? She's not telling me something. She's watching me, her mouth set into a hard line, her eyes drilling into me.

'I'll get him, Michelle.'

'What? Who?' My voice sounds like a gargle through my shock.

'Aiden. I'm going to find him, and I am going to get him.'

'Kelsey, no. Stay out of all this.'

'Men like that deserve to die. You taught me that.'

She stands and walks away. I call out to her, but a guard gives me a hard shove, forcing the sound out of my lungs.

I am taken back to my cell, adrenaline coursing through my veins. I want to run; to scream. I want to keep talking to Kelsey.

My cell door slams behind me with a thunk.

My eyes are immediately drawn to my bed. My sheets remain neatly made, creating a pale canvas for the blood-red gift that wasn't there when I left.

A red rose.

LIKE WHAT YOU READ?

There's more!

For free books, competitions, news on the author and general silliness, sign up to the mailing list HERE

Or join in the fun on Facebook by searching for '**C.L. Sutton Author**'

Alternatively, drop me an email at **hello@clsutton.com** and I will endeavour to reply to you personally.

Thank you from the bottom of my heart

It means so much to me that you have taken the time to read my book. A monumental amount of time, effort, and love is poured into every book written and I think I speak for all authors when I say we are grateful for your support.

If you want to help give my book a boost, please consider leaving a review and recommending me to your friends. It's a HUGE help.

About the Author

Being a bookkeeper in her former life made Clare's creative juices wither away and die. After giving birth to twins and relishing storytime, she soon learnt that the art of story was calling to her.

Now a writer of Psychological Thrillers and loving life, when you can't find her elbow-deep in a plot, you'll find her trekking around the New Zealand bush with her family.

Acknowledgments

My first book – oof!

When I embarked on this journey, I didn't expect it to be such a whirlwind. I mean, think of a story and put the words on paper. Right? Ha!

First and foremost, I need to thank my husband. Not once did he laugh at my ridiculous dream. Forever sweet, always encouraging. My rock. (And not bad-looking either).

I would also like to thank the writing community as a whole for being so supportive and a constant source of generous knowledge. A particular thanks to Ali, the leader of the gang.

My editors, Emma Mitchell from Creating Perfection for the developmental edit and Erin Driessen for the brilliant line edit. Both scrubbed and polished my manuscript and believed in me when I just couldn't. Message me for their details, fellow writers!

Good beta readers are hard to come by, and you, Chelsea Stevenson, were exceptional. Expect my next manuscript in your inbox soon!

And finally, my experts, Emma and Sarah, for giving me titbits on how social services function. In my eyes, you're both heroes for the jobs you do. With hearts that big, you were born to help people, me included.

Manufactured by Amazon.ca
Acheson, AB